M   R

LESLEY COOKMAN

Published by Accent Press Ltd – 2013

ISBN 9781909335929

Cover Design by Sarah Davies

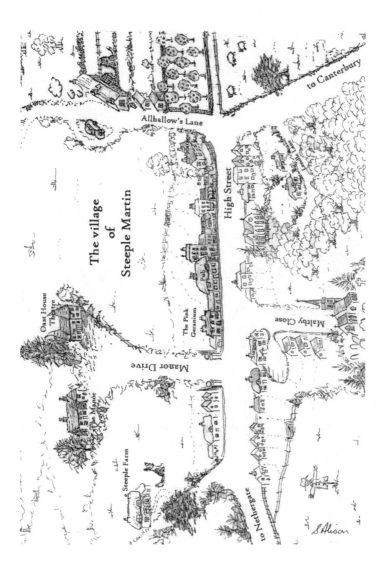

The village
of
Steeple Martin

Allhallow's Lane

to Canterbury

High Street

Oast House
Theatre

The Pink
Geranium

Maltby Close

Manor Drive

The Manor

Steeple Farm

to Nethergate

S.Alison

Acknowledgments

More acknowledgments than ever this time, as I've been helped by so many people. Firstly, once again, my son Miles, who gave me the original idea, and who also introduced me to Helen and Sean Sullivan, who let me poke around their beautiful house, Bogle.

Next, Richard Platt, whose *History of Smuggling* and terrific website www.smuggling.co.uk were of inestimable value, as were the pamphlets *Whitstable and the French Prisoners of War* and *The Seasalter Company* by the late Wallace Harvey.

Val and Stuart Tilley also gave me a lot of help on Whitstable's past, and Christchurch University Canterbury's project on the Battle of Maidstone was also a great help.

When the book was nearly finished, in the course of ongoing research I came across a book by a friend of mine, Catherine Aird, called *A Most Contagious Game*, which, although written forty-five years ago, has so many similarities in the background, as it were, that I was stunned. It is the only novel published outside her Inspector Sloan series, and lay almost forgotten until recently reissued by the Rue Morgue Press. I recommend it highly.

Thanks once more to my publishers, Accent Press, who this year celebrated their tenth birthday (with my help!) and to my lovely editor, Bob Cushion. Love you all.

It may be noticed that I've actually mentioned some real places in this book, but don't try and find any of the Steeple villages or Nethergate. I've sort of zipped Kent open to insert my little corner of it, so no one will ever find it. Only Libby and me.

Lesley Cookman, 2013

WHO'S WHO IN THE LIBBY SARJEANT SERIES

Libby Sarjeant
Former actor, sometime artist, resident of 17, Allhallow's Lane, Steeple Martin. Owner of Sidney the cat.

Fran Wolfe
Formerly Fran Castle. Also former actor, occasional psychic, resident of Coastguard Cottage, Nethergate. Owner of Balzac the cat.

Ben Wilde
Libby's significant other. Owner of The Manor Farm and the Oast House Theatre.

Guy Wolfe
Fran's husband, artist and owner of a shop and gallery in Harbour Street, Nethergate.

Peter Parker
Ben's cousin. Free-lance journalist, part owner of The Pink Geranium restaurant and life partner of Harry Price.

Harry Price
Chef and co-owner of The Pink Geranium and Peter Parker's life partner.

Hetty Wilde
Ben's mother. Lives at The Manor.

Greg Wilde
Hetty's husband and Ben's father.

DCI Ian Connell
Local policeman and friend. Former suitor of Fran's.

Adam Sarjeant
Libby's youngest son. Lives above The Pink Geranium, works with garden designer Mog, mainly at Creekmarsh.

Lewis Osbourne-Walker
TV gardener and handy-man who owns Creekmarsh.

Sophie Wolfe
Guy's daughter. Lives above the gallery.

Flo Carpenter
Hetty's oldest friend.

Lenny Fisher
Hetty's brother. Lives with Flo Carpenter.

Ali and Ahmed
Owners of the Eight-til-late in the village.

Jane Baker
Chief Reporter for the *Nethergate Mercury*. Mother to Imogen.

Terry Baker
Jane's husband and father of Imogen.

Joe, Nella and Owen
Of Cattlegreen Nurseries.

DCI Don Murray
Of Canterbury Police.

Amanda George
Novelist, known as Rosie.

Chapter One

The white-rimed undergrowth crackled and the grass crunched underfoot. In the moonlight, shapes loomed up on either side, threatening. The murderer paused, listening, but all was quiet. He then turned and crept from the scene, leaving the victim on the ground, staring silently and sightlessly through the branches at the stars.

Adam Sarjeant glanced over his shoulder at the creeping mist. Through it, the trees were vague outlines, giants moving noiselessly towards him.

'Mog,' he called. 'We can't go on much longer in this, can we?'

His employer pushed back lank dark hair and looked up from the paving slab he was lining up. 'No. Just bring the tarp over and we'll cover it all. With any luck it'll be better tomorrow.'

Adam turned away from the new swimming pool he and Mog had been landscaping towards the covered pile of materials at the edge of the lawn. Beyond a wall, the house swam eerily like a great half-timbered ship. There was rustle over to his right, and a figure burst through the hedge.

''Ere, Adam! Mog!'

'Johnny?' Mog stood up. 'What is it?'

'Bleedin' body, innit? Fuckin' 'ell.' Johnny suddenly bent double, his stringy grey pony tail swinging forward over his shoulder.

'Johnny?' Adam ran towards him. 'Are you all right? What do you mean a body?'

Johnny lifted his head. ''Course I'm not bleedin' all right. Call the cops.'

Mog arrived at Adam's side. They looked at each other.

'Had we better check?' said Mog.

'It's a bleedin' woman, I tell yer. Dead as a dodo. Call the cops.' He sat down suddenly on the ground, his head in his hands.

Mog pulled out his phone and pushed buttons, while Adam ineffectually patted Johnny's shoulder.

'Yeah,' he heard Mog saying. 'No, I'm just working on the garden. The caretaker, he found it. Dark House, Dark Lane, between Steeple Cross and Keeper's Cob.'

'They say to stay here.' Mog looked nervously towards the gap in the hedge where Johnny had burst through. 'Where is it, Johnny?'

'Just outside the grotto. They won't make me go back, will they?'

'I don't know,' said Adam. 'They might.'

'I can't.'

'Did they say how long they'd be?' asked Adam.

'No, and let's face it, this house isn't exactly on a major road, is it?' Mog felt in his pocket for his tobacco. 'Want a rollie, Johnny?'

'Yeah. Ta.' Johnny looked up and watched as Mog rolled two slim cigarettes.

'It's going to be dark soon,' said Adam. 'Have we got a torch, Mog?'

'Don't know. Might have in the van.'

'Shall I go and see? If I walk about at the front the security light will come on and the police might see it.'

Mog nodded, leaning down to light Johnny's cigarette.

Adam walked towards the gate in the hedge which led to the lawns at the back of the house and made for the drive at the side. The security lights came on and he walked to the gateway to see if he could see anything coming, but the lane, narrow as a cart track, twisted away in both directions, shrouded in unbroken mist.

He fetched the big wind-up torch from the van and went back to Mog and Johnny.

'You know, I don't suppose we actually need to stay out

here. I'm sure we could go in to the house.'

'Haven't got the key.' Johnny shook his head.

'But I thought you were the caretaker?' said Mog.

'Yeah, well. Just here to keep an eye on things. The cleaner's got a key. Missis calls 'er and me when she's coming down and the cleaner comes and gives the place a once over. I just locks and unlocks the gates.'

'We could sit in the van,' suggested Adam.

Mog nodded. 'Come on, Johnny. We can all squeeze in.'

But as they approached the van, they heard an engine and within seconds a police car had pulled up in the lane.

'You reported finding a body?' The first uniform climbed out of the driver's seat.

'Yes,' they said together.

'That was quick,' said Adam.

'Diverted from traffic.' The other uniform came up. 'We were near the turn off on the Canterbury Road. Better take a look.'

'I can't go back,' whined Johnny.

'You found it, did you, sir?' First Uniform looked Johnny up and down. 'Point me in the right direction.'

'You'd never find it,' said Adam, with a sigh. 'We'll show you where the grotto is and you can take it from there.'

'Grotto? Bloody Father Christmas got here early?' said Second Uniform. Adam and Mog just looked at him.

'Come on, Johnny,' said Mog.

Adam led the way back to the hedge and pointed through at the Victorian stone grotto.

'Johnny has to come through the grotto from his place,' he explained.

The Uniforms peered in to the grotto, with its mock bridge and tumbling "ruins", planted with a variety of ferns.

'Bit weird,' sniffed First Uniform.

''S'artistic,' muttered Johnny.

'So where's this body, then?' asked Second Uniform, swinging his torch across the empty space.

'Other side of the bridge.' Johnny turned his back. 'I don't want to see it.'

'All right, sir, all right. You stay here.' Second Uniform stepped into the grotto, leaving First Uniform with Adam, Mog and Johnny.

'Ain't you going?' said Johnny.

'No, he's got to look after us,' said Mog.

'Quite right, sir. Now,' First Uniform got out his notebook. 'Can I have your names and addresses, please?'

He had just finished writing them down when Second Uniform reappeared talking into a radio.

'Better go and have a look, Steve,' he said, as he ended the call. 'I'll stay here.'

First Uniform went through into the grotto and turned on his own torch.

'Now, sir,' said Second Uniform. 'Did you touch anything?'

Johnny looked as though he was going to be sick. 'No, I fuckin' didn't!'

'And you don't know the deceased?'

'No.'

'So she's not one of the family who live here?'

'No. Oh gawd, I'd better tell 'er, 'adn't I?'

'He means Mrs Watson, one of the owners,' said Mog.

Second Uniform swung towards the house. 'She not in?'

'She'll be in London,' said Adam. 'She's not here that much.'

'So you look after the place?'

'Johnny does. We're just landscaping round the new swimming pool.'

Second Uniform's eyebrows rose to his hairline. 'Strewth! And she's not here much?'

Adam and Mog both shook their heads.

'Enjoys 'aving things done about the place,' contributed Johnny. 'It's 'er 'obby, like.'

First Uniform came back through the grotto. 'I can hear the cars,' he said. 'You go, I'll stay here.'

After a moment a group of men rounded the side of the house and came across the garden.

The first man stopped in front of them.

4

'Oh, no, Adam, not you,' said Chief Detective Inspector Connell.

Chapter Two

'Oh, no, Adam, not you!' said Libby Sarjeant.

'Yes, Ma, I'm sorry. Ian said he's very sorry, too, but he couldn't do much else, could he?'

'He could have let you go home and called you in tomorrow!'

'No, Ma, he couldn't,' said Adam patiently, 'you know that really. So what I was wondering was, could you come and get me? Mog needs to get home, and he doesn't really want to go all the way out to Steeple Martin first.'

Libby looked at her watch. 'All right. I'll just call Pete and ask him to take the panto rehearsal –'

'Oh, I forgot! Look don't worry, I'll get the bus.'

'Don't be daft. Ben's already gone to the theatre, or I'd get him to come with me. Will you be in the reception area?'

'I expect so,' said Adam. 'Thanks, Ma. Bit much, still having to rescue me at my age, isn't it?'

'You're still my baby,' said Libby. 'You all are.'

'Shall I send Ben back to you?' asked Peter Parker when she called him. 'Can you wait?'

'No, I'm fine, Pete. Sorry to have to ask this, but I suppose it is a bit of an emergency.'

'Ian should have sent him home in a police car,' grumbled Peter.

'The village would have had a field day,' laughed Libby. 'No, I'm going. I'll speak to you later.'

Libby decided that Ben's new 4x4 was a better bet than her crumbling Romeo the Renault, and accordingly set off for Canterbury in it.

To her surprise, Chief Detective Inspector Ian Connell, old friend and sometime adversary, was in the reception area of the police station with Adam.

'I'm sorry about this, Libby,' he said, coming forward to take her hand. 'But however much I know that neither Adam nor Mog could have had anything to do with this, we have to go by the book.'

'I know.' Libby looked at Adam, who looked pale. 'Are you all right, darling?'

'He had to view the body, I'm afraid,' said Ian.

'It was OK,' said Adam, valiantly. 'They had to see if anyone knew who she was.'

'And no one does?' asked Libby.

Adam shook his head.

'The owner of the property is coming down tomorrow, and we'll ask her, of course.' Ian patted Adam's shoulder. 'Go on. Go home and have a good strong drink.'

'It wasn't very nice, Ma,' said Adam as they climbed into the car. 'I think her throat had been cut.'

Libby's stomach lurched. 'Oh, darling, I'm so sorry. Didn't they cover her up?'

'We had to look while she was still in the garden,' said Adam. 'Mog hated it.'

'Of course, both of you did,' said Libby, turning the car round in the car park. 'Come on, let's get you home. Do you think Harry will let you have something to eat in the flat?'

Adam lived in a flat over The Pink Geranium restaurant, owned by Peter and his partner Harry Price, and run by Harry himself. He pulled a face.

'I expect he would, but it's Monday. He's closed. Anyway, I don't think I'm hungry.'

'What do you want to do, then? Come home with me?'

'No, I'm going to go to the pub. You go on to rehearsal and have a drink with me afterwards. I don't want to sit in the flat on my own.'

'If you're sure.'

'I'm sure,' said Adam. 'I can have a pie in the pub if I feel

7

like it.'

Libby dropped Adam in the high street, drove up The Manor drive and parked outside the theatre. She pushed open the glass doors and heard faint sounds of laughter from the auditorium.

She found Peter on the stage himself, giving a very good impression of a principal boy, while the rest of the cast hooted with laughter.

'Going to take it on, are you?' she asked when the laughter had died down.

'I was just demonstrating to Olivia,' Peter said, somewhat sheepishly. 'I didn't expect you back.'

'Olivia, you've now seen just how outrageous you can be in panto,' Libby said to the young woman hovering at the side of the stage. 'The rest of you, take five while I have a word with Peter.'

'How's Adam, Libby?' called someone from the back. Ben Wilde, Libby's significant other, suddenly appeared from backstage.

'Yes, how is he?' he asked.

'He's fine, thanks,' said Libby. 'Well, a bit shocked, you know, but OK otherwise.'

'So, how is he really?' asked Peter as they sat down in the stalls.

'Shocked, as I said. He's gone to the pub. Is Harry at home? Because I think Ad could do with some company. I'll go down at the end of rehearsal.'

'I'll give Hal a call,' said Peter. 'And you can carry on with the rehearsal. We'd just got to where the Prince and Dandini enter the forest.'

Libby called the rehearsal to order and went back to the beginning of the scene. The theatre, an old oast house owned by Ben's family at The Manor, had been converted by him with help from Peter, his first cousin. Ben, Peter and Libby now ran it as a charitable trust, staging their own productions such as the annual pantomime, visiting companies' productions — amateur and professional — and the occasional musical or comedy one-nighter.

When the Prince and Dandini finally ran out of steam and the disguised Fairy Godmother had given her bewitched sticks to Cinderella, Libby called a halt and, after locking up, led a Hamelin-like procession down the Manor drive to the pub. It seemed the entire cast wanted to know what had happened to Adam.

They found him ensconced at the table by the fire with Harry, an empty plate before him and a pint in his hand.

'I was hungry after all, Ma.' He grinned up at his mother.

'So I see. Sorry about this lot,' said Libby, sitting down and gesturing at the crowd behind her, who all pressed forward with questions, which Adam answered briefly but patiently. Eventually, he was left alone with Libby, Ben, Peter and Harry.

'So do they think this Watson person had something to do with the death?' asked Ben.

'I don't know. I don't know if someone's gone to London to interview her or what.'

'Ian said she was coming down tomorrow,' said Libby, 'but I can't imagine they wouldn't have sent someone round to see her straight away.'

'I wouldn't have thought it was someone she knew,' said Harry. 'Daft to leave a body on your own property.'

'Not if you thought it was going to be undisturbed for a while,' said Peter.

'But Mrs Watson would have known Johnny was likely to find a body. She employed us to do the landscaping round the swimming pool.' Adam shook his head. 'In this weather. I ask you.'

'Had you worked for her before?' asked Libby.

'No, Lewis knows her. He recommended us.'

'I think Lewis must know everyone with money in the county,' said Libby.

'He helped her with the interior of Dark House,' said Adam. 'You know, she's one of these people who has to have celebrity designers. And we're almost as good because we work with him.'

Lewis Osbourne-Walker, a television celebrity handyman

9

with his own show, owned Creekmarsh Place, where Mog and Adam were restoring the gardens.

'What else do you know about her?' asked Peter. 'Is there any other family?'

'There's a husband, but he works abroad.' Adam shrugged. 'Lewis would know more.'

'Perhaps we should tell Lewis,' said Libby thoughtfully. 'After all, this Watson woman is a friend of his.'

'Is that wise?' asked Ben.

'Wise?' scoffed Harry. 'Applied to our Lib? Don't be daft.'

'Actually, I think I will,' said Adam. 'After all, he got us this job.' He fished his mobile out of his pocket and swiped the screen. As Lewis answered, he got up and moved away from the table.

'Did you find anything out from Ian?' asked Ben.

Libby shook her head. 'But they had to view the body to see if they knew who it was. Her throat had been cut.'

A murmur went round the table.

'There was a sort of caretaker there – he found the body. Ad said he was beside himself.'

Adam came back. 'Lewis says he'll call Adelaide Watson. Her husband worked for that big company that closed down near Felling, that's why they've got the house here, but now he's got a job in Brussels and she's bored. Both their kids are grown up and moved away.'

'So no one from the family was anywhere near the house?' said Libby.

'Doesn't look like it,' said Adam. 'I've never even met Mrs Watson.'

'Adelaide,' murmured Harry. 'Parents fans of *Guys and Dolls* were they?'

'Eh?' said Adam.

'Adelaide was a character in the musical *Guys and Dolls*, ignoramus,' said Harry.

'Well,' said Peter, 'let's hope she isn't married to a gambling gangster.'

'Eh?' said Adam again.

10

Four faces turned towards him.

'Adam!' they said.

The next morning Libby was unsurprised to receive a phone call from Lewis.

''Allo, me old mate.'

'Lewis! How are you?'

'I'm fine. Look, Lib, about this body.'

'Yes,' said Libby warily.

'I'm stuck in London and I'm filming in Somerset tomorrow, or I'd come down, but Adelaide's got to come down to have a look at it. Wondered if you'd go and hold her hand?'

'Me? Why me? I don't know her from Adam!'

'Ha, ha. He doesn't know her either.'

'What about her husband? Her children? She must have local friends.'

'I don't know that they have. When Roland worked at Felling he never had much time for socialising, and she's not exactly the WI type.'

'I can't just barge in,' said Libby. 'And Ad and Mog have been told to stay away. Mog's furious.'

Lewis sighed. 'She's just told me she doesn't want to stay down there on her own. I suggested she took one of her London friends with her, but she sort of gave the impression that would be a no-no.'

'Well, even if I pop in to do a bit of hand-holding, I'm not staying there. I have got a life, you know, Lewis.'

'I know, and you'll be deep in panto rehearsals by now, won't you?'

'Yes, and I had to leave one to pick Ad up from the police station last night.'

'Well, can I just give her your number? Then if she wants a bit of company she can ring.'

'Landline only, Lewis,' warned Libby. 'I'm not having her interrupt rehearsals.'

'I promise.' Lewis sighed again. 'I'm sorry, Libby. Looks like Ad and I have got you mixed up in another murder.'

11

'You bloody haven't!' said Libby, horrified. 'Ad just happened to be there when the body was found, that's all.'

'And I know the owner of the property. Who, let's face it, might be up to 'er bleedin' neck in the whole thing.'

'Bloody hell,' sighed Libby.

Chapter Three

Adam appeared in the doorway a little later in the morning looking harassed.

'What's up?' asked his mother, going to put the kettle on.

'The police want to talk to me again.' He followed her into the kitchen and perched on the corner of the table.

'Why?'

'How should I know? Ian said he knew Mog and I hadn't anything to do with it.'

Libby frowned. 'I suppose knowing a person doesn't preclude them from being a suspect. I expect this is the superintendent or someone asking why you haven't been put through it a bit more rigorously.'

Libby's phone rang.

'Libby, look, you mustn't be worried about Adam –'

'How did you know he was here?'

'I didn't, but I knew he'd have told you we want to see him again. I'm afraid the powers that be don't see it quite like I do, and they're now talking time of death alibis.' Ian sighed heavily. 'Although no one seems quite sure when that was.'

'So how can anyone provide an alibi?'

'It has to be during the previous night. And Adam, Mog and this Johnny person were really the only three people we know about who were aware of the property being empty.'

Libby's heart jolted. 'What about the cleaner? And you know villages – they always know everything …'

'Dark House isn't really in a village, though, is it?' said Ian.

'And Lewis says they don't have any local friends.'

'Lewis?' Ian's voice sharpened.

'You did know he introduced Ad and Mog to the Watsons, didn't you?'

'So he knew about the house?'

'Oh, come on, Ian! Lewis was in London and filming in Somerset. And yes, he did the interior design for Adelaide Watson.'

'And they had no local friends.' Ian fell silent.

'Well, you can ask her, can't you. She's coming down.'

'How do you know?' asked Ian.

'Lewis told me,' sighed Libby. 'Look, I seem to be getting involved again, and I really don't want to. I just think it's daft to imagine Ad –'

'I don't imagine anything,' said Ian sharply. 'We just need to see him again. Is he still without transport?'

'Yes,' said Libby, 'but –'

'No, you won't bring him in,' said Ian. 'We'll come to him. Shall I speak to him? Oh, and this is strictly off the record.'

Libby handed the receiver to a nervous Adam and turned to pour boiling water into the teapot.

'He says he and someone else are going to come and see me in about an hour. What did he tell you?' Adam handed back the phone and Libby repeated her conversation.

'So where were you the night before last?' she asked, fetching milk from the fridge.

Adam looked half irritated, half amused. 'Why, do you suspect me, too?'

'Don't be stupid.'

'I was home alone after I came back from lunch with you and Hetty.'

'Sunday, of course,' said Libby gloomily. 'There wasn't even anyone in the restaurant who might have seen or heard you.'

'Mother, dear, you are making me paranoid.' Adam took his mug. 'I'm sure Ian will make sure I don't get banged up for it, but it's horrifically worrying, nevertheless.'

'Best thing to do is find the real murderer,' said Libby. 'Come on, I'll light the fire.'

By the time Ian arrived, Libby was making a pot of soup for lunch.

'This is DC Robertson,' Ian introduced the young man standing nervously behind him. 'This is Mrs Sarjeant and her son Adam.'

'I'll go back in the kitchen,' said Libby, waving her wooden spoon.

'No need,' said Ian easily. 'As long as you don't interrupt.'

Libby looked at Adam. 'Would you rather I went away?'

Adam didn't look at her. 'I don't mind.'

'Take a seat, then.' Ian sat in the armchair opposite Adam on the sofa, while DC Robertson took a chair by the table in the window. Libby hovered in the kitchen doorway.

Having established once more that Adam had no idea who the dead woman was, Ian proceeded to ask about his movements over the whole of Sunday.

'So,' he said finally, glancing at his notebook, 'after you left Hetty's on Sunday you went back to the flat and that was it?'

Libby caught DC Robertson's surprise at the informality of the question.

'I popped to the pub for a pint –'

'You didn't tell me that!' Libby burst out.

Adam scowled. 'And I called Sophie, but that won't help, will it?'

DC Robertson was looking even more bewildered. Ian took pity on him.

'I know the family,' he said. 'Adam, did you call Sophie on your mobile?'

'Yes.'

'Then it will show up in both your phone records. Sadly, that doesn't help, because your mobile could be used anywhere. And we know there's a signal at Dark House, because Mog called 999 from there.'

Adam nodded morosely.

'Don't worry.' Ian got up and put a hand on his shoulder. 'I know you didn't do it, but we've got to go through the motions.'

'Any idea who it is yet?' asked Libby.

'We're going through a few people reported missing over the last few days, but no luck so far,' said Ian. 'Cheer up, both of you. You've been close to murder investigations before.'

'But we haven't been suspects,' said Libby.

Ian sighed. 'No.'

Libby saw them both out and went back to Adam. 'He's right, Ad. He knows you didn't do it, but he's got to go through the motions.'

'Suppose one of those missing persons turns out to have some sort of link to me?' Adam looked up, his face pinched.

'Then you'd have recognised her, wouldn't you? Come on, the soup's ready. Nothing like soup for cheering up a winter's day.'

Adam had gone back to the flat to get ready for an evening helping out in The Pink Geranium when Libby's landline rang.

'Mrs Sarjeant?' asked a soft female voice.

'Yes?'

'Lewis suggested I call you. You know – Lewis Osbourne-Walker?'

'I know Lewis. You must be Adelaide Watson?'

'I – ah – yes. I'm Adelaide Watson.'

'What can I do for you, Mrs Watson?'

'I don't really know.' Libby visualised the woman twisting her hands together. 'Lewis thought …'

'He told me you would be on your own and might not want to be,' said Libby. 'I don't know what good I'd be, but I'll happily come over this evening for a while, if you would like me to. I might bring my son with me to navigate.'

'Your son? Oh, yes, he's one of my landscapers, isn't he? The good-looking one.'

Libby laughed. 'Well, I think he is. Yes, that's the one, Adam. If he's free, of course,' she added, remembering Adam was working tonight.

'I could do with some company, actually. You see, I don't really know many people round here, and I didn't want to intrude on anybody …'

'That's fine,' said Libby cheerfully. 'I'll feed my other half,

16

then I'll come over. It'll probably be about half past seven. Is that all right?'

Ben looked grumpy when Libby told him she was going to help the needy, but didn't offer to come too, and Adam, as she'd feared, was up to his armpits at the restaurant.

She took Ben's car and drove out of Steeple Martin towards Canterbury. After a mile or so, she took the road that would lead to Steeple Cross and the villages and woods beyond.

'Keeper's Cob,' she muttered to herself. 'That's what I've got to look for.'

But beyond Steeple Cross she could see no signposts for Keeper's Cob. On her right, however, stood a pub, smartly painted cream and shining in the darkness. She parked, got out and went inside.

There were three men standing at the small central bar, all of whom turned round and stared at her. To her right and left, the rooms were laid out as dining rooms, although no one was eating. She cleared her throat and approached the bar.

'Excuse me, but I'm looking for Keeper's Cob,' she said.

'Easiest way's straight on, then turn right at the crossroads,' said one man, ostentatiously "country" in a Barbour jacket and wellingtons.

'Dark Lane's direct, though,' said the second, in Tattersall check shirt and pale cord trousers.

'Not easy, Dark Lane,' said the third, leaning on the bar and staring into his pint.

'That's actually where I'm going, to Dark House,' said Libby. 'How do I get there?'

All three turned to face her, identical frowns on their faces.

'Journalist?' they said together.

Libby was taken aback. 'No! I'm a friend of Mrs Watson's, but I've not been here at night before,' she crossed fingers, 'and I'm a bit lost.'

'Ah,' said the first man, still suspicious.

'She's had to come down here – well, she had to, and she wanted company.'

They all nodded. 'Murder.'

17

Libby sighed. 'Yes. So will you tell me where I am?'

'On the corner of Dark Lane,' said Tattersall check. He pointed. 'Up the side of the pub.'

'Dodgy though,' said the third man. 'Gets a bit rough further along. Take it slow, like.'

Libby thanked them and went back to the car. Obviously the murder was known about and the locals protective of their own. Well, she couldn't blame them for that, but Adelaide Watson wasn't supposed to have any friends in the area. She supposed it was just solidarity at work.

Woods pressed in on her left as she turned into the narrow lane. On the right the few houses soon petered out, giving way to small fields, beyond which more trees could be seen wavering above the mist. Ahead, the lane twisted into the fog and became almost a cart track, covered in a carpet of what appeared to be undisturbed leaves from the trees which now pressed in on both sides, becoming a dark and ghostly tunnel.

'This can't be right,' Libby said out loud to herself, trying to hold panic at bay. 'No one lives here.'

But the darkness lightened, the trees thinned and there was a gateway. Aware that she was actually shaking, Libby turned in and drew to halt, resting a thumping head on the steering wheel.

'Mrs Sarjeant?'

She looked up to see a worried face at the car window and gave a weak smile.

'I know it sounds pathetic,' she said as she climbed out, 'but your lane is really scary!'

'You came from the Steeple Cross end, didn't you? By The Dragon pub? I always come in from the Keeper's Cob end, it's slightly easier.' The woman held out her hand. 'I'm Adelaide Watson.'

Libby took the proffered hand and looked properly at her hostess. Adelaide Watson was small and unremarkable-looking, except for her obviously expensive clothes and haircut.

'I'm sorry you've had all this trouble,' she said. 'I shouldn't have asked you here.'

'That's fine,' said Libby. 'I don't think I'd like to be out here on my own, either. Is your husband going to come home?'

Adelaide frowned as she turned to go into the house. 'He hasn't said so, but I think the police want him to.'

'To see if he knows the woman?' said Libby. 'Unlikely, if you don't.'

'Oh, no. You see, there were over two thousand employees where he worked at Felling. It could be someone from there.'

She led Libby into a low-ceilinged, wood-panelled room which had a log fire burning in one of the largest inglenook fireplaces Libby had ever seen.

'Please sit down. I've made coffee as I didn't think you'd want a drink.'

Libby sank into a huge squashy sofa and accepted coffee.

'So what have the police told you so far?' she asked.

'Only that Johnny found the – the body yesterday afternoon, and the – er – your son and … and –'

'Adam and Mog, the landscapers,' Libby said.

'Yes, that they were here too. None of them know who she is. Was.'

'No, and you didn't either?'

'No.' Adelaide shuddered. 'They showed me pictures.'

'And did they ask who knew you wouldn't be in residence?'

'Well, yes, they did, but I don't really know many people locally. We used to see people when Roland worked in this country, and we know a few people from across the county, but not here. Most of my friends are in London.'

My friends, noted Libby. Not *our* friends.

'So the only people who knew you weren't here were my son and his boss, Johnny and your cleaner?'

'Marilyn, yes. She's not exactly my cleaner, though. She just keeps an eye on the place and opens up now and then. She could have told any number of people, of course. She lives in Keeper's Cob and comes here in her son's Land Rover. He farms over there.'

'Do you use any of the local shops? Order anything from farm shops?'

Adelaide shook her head. 'I go to Waitrose in Canterbury.'

You would, thought Libby.

The newest model smartphone that lay beside Adelaide began to warble. She picked it up.

'Carl? What?' She shot a scared look at Libby, and switched to speakerphone.

'Ramani? No, I haven't … I've only just got here. And I've got someone with me.'

'Of course, you haven't met her, have you?' A man's voice floated out. 'It's just that I've got home and she's not here.' The voice sounded scared. 'And I don't know where she is.'

Chapter Four

'Police,' mouthed Libby.

Adelaide stopped looking horrified and obviously tried to pull herself together.

'Have you told the police, Carl?'

'N-no. I don't know how long she's been gone, you see. She might have only popped out.'

'Have you been away?' asked Adelaide at another mouthed prompt from Libby.

'Yes, I went away on Sunday. Two-day conference in Hertfordshire. So you see, she could have just gone out for the evening.'

'Why did you ring here?' asked Adelaide, off her own bat, this time.

'I don't really know,' said the unknown Carl. 'She doesn't know many people, and I thought she might have … well, you see, I can't think where she'd have gone. You know she doesn't go out much.'

'I think you should tell the police,' said Adelaide firmly. 'Let me know what happens.' She rang off.

'Who is he and why did he ring here?' asked Libby, sitting forward.

'He's our local doctor. We've met him socially a few times, but never his wife. She's Asian – and you heard him say I've never met her. I can only think he thought of me because I'm often on my own here and she might have come here.' She looked up at Libby. 'You don't think …?'

'Was the picture the police showed you of an Asian woman?'

'I – I think so.'

The women sat looking at one another.

'Should we phone the police?' asked Adelaide eventually.

'I wouldn't,' said Libby. 'They'll probably want to talk to you again anyway, so wait until they do.'

'But suppose Carl doesn't call them?'

'You can always call him back and ask what the police said.'

Adelaide's phone rang again.

'Carl?' she said, switching again to speaker.

'The car's gone,' he said flatly.

'Her car?'

'Ours. We only have one. I was picked up by a colleague on Sunday evening so I could leave the car for her, although she hates driving.'

'Phone the police,' said Adelaide. 'Do it now.'

'All right.' There was something suspiciously like a sob in the man's voice.

'Poor bugger,' said Libby, after Adelaide switched off the phone.

'Do you think I should go and see him?' Adelaide said after a moment.

'No. The police will probably go and see him straight away once he's given them a description. He's got no transport now and if he lives in the back of beyond like this …'

Adelaide sighed and nodded. 'Well, not quite so bad. He lives behind The Dragon.'

'I haven't cheered you up much, have I?' said Libby. 'Perhaps we ought to talk about something else.'

They both tried, but neither of them could forget why Libby was there, nor the call from the doctor. When Libby's phone rang in her pocket, she was relieved at the interruption, but alarmed when she saw who it was.

'You said Lewis told you about Adelaide Watson. I've just called your home number and no one was there. Are you rehearsing?'

'Er – no.'

'At Dark House, then.'

'Yes, I am. Mrs Watson wanted company.'

Ian sighed. 'And I suppose you were there when she received a phone call from Doctor Oxenford?'

'Two, actually.'

'Two?'

'One to ask if his wife was here, and the second to say their car had gone.'

'So it was you who encouraged him to call the police.'

Libby's eyes widened. 'Shouldn't I have done? Under the circumstances –'

'Under the circumstances you may well have frightened the poor man into the middle of next week for nothing,' interrupted Ian.

'But,' said Libby, looking over at Adelaide to see if she was understanding any of the conversation. Libby's phone was too ancient to have speakerphone. 'If it is her, then the quicker you find out the better, isn't it?'

'I'll need to speak to you both shortly. How long are you going to be there?'

Libby looked at her watch. 'It's nine now,' she said. 'I wasn't planning to stay after ten. It's a horrible night.'

'I'll get someone to you as soon as possible. Warn Mrs Watson.'

'Oh, dear,' said Adelaide, after Libby had relayed the conversation to her. 'But I heard what you said about the sooner the better. So they think it's Mrs Oxenford, then?'

'Well, if it isn't, they won't need to see us, will they? I expect they'll go to see the doctor, get a photograph and cart him off to the morgue to have a look. Then he'll be in for it.'

'Why?' asked Adelaide, shocked. 'He didn't do it!'

'They always look at the nearest and dearest first. And how do you know he didn't do it?'

'He said he was picked up on Sunday evening by a colleague. He couldn't have been dumping her body in my grotto in the early hours if he was in Hertfordshire.'

'That's true,' said Libby gloomily. 'And he didn't have any transport, either.'

Adelaide sighed and stood up. 'I'll make fresh coffee,' she

said. 'At least that gives me something to do.'

Libby wandered round the room looking at paintings, wondering if Lewis had helped choose them, or if they were already treasured possessions of the Watsons. She heard Adelaide's phone ring again from across the hall.

'Would you believe it?' Adelaide came in with an exasperated expression and a tray. 'That was Roland. He's just got off the Eurostar at Ashford and wants me to pick him up.'

'Oh, dear,' said Libby.

'I told him I couldn't, I was waiting for the police,' said Adelaide triumphantly. 'He'll have to get himself home.'

'Is that how he always goes to and from work?'

'Yes, but he won't drive himself to the station because he says the parking costs too much when he has to be over there for at least a week at a time, and mostly longer.'

'Ah,' said Libby, thinking that the Watsons were probably as selfish as each other and wondering if their sons were the same.

'Are your boys coming home?' she asked.

'No, and I don't see why they should. The police have been to see them both, though. Such a cheek.'

'The body was found here, though. They must have wanted to see if either of them – are there two? – knew her.'

'Yes, two. One in Leeds, the other in London. Ridiculous. How could either of them have got here in the middle of the night?'

Privately, Libby thought it was perfectly possible overnight, as long as you had a decent car. And no one was there at night except Johnny, who lived beyond and out of sight of the grotto, apparently, whatever that was.

'I was thinking about your grotto,' she said aloud. 'It sounds intriguing. Did you have it built?'

Adelaide's face brightened. 'No, it was built by the people who lived here in the late eighteen hundreds. They seem to have liked ruins.'

'And ferns,' said Libby. 'They loved ferns.'

'Oh, yes, the grotto's covered with ferns. It was one of the things we liked about this house. No one else we know has anything like it.'

That would be it, thought Libby. Not your own taste, then.

It was just after ten o'clock when the doorbell rang.

To Libby's surprise, Ian and DC Robertson walked in.

'I'm sorry to bother you so late, Mrs Watson, but I just need to confirm what Doctor Oxenford told me this evening.' Ian smiled his most charming smile and Libby watched Adelaide almost simper.

'Of course,' she said, her voice dropping by at least two tones.

'Is it Ramani Oxenford?' asked Libby.

Ian scowled at her. 'Doctor Oxenford's being taken to view the body,' he said. 'Now, Mrs Watson, he called you when?'

'Not long after you got here, wasn't it?' Adelaide looked at Libby.

'Yes, about eightish or just after. Then again about ten minutes after that.'

'And can you remember exactly what he said?'

'Well –' Adelaide looked at Libby again. 'He just said had she come here?'

'Even though you'd never met her,' put in Libby.

Ian turned another ferocious scowl on her, but Adelaide said, 'No, Inspector, she's right. And I put him on speakerphone, you see. And then he phoned again and said their car was gone.'

'Anything else?'

'He said he'd been picked up by a colleague Sunday evening,' said Libby. 'To go to a conference in Hertfordshire.'

'Yes,' said Ian. 'And nothing else?'

Both women shook their heads.

'So what can you tell me about Carl and Ramani Oxenford, Mrs Watson? Have you known them long?'

'No, not long. Carl is our doctor down here, and, as I was telling Libby, we've met him a few times socially. I don't think his wife goes out much. I think that's why he thought she might come here, as she knows I don't go out much here, either.'

'But how would she have known you were here?' asked Ian.

Adelaide looked bewildered. 'But she didn't. She didn't

come here.'

'He means why would the doctor think his wife knew you were here,' explained Libby.

'A stab in the dark,' said Adelaide, then covered her mouth with her hand in horror. Ian's own mouth twitched.

'Happens all the time, Mrs Watson,' he said. 'So there's nothing more you can tell me about the Oxenfords?'

'Nothing. I've never been to their house – except to the surgery a couple of times.'

'And you, Mrs Sarjeant?' Ian asked. Libby's mouth fell open. 'Well?' he prompted.

'I don't know either of them. And I don't know Adelaide, either, really. She's a friend of Lewis's, I told you.'

The sound of a door being thrust back hard and a muttered swear word brought Ian and DC Robertson to their feet. Adelaide momentarily closed her eyes.

'That'll be my husband,' she said.

Chapter Five

Roland Watson came into the room looking thunderous. Ian stepped forward and calmly held out a hand.

'I'm Detective Chief Inspector Connell, sir, and this is DC Robertson.'

'And why are you here?' boomed Watson. 'Come to harass me, now, have you? Fetching us all down here in the middle of the night?'

'No, dear, they came to talk to me and Mrs Sarjeant here.' Adelaide stood and indicated Libby. Roland Watson swung a huge head towards her like an angry bear.

'And who the bloody hell are you?'

'This is Mrs Sarjeant, a friend,' interrupted Ian smoothly, 'and they are both witnesses to something that happened this evening.'

'What?' The head swung back to Ian. 'Another body?'

'No, sir.' Ian waved a hand. 'If we could sit down?'

Libby stood up. 'Shall I go and make fresh coffee?' she asked Adelaide, giving up all idea of being home before midnight.

'Oh, please. We'll run out of the ground stuff if this goes on.' Adelaide gave a half-hearted titter and subsided at a look from her husband.

Libby enjoyed pottering in the huge kitchen which had obviously been added quite recently and tastefully. The coffee things had been left on the counter when Adelaide made the last pot, and Libby found more cups and then carried the lot back into the sitting room.

'... seen the woman in my life,' Roland was saying. 'Neither has my wife.'

'Your sons say the same,' put in DC Robertson, the first words he'd spoken that evening.

'My sons? What the bloody hell do you want to bother them for?'

Ian gave an almost imperceptible sigh as Libby handed him a cup of coffee.

'The body was discovered on your premises, sir. Everyone who has a connection here will have to be questioned. We've spoken to your cleaner –' he looked down at Robertson's notebook, thrust helpfully under his nose ' –Marilyn Fairbrass, your odd job man –' he looked down again '– John Templeton and your gardeners, Maurice Legg and Adam Sarjeant. We shall naturally have to question anyone who might have known the premises were empty at the present time.'

Libby was thinking. 'What about the car?' she said.

Everyone turned to look at her in astonishment, but Ian's expression softened.

'Yes, Libby, we've thought of that.'

Adelaide and Roland Watson stared at them both and Libby coloured.

'Well, you don't need my company now, Adelaide,' she said and put her coffee cup back on the tray, 'so, if Chief Inspector Connell doesn't need me any more – '

'Hold on a minute, Libby, and you can follow us back to the Canterbury Road.' Ian stood up and DC Robertson followed suit. 'Mr and Mrs Watson, I'd be pleased if you didn't talk about this to anyone until we've taken formal statements from you both. Will you come in to the police station in the morning?'

'Come in –?' Roland looked even more furious. 'Why the hell should we?'

'Because I shall have to bring you in if not, sir,' said Ian, still calm. 'Thank you for the coffee, Mrs Watson.'

'Bloody hell!' Libby burst out as soon as they were safely outside. 'I don't know how you didn't blow up. I'd have slapped the handcuffs on him after the first five minutes.'

Ian laughed. 'Which is why you're not a police officer. Now, come on, have you got room to turn that beast round? If you drove up here from Steeple Cross it can't have been pleasant.'

'It wasn't. It feels like the back of beyond here, as though no one ever comes near. And it was foggy.'

'It's cleared a bit now,' said DC Robertson. 'And most of the locals use the other end of the lane from Keeper's Cob.'

'So Adelaide told me.' Libby unlocked the car door and climbed in. 'Am I just to follow you? You're not going to tell me anything else?'

'Not tonight, I'm not, but I expect we shall have to talk to Adam again now.'

'Now you know who it is, you mean?'

'I didn't say that,' said Ian. 'I'll probably speak to you tomorrow.'

Libby followed the reassuring lights of the unmarked police car down Dark Lane. They led her back to the Canterbury road and, with a wave, sped off.

Ben was waiting with a sustainingly large whisky.

'I don't know why you say yes to these things,' he said, sitting opposite her after throwing a log on the fire.

Libby sighed. 'Neither do I.'

'Sheer nosiness, probably.' Ben grinned at her.

'Probably. And I'm a bit worried about Ad.'

'Why? He didn't do it.'

'But they'll keep after him as one of the people who knew about the house and the grotto and the fact that the owners weren't there.'

'They'll keep after Mog and the caretaker, too. And – I've just thought of this – Lewis, too.'

'Lewis?'

'He knew. He sent Adam and Mog there, and he's worked on the house.'

'Oh, bother, I told Ian about that.'

'Oh, I expect they'd have worked it out for themselves,' said Ben. 'So tell me what exactly happened.'

When Libby had finished recounting the details of her

29

evening, Ben looked thoughtful.

'Funny how both the Watsons knew the doctor yet not the wife.'

'It sounds as though she might be a typical Asian woman who doesn't go out except in a burkha,' said Libby.

'That's a terrible generalisation. And if she was one of those women, why is she married to a white Englishman?'

'We don't know that's what he is. Carl isn't a very English name.'

'But Oxenford is.'

'Hmm.' Libby stared into the fire. 'It's a real puzzle.'

'You're used to puzzles. Come on, finish that whisky and let's get to bed. It's gone midnight.'

Libby was woken the following morning by Ben with a mug of tea.

'Fran phoned,' he said. 'I managed to pick it up before it woke you.'

'What's the matter? This time in the morning?'

'I think she's had one of her "moments",' said Ben, 'but she wouldn't tell me.'

Libby struggled to sit up and took her tea.

'I'll call her in a minute,' she said. 'Did she say it was urgent?'

'No, because when I said I'd wake you she said it wasn't.'

'Right. I'll come downstairs.'

'Finish your tea first,' said Ben. 'It's only a quarter to eight.'

Ten minutes later, leaning against the Rayburn and watching Ben eat toast, Libby called her best friend, Fran Wolfe.

'Bit early, isn't it?' she began.

'Sorry, Lib, but I woke up with this – this sort of picture in my head.'

'Oh?'

'It was like a ruin. And it was dark. But I was staring up at the sky, or what I could see of it, and I couldn't move or call out. Any ideas?'

'Oh, yes,' said Libby heavily. 'I'd better tell you about it.'

'I'll come over,' said Fran. 'Make a big bowl of soup.'

'She didn't even ask what it was,' said Libby as she switched off the phone.

'Of course she didn't,' said Ben. 'She phoned here because whatever it was she saw or felt connected somehow to you. So now she knows you've more to tell her than a simple telephone call would take.'

'OK.' Libby pushed herself away from the Rayburn. 'I'll go and have a shower.'

By the time Fran arrived just after ten o'clock, Libby had chopped piles of vegetables for soup and had a new recipe for quick bread ready to go in the oven.

'Coffee?' she asked. 'Too early for lunch.'

When they were both seated by the fire in the sitting room, with Sidney the silver tabby sitting bolt upright on the hearthrug between them, staring into the flames, Libby began her story.

Fran let her go on to the end without interruption, although her eyes widened when Libby mentioned the grotto.

'So Adam's a suspect?' said Fran slowly, when Libby had finished.

'Well, not really, but they have to look into him.'

'Ridiculous.' Fran shook her head. 'Whoever it was planned this. If Adam ever hurt anybody it would be on the spur of the moment in self-defence.'

'How do you know it was planned?'

Fran looked surprised. 'I'm not sure. It just was. I don't know how I knew that any more than I know why I had the dream. Although I suspect that was because you and Ad have a close connection with it. Why haven't you told me before?'

It was Libby's turn to look surprised. 'Do you know, I have no idea. Normally I'd have told you immediately.'

'There was probably a reason.' Fran looked mysterious.

'A psychic one?'

'Probably.' Fran looked up and smiled. 'Anyway, now we need to know what the dream was about.'

'The body, of course,' said Libby. 'Only you dreamed it was you.'

'It doesn't help, though. After all, you know that the body

was found in the grotto with its throat cut.'

'Yes. And Ian says it was probably put there the night before.'

'Probably?'

'Well, I can't see someone carrying it in there in broad daylight.'

'What about time of death?'

'I don't know. Late Sunday night or early hours of Monday morning, I suppose. That's not the sort of thing Ian would tell me, but those seem to be the times the police are concentrating on for the alibis.'

Fran frowned. 'Was she killed where she was found?'

Now Libby really looked bewildered. 'I've no idea! Why?'

'Just wondering ...' Fran stared pensively into the fire.

'But what about?'

'About her. The victim. Why didn't I feel that darkness – you know? The suffocation.'

'Because she wasn't suffocated, I suppose.'

'Mmm,' said Fran doubtfully.

'Oh, let's forget it for now.' Libby stood up. 'I'll go and start lunch.'

'It's much too early for lunch.'

'Yes, but the bread's got to bake and the longer the soup's on the better it will be.'

Fran followed her into the kitchen.

'How's the panto going?' she asked.

'Oh, same old, same old. We have a new principal boy, Olivia, who read Drama and English at Kent uni. She's not bad. How's life down beside the seaside?'

Fran lived with her husband Guy in Coastguard Cottage on Harbour Street in Nethergate. Guy's art gallery-cum-shop was a few doors along, over which was a flat in which his daughter Sophie occasionally stayed.

'Oh, much the same. Did I tell you Chrissie's latest plan?'

Chrissie was one of Fran's daughters, married to the rather stuffy Bruce.

'Go on, what's she up to now?'

'She wants to move them all to France.'

'France? What for?'

'Because baby Montana will learn to be bi-lingual and they can start a vineyard. *Start*, mind.'

Libby exploded with laughter. 'From scratch? Can you just imagine! And what does Brucie-baby have to say about this?'

'This hasn't so far been revealed. I can't help feeling sorry for him.'

'I know what you mean.' Libby added stock to the softened vegetables in the pan. 'Now, do you want another coffee?'

'Are you going to have to get more involved with this?' asked Fran, when they had returned to sit by the fire.

'You mean the Dark House business? I will if they continue to suspect Adam.'

'Of course they won't,' said Fran. 'But they might make it uncomfortable for him.'

'And for Mog. And for that poor Johnny, who I suppose is at the top of the list.'

'What do you know about him?'

'Nothing really. Ad thinks he's an old hippy who's found himself a comfortable billet.'

'Does he drink?'

'Just because he's an old hippy? I'd have thought he was more likely to be going round in a fug of dope. Why, anyway?'

'I thought about the local pub. Wouldn't they know about what goes on up there?'

'I called in there when I was looking for Dark House,' said Libby, frowning at the memory. 'I wouldn't have thought it was an old hippy's favoured drinking place. Rather more "county" than "country", if you know what I mean. And it's not really near the house.'

'From what you say, the house isn't really near anywhere.'

'No.' Libby shook her head. 'But I don't know the area. There might be another pub, or even another village, nearer than Steeple Cross.'

'What about Keeper's Cob?'

'I don't know. I've never been there.' Libby noted the look

33

on Fran's face. 'What? Are you thinking what I think you're thinking?'

Fran beamed. 'Of course I am. Hurry up with the soup.'

Chapter Six

'If we go in from Keeper's Cob,' said Fran, peering ahead at the road where Dark Lane led off to the right past The Dragon, 'we go straight along here and turn right at the crossroads.'

'I think so,' said Libby nervously. 'It was dark and foggy. I didn't really know where I was going.'

'It's foggy now,' said Fran. 'Eerie.'

'You wait till we get into that lane,' said Libby. 'It's proper scary.'

Sure enough, at the crossroads a signpost pointed right towards Keeper's Cob. This lane, too, grew narrower and headed slightly downhill. Fran kept in low gear, and as they rounded a bend. Libby pointed.

'There. There's Dark Lane.'

'But no village,' said Fran. 'It must be further on.'

She drove on, going further downhill until another lane branched off to the right with an old-fashioned and battered fingerpost, which read "Keeper's Cob ½". Cautiously, she turned in.

Here, the road surface was covered in fallen leaves the way Dark Lane had been, and the trees once more closed in around them, wavering in the mist.

'Told you,' said Libby. 'Scary.'

A small house, originally painted white, appeared on a slight rise to their left. A thick-set man stumped around the corner leading a flock of noisy hens and didn't spare them a glance. Fran ploughed on.

At another bend in the road stood a short row of terraced cottages, two with smoke issuing from the chimneys, and almost opposite them a lowering building with dilapidated thatch. Fran stopped the car, and they could hear a faint squeak from an indistinguishable sign swinging from a rusty arm.

'Pub,' they said together.

'Do you think this is Keeper's Cob?' asked Libby. 'There's not much of it.'

'Perhaps there's more further on,' said Fran. 'And this can't be the only way in.'

'Let's go and ask in the pub,' said Libby. 'We can always say we're lost.'

'Which is true,' said Fran. 'I don't think I could find my way back.'

She pulled in to the side of the road and switched off the engine. 'God, this is isolated.'

'And yet if you look on a map it's densely populated. Big commuter area.' Libby got out of the car.

'This doesn't look like commuter heaven.' Fran looked round at the terrace of cottages and back up towards the small white house.

'Come on, let's find out.' Libby led the way towards the black door of the pub, pausing to look up at the sign. 'Can you see what it says? I suppose it *is* a pub?'

'The Feathers,' said Fran, squinting. 'See? You can just make out the three feathers.'

'Hmm,' said Libby and pushed open the door.

To their surprise, the tiny bar was full. The all-male crowd fell silent as they walked in, and Libby clutched Fran's arm.

'Excuse me,' she said in a quavering voice, and cleared her throat.

'Is this Keeper's Cob?' Fran asked in a much stronger voice. Libby glanced at her admiringly.

'Aye.' A few voices answered.

'And is this the only pub?' asked Fran, improvising wildly. 'Only we were looking for The Dragon.'

'Don't know how you come 'ere, then,' said one large, red-faced man with watery blue eyes. 'Dragon be down t'other end of Dark Lane. Steeple Cross.'

'Ah. Could you tell us how to get there, only we appear to be lost,' said Libby, feeling better and backing Fran up. 'Where's Dark Lane?'

'Back up along,' said another. 'Do be a bit difficult.'

'Best go through village,' someone else offered. 'Towards Canterbury.'

'Towards *Canterbury*?' echoed Fran and Libby together.

'Aye.' Several faces looked surprised.

'Through village,' the landlord came out from behind the bar and pointed. 'Carry on and you'll see a signpost for Steeple Martin and Canterbury. Go towards Steeple Martin and then you'll see a sign for Steeple Cross.'

'Oh, I know,' said Libby. 'Thank you so much.' She turned and almost pushed Fran out the door.

'You know where we are?' said Fran, as they made their way back to the car.

'No, but I know what we've been doing. Going round in circles. I bet there's a whole network of tiny lanes criss-crossing each other. Designed to confuse the unwary traveller, I reckon.'

They got into the car.

'Confuse, why?' asked Fran as she started the engine.

'Smuggling,' said Libby. 'This part of the world was where the eighteenth-century smuggling gangs brought their stuff up from the coast. I bet you anything you like that pub back there was one of the meeting places.'

'Perhaps Dark House was, too. Perhaps there's a tunnel. Didn't you say something about a grotto?'

'Yes, but that's Victorian. Although I suppose it could conceal an older tunnel.' Libby peered around her as the lane broadened out and took them through a few more houses. 'I also bet there's a short cut from that pub, or near it, to Dark House. It must be almost behind, as the crow flies. And,' she turned to Fran, 'I bet that Johnny was in there.'

'Why?'

'There was a particularly shifty-looking individual who melted back into the shadows as soon as we came in. Didn't you notice?'

'Ah. With a pony tail.'

'That's the one. But why did he? He doesn't know who we are.'

'We don't know who he is, either,' Fran pointed out.

'No, but he seemed uncomfortable.'

'You're letting your imagination run away with you,' said Fran as they emerged on to the Canterbury Road. 'We might as well go back to yours now. I don't fancy driving back along those lanes again.'

'I know. I suppose they might be better in summer.'

'When the woodland would be denser? No thanks. Spring maybe, as long as the sun was out. I'd hate to live up there.'

'Me, too,' said Libby with a shudder. 'Come on, time for a nice cup of tea.'

Lights were twinkling in Steeple Martin as they approached. Late November, and the sky was already darkening. The mist drifted down the high street and swirled into Allhallow's Lane, almost obscuring the track at the end.

'Will you be all right driving home in this?' asked Libby, as she let them in to number 17.

'It's main road all the way,' said Fran, 'and I'm not that much of a wimp.' She frowned. 'It was just those lanes. That whole area. Weird.'

'I'm glad it's not just me,' said Libby, going to move the kettle onto the hotplate. 'Now, I'm going to see if there's any life left in that fire.'

'What I can't imagine is why anyone, especially people like the Watsons, would choose to live there,' said Fran.

'You didn't see the actual house,' said Libby, giving the grate a good riddle. 'It's quite lovely, but just so isolated. Although, if I'm right, The Feathers and that little collection of cottages aren't that far behind it. We must see if we can find out.'

'When will Adam and Mog be allowed back?'

'No idea. If they're still suspects they won't be allowed back until they're cleared. I wonder how Ian's getting on with Carl Oxenford?'

38

'Yes,' said Fran, 'you didn't really say much about him.'

'There wasn't much to say. I don't know if he identified the body as his wife.'

'Ah, yes. What was her name?'

'Ramani.'

'I think it's almost definitely her,' said Fran. 'That kettle's boiling.'

'Well,' said Libby, five minutes later when they were sitting down with large mugs of tea, 'what shall we do now?'

'There isn't anything we can do,' said Fran. 'No one's asked us to interfere.'

'I could ring Adelaide and ask if she's all right.'

'It'll sound like morbid curiosity.'

'No it won't. She asked me to go over last night. It'll be a perfectly legitimate enquiry.'

Fran looked doubtful. 'All right. You know best.'

'That's the first time you've ever said that,' said Libby with a grin. 'Oh, bugger.'

'What?'

'I haven't got the Watsons' number. She rang me last night. I didn't ring her.'

'Lewis will have it.'

'He's on a shoot in Somerset, I can't really disturb him.'

'What about Adam?'

'I suppose Mog might have it.' Libby picked up her phone and pressed speed dial. 'Ad? How are you? Won't they? Oh, dear. I bet Mog's not best pleased. Listen, Ad, have you or Mog got the Watsons' number? She called me last night and I went over there, and I want to see if she's OK. Yes, yes, I'll tell you all about it. Come to supper – or are you working tonight?' She looked at Fran and made a face. 'Oh – thank you, darling. Now what about supper? OK, see you then.'

She put the phone down and scribbled something on the edge of the television listings magazine. 'In case I forget,' she said.

'You got the number, then?'

'Yes. Ad and Mog can't go back to the house because the garden is completely out of bounds and they're even digging up part of what they'd already done. Mog's furious, apparently.'

'Go on, then. Ring the lady up.' Fran sat back in the armchair and cradled her mug. 'Let's see you do your caring stuff.'

Taking a deep breath, Libby picked up the phone again and keyed in the number.

'Oh, hello, Roland,' she said screwing up her face in distaste. 'It's Libby Sarjeant here. I was just calling to see how Adelaide was. Yes? Oh, thank you.' She turned to Fran. 'I thought he wasn't going to let me speak to her. Oh, Adelaide. How are you this morning? Adam tells me they're digging up the garden?' She listened for a while, making various affirmatory noises until she suddenly sat upright. 'They have? Who? And why? Oh, so it was Ramani. Oh, dear.' She went quiet again, and Fran leant forward, trying to catch what was being said.

Eventually, Libby nodded. 'Yes, of course. I can't come today, but I'll pop round in the morning. No, no trouble. Or would you like to come here? You would? Right, I'll give you directions.'

'So what's happened?' asked Fran when Libby had ended the call.

'Quite a lot,' said Libby. 'They've got another suspect.'

'Really? Who?'

'Someone who called at the Oxenfords' house asking for Ramani. That's all Adelaide knows, but the body was her. Carl's distraught.'

'And she's coming here tomorrow?'

'She wanted me to go today, as you heard, but I thought it might do her good to go somewhere else. If the police need her Ian knows where she'll be.'

'Did she say anything about her husband?'

'No. I shall grill her tomorrow. I suppose you want to be here?'

Fran raised her eyebrows. 'Now, why would you think that?'

Later, Adam came to supper and Libby told him all she knew.

'Not much, really,' she said, as she and Ben cleared the kitchen table. 'But we'll find out more tomorrow. Now, we're off to rehearsal, but as it's Wednesday, Patti and Anne will be in the pub later. Are you coming?'

'They're booked in at the caff,' said Adam. 'I'll see you later. I'll pootle along with them.'

The Reverend Patti Pearson drove to Steeple Martin every Wednesday afternoon from her parish of St Aldeberge to have dinner with her friend Anne Douglas in The Pink Geranium. After dinner, they usually met up with Libby, Ben and Peter in the pub. It was so that evening after a fairly disastrous pantomime rehearsal.

'I'm really not happy about our new Dame,' said Libby when asked by Anne what she was looking fed-up about. 'Tom, our usual Dame, has gone and moved away, bother him, and we've had to find a new one.'

'What's wrong with the new one?' asked Patti.

'I shouldn't say this, really,' said Libby, looking uncomfortable, 'but he's an Ac-Tor, dahling. Happier doing gritty drama, but thinks if Sir Ian McKellen can play a Dame, he can. Not always the way.'

'A Dame,' pontificated Peter, 'is always a bloke in a dress. She is not a drag queen, although there have been notable exceptions to that, but then, they were incomparable drag queens. The humour comes from this big, down to earth guy wearing the most outrageous costumes and not even attempting to appear feminine.'

'I love a good Dame,' sighed Harry theatrically. He had accompanied Adam, Patti and Anne to the pub after closing the restaurant. 'I'd make a very good Dame.'

'Too camp, ducks,' said Peter fondly. 'You could do it, Ben.'

'I have in the past,' said Ben surprisingly.

'Really?' All eyes turned to him.

'I didn't know that,' said Libby.

'When I did that TIE tour, remember? I told you that.'

'TIE?' asked Patti. 'What's that?'

'Theatre in Education,' said Libby. 'You know, those small troupes who go into schools and teach sensitive subjects by performing plays about them.'

'Or even proper plays,' said Ben. 'And pantomimes.'

'So it was pro, then?' said Adam. 'Paid?'

'A pittance, but yes, paid,' smiled Ben.

'Why don't you take over, then?' asked Anne.

'Not done,' said Libby with sigh. 'Remember we agonised over that panto director the other year? We didn't know how to sack him, but in the end we didn't have to. He admitted defeat and left of his own accord. But we'd need a bloody good reason to get rid of Sir Larry.'

'Is that his name?' Anne's eyes were round.

'No, just what we call him,' explained Ben with a grin.

'Let's not talk about panto,' said Harry, leaning his elbows on the table. 'I want to hear all about this latest murder.'

Chapter Seven

Fran was once more sitting by Libby's sitting room fire when Adelaide Watson arrived the following morning.

'This is my friend Fran, Adelaide,' said Libby. 'She and I have – er –'

'Yes, I know.' Adelaide's smile was a little strained. 'You're the psychic. Lewis told me.'

'Ah, yes.' Libby exchanged a quick look with Fran. 'Do sit down. I've got the coffee on – or would you prefer tea?'

'Oh, coffee, please. Thank you.' Adelaide perched on the sofa and looked round. 'Lovely cottage.'

'Thank you. Not as grand as your place, though.'

'No,' said Adelaide, sounding wistful.

'How are you feeling, now?' asked Fran. 'It must have been such a shock.'

'It was,' said Adelaide. 'And it keeps getting worse.'

'Worse?' Libby came back with a tray of mugs, cafetière, and milk.

'Well, it's the questions. Roland's had to go into Canterbury again today, and both the boys have been interviewed. The police seem to think someone in the family must have killed her, even though the boys had never even met her.'

'I thought you said there was a new suspect?'

'Yes.' Adelaide took the mug Libby held out to her. 'This man who came to Carl's door to ask for Ramani. Carl had never seen him before.'

'So who was he?'

'Carl doesn't know. The police were at his house at the time, and they whisked this person off straight away.'

'Unlikely to be the murderer,' said Fran. 'Going to the victim's house and asking for her. Why draw attention to yourself in that way?'

'Double bluff?' suggested Libby.

'Or perhaps the police already knew something about him?' said Fran.

'I don't know. And I can hardly ask, can I?' said Adelaide.

'So why have they asked Roland back again?' asked Libby. 'I know he had to go in yesterday.'

'And he wasn't pleased.' Adelaide sighed. 'He wouldn't tell me why he had to go back today. They haven't wanted to talk to me again.'

'You're not likely to have cut someone's throat,' said Fran. 'They obviously think this is a man's crime. Do we know the results of the post mortem?'

Adelaide looked bewildered.

'They aren't likely to tell anyone that unless it throws something up,' said Libby. She turned to Adelaide. 'Are you sure you're happy about staying out there?'

'No, I'm not.' She shrugged. 'Oh, it's a lovely house, but it's so remote. You wouldn't think you were in the south-east commuter belt, would you? I never wanted it in the first place.'

'But you keep spending money on it,' said Libby.

'I know. To try and make it more – oh, I don't know. More homely, I suppose.'

'That's why you spend so much time in London,' said Fran.

'Yes. It was different when Roland worked locally, but even then – I think he only bought the house to impress people.'

'That sounded bitter,' said Libby.

Adelaide smiled. 'I suppose it was. I'd sell the bloody place if it was up to me.' She put her mug down and sat up straight, looking determined. 'Now, what I wanted to say was would you look into this murder for me? I know you've done it before.'

Libby and Fran exchanged wary looks.

'We can't go round asking questions, you know,' said Libby. 'The police get very upset.'

'But you know the chief inspector, don't you? Couldn't you

find out things from him?'

'No.' Fran was firm. 'He's not allowed to tell anyone what goes on in an investigation unless that person is relevant. And he hates us interfering.'

'But you must be able to find out something?'

'Well, I don't know what,' said Libby. 'Unless there's something you could tell us that, perhaps, you wouldn't want to tell the police?'

Adelaide shifted on the sofa and her eyes slid sideways. Libby gave Fran a significant nod.

'Well,' began Adelaide, 'there is something ...'

'Yes?' prompted Libby, after a moment.

'I shouldn't really say this.' Colour had seeped up Adelaide's neck and appeared mottled in her pale face. 'But, you see ... well, if I told the police, Roland would know. And he – he's not – I mean – '

'Just tell us,' said Fran. 'We're not likely to tell Roland, are we?'

'I think Roland had an affair with Ramani.' Adelaide's words came out in a rush. Libby and Fran sat in silence staring at her. 'You see why I don't want to tell the police?'

Fran nodded slowly.

'Do you think he killed her?' asked Libby.

The colour left Adelaide's face as quickly as it had arrived. 'God, no! He'd never do that, and anyway, he was on the other side of the channel.'

And, thought Libby, look how quickly he got home on Tuesday.

'But if you tell the police what you think they would question him about it, and your life would become unbearable?' guessed Fran.

'Yes, because he would know I'd told them.'

'What makes you think they *did* have an affair?' asked Libby. 'I thought you said you hardly knew Carl or Ramani and had never even seen her.'

'Well, yes,' said Adelaide.

'Your husband said neither of you had ever laid eyes on the

45

woman. Although I didn't actually hear all of that conversation as I was making coffee.' Libby frowned. 'Ian hadn't confirmed that the body was Ramani's, so how could Roland be saying that? He shouldn't have known who the body was.'

'That was me. He wanted to know why you and I were witnesses to something, so I told him. I don't think your inspector was too pleased.'

'Oh, right. So carry on. Why did you think they were having an affair, and when did you see her? And,' said Libby, with a flash of inspiration, 'why didn't you recognise the body?'

Adelaide sighed, and Libby poured her more coffee. 'I've always known when Roland has an affair. There's something about him, and I know when he worked here he was known in the company as a –' she paused.

'Randy old sod?' suggested Libby.

'Yes. He was always so – oh, you know – hail fellow, well met. One of the lads. Loved being Captain of the local golf club, and always a great one for the ladies, as they say.' She sighed. 'Anyway, I was used to it, so I knew there was someone in his life over the last few months. I assumed it was someone in Brussels, it would be easy for him to have someone over there, but then one day I was driving up to Keeper's Cob and I saw … I saw …' She lowered her eyes.

'Roland and Ramani?' Fran said gently.

'Yes. In Roland's car. I almost didn't see it – you know what these lanes are like and it was parked in the trees. I'm afraid I drove past and then stopped and walked back. They didn't see me.'

'How did you know it was Ramani?' asked Libby.

Adelaide's colour came back. 'I had to go to the doctor for a routine matter and I saw her then. She came into the surgery briefly.'

'But you didn't recognise the body?'

'No. I only saw her head, and her hair was concealed somehow. When I saw her with Roland (and I saw her again when I dropped him off at Ashford one time) she looked a real glamour girl.' The corners of Adelaide's mouth turned down. 'I

46

think sometimes he pretended he was going to Brussels when he wasn't and she would pick him up. I suppose while Carl was in surgery so she could have the car.'

'Do you think that's why Carl called you? Did he know, too?'

'I don't know.' Adelaide's expression was agonised. 'That's what I thought straight away. And especially when he said the car had gone.'

'I think he probably did know – or suspect, at least,' said Fran. 'It makes sense. And he will probably tell the police, too.'

'I suppose he will,' said Adelaide with a sigh. 'Perhaps that's why they recalled Roland this morning.'

'I don't suppose there's anything we can do, then,' said Libby. 'They'll start making enquiries immediately. They'll check where he was on Sunday night and we can't do that sort of thing.'

'I suppose so.' Adelaide put down her mug. 'But I do feel better for talking about it.'

'Any time,' said Libby. 'And if I were you, I'd force your husband to sell that house.'

'I don't think I care what he does with it now. I'm going to move back permanently to London.'

'What about the garden and the swimming pool?' asked Libby.

'Oh, I hope they'll be allowed to finish that. It would add to the value. After all, if it is sold, I'll get half.' Adelaide stood up. 'Thank you for listening, and if you get any sort of inspiration,' she turned to Fran, 'I hope you'll let me know.'

'Do you think she means she's going to leave him?' said Libby as she watched her guest turn her car and drive slowly towards the high street.

'It sounds like it,' said Fran. 'And not a moment too soon, as far as I can tell.'

'But she's so scared of him. She wilts when he's there. And he's quite horrible – I don't know how he's managed to have affairs.'

'You saw him at his worst, don't forget. He wasn't out to

47

impress you, he was just angry.'

'I suppose so.' Libby collected the coffee tray and took it into the kitchen. 'That was a bit of a facer, though, wasn't it? I had no idea she was lying on Tuesday night. Do you want more coffee?'

'No thanks. What do you think we ought to do?' Fran perched on the edge of the table.

'Do? Well, nothing. As I said, the police already know by now that Roland was having an affair with Ramani, if we assume Carl suspected it as well as Adelaide, so they'll be looking in to his alibi. We can't help.'

'No.' Fran looked thoughtful. 'I do hate being hamstrung, though.'

'We've got so used to being able to investigate, that's the trouble. This time, we can't.'

'Unless I have any further – what did she call it? – inspiration,' said Fran.

'We didn't tell her about the first one. But she obviously knows all about you.'

'I'm still a bit confused about that, you know. The victim was alive, I'm sure of it.'

'I'm not sure what that means. For some reason I assumed she'd been killed somewhere else and dumped there, but you think she was killed in the grotto?'

'Otherwise, why was I staring up through the trees? Do you think I should tell Ian?'

'I don't think so. After all, they'll be a bit nearer actual time of death now, and they'll know if she was killed *in situ*.'

'Maybe. But it's frustrating.'

Fran slipped off the table and went back into the sitting room just as Libby's landline rang.

Wiping her hands on a tea towel, Libby picked up the phone.

'Libby, it's Ian. Listen, I know this is slightly unconventional, but I need your help.'

Chapter Eight

'You what?' Libby looked across at Fran and mouthed "Ian".

'We're sure that there was something between Mr Watson and the victim, but neither Mr Oxenford, Mrs Watson or Mr Watson himself will tell us.'

'Why do you think there was? Did someone tell you?' Libby perched on the arm of the sofa, eyebrows waggling furiously at Fran.

'Under questioning they've all avoided certain themes, although I can't think why. But when Mrs Oxenford's things were searched there was a distinct discrepancy between what we had been told about her personality and the clothes she owned. And Mr Watson inadvertently said something that made us think he knew that side of her personality.'

'What did he say?'

'I can't tell you that, Libby. But I want you to see if you can get anything out of Mrs Watson that she might not be willing to tell the police.'

'Spy on her?' Libby bit her lip.

'Helping the police,' corrected Ian.

'I'll see what I can do. Oh, and Ian, have you got a time and place of death, yet?'

'Well, yes,' said Ian, sounding surprised. 'She was killed where she was found, but the time of death's quite a lot later than we thought. Why?'

'Will you have a quick word with Fran, then?' Libby handed over the phone and listened to Fran explaining her dream to Ian. She handed the phone back.

'Interesting,' he said. 'I'll talk to the pathologist. It could be very helpful. So will you see what you can get out of Mrs Watson?'

'I've said, I'll see what I can do. I'll be in touch.'

'What did he want?' asked Fran. Libby told her.

'Well, we can legitimately look into it, now,' said Fran, 'but I don't see how we can split on Adelaide when she told us all that in confidence.'

'That's what I thought. Oh, bum. I meant to ask about the new suspect. How can we find out about him?'

Fran thought for a moment. 'Adelaide said she saw Ramani and Roland at Ashford International. That looks as though sometimes Roland wasn't going to Brussels when he said he was. It also means they meant to be together for a while.'

'But not long, or Carl would miss Ramani.'

'Right. So, a hotel near Ashford International?'

'There are hundreds – thousands.'

'Not thousands, Lib, although more than there used to be. Now, what's more likely, a town or country hotel?'

'Town – more impersonal. One of the chains. But how's that going to help us find the other suspect?'

'It isn't. I'm just trying to think of a way to point Ian in the right direction without betraying Adelaide.'

'And that would be how?'

'If we could identify them together at a hotel.'

'Fran! Have you run mad? What do you propose we do? Trail round every hotel in the vicinity of Ashford and ask if they've seen a white British male in his fifties with an Asian woman in her thirties? Don't be daft.'

Fran sighed. 'No, you're right. We'll just have to persuade Adelaide to tell Ian what she suspects.'

'I wish we could talk to Carl,' said Libby. 'How could we do that?'

'We can't,' said Fran.

'No.' Libby sighed. 'Oh, well. I'll give Adelaide time to get home, then ring her.'

'It would be better to speak to her face to face.'

'Oh, I can't face another drive over there.'

'Come on, I'll drive. And we'll go straight up Dark Lane this time, no faffing around Keeper's Cob.'

There was no fog around that day, although it was still cold under a threatening sky. Fran drove off the Canterbury Road and down towards The Dragon, where she turned right into Dark Lane.

'Fran, look! Stop!' Libby pointed to the ginnel which ran behind The Dragon. To where, on the steps of a white-painted house, hand raised to knock on a blue painted door, stood Adelaide.

'The doctor's house?' murmured Fran, but Libby was already out of the car running towards Adelaide.

'I'm so glad we caught you,' panted Libby, as Adelaide turned, startled, just as the blue door opened and a slight, dark-haired man stood there, looking equally startled.

'Carl – I'm s–sorry,' stuttered Adelaide.

Libby, trying to breathe calmly, stepped forward and held out her hand. 'Doctor Oxenford? I'm so sorry for your loss. My friend and I were just trying to catch up with Adelaide. It's fairly urgent.'

'This is Libby Sarjeant,' mumbled Adelaide. 'I suppose I'd better see what she wants.'

'Right.' Carl Oxenford nodded a bewildered understanding. 'Did you want to come in?'

'No,' said Adelaide hastily. 'I mean, I'll just see what Libby wants and then I'll come back.'

'Oh, right. Yes.' Carl nodded again, and leaving the door open retreated into the house.

Libby led the other woman down the steps.

'What do you mean by assaulting me like that?' hissed Adelaide.

'Assaulting you? What on earth do you mean?' Libby was indignant. 'We're trying to help you, that's all.'

'Help? How?'

'Look,' said Libby, anger suddenly coming to the surface. 'Twice now you've asked for my help – from me, a total stranger. And, when I'm continuing to do that, you accuse me of assaulting you? Honestly. You're not worth it.' And she turned away. Almost immediately, to her relief, she felt a hand on her arm.

'Libby, I'm sorry. I wasn't thinking.'

'No, you weren't. And unless you want us to go straight to the police with what you told us this morning, you'd better listen.'

Fran had got out of the car and come over to them.

'What are you so scared of, Adelaide?' she said now. 'Apart from your husband, that is.'

'My – ' The words stuck in Adelaide's throat and she shook her head.

'Well listen,' Libby went on. 'Just after you left, I had a call from Chief Detective Inspector Connell. He's sure there was something between Roland and Ramani, but no one will tell him anything, not you, Roland or Carl. Now we know that you have evidence, and when he asked Fran and I if you had told us anything,' not quite true, but nearly, 'we had to decide whether or not to tell him. We decided not to, but to try and persuade you to go to him voluntarily.'

Adelaide looked hunted. 'I can't.'

'Then we will have to tell him,' said Fran. 'We could be charged with withholding information if we don't.'

'Look, we know that you think Roland will know if you tell the police, but all you'll be doing is confirming what they already suspect.' Libby put her head on one side. 'If that makes sense.'

'I –' began Adelaide and stopped. Looking over towards the blue door, she said 'Will you come in and explain that to Carl? It affects him, too.'

Libby raised her eyebrows. 'So you know him better than you admitted, too?'

Adelaide's blotchy colour rose once more. 'No – well, yes. Will you come in?'

'I'll just lock the car,' said Fran.

Libby waited for Fran, then they followed Adelaide down a short corridor and into what appeared to be a library at the back of the house overlooking a high-walled garden. Carl Oxenford stood in the middle of the room, and from a winged armchair beside him rose a tall, distinguished black man.

'Um, Libby thinks I ought to tell the police,' said Adelaide.

Carl Oxenford looked slightly perplexed, as well he might, thought Libby, feeling increasingly uncomfortable.

'About what?' he asked eventually.

Libby flicked a glance at the other man, wondering why he was to be privileged to hear this conversation.

'The police suspect there was a relationship between your late wife and Mr Watson,' she said baldly. 'I know you both suspected there was, all I'm asking is that Mrs Watson tells the police of any confirmation either she or you might have.'

Carl Oxenford sighed and gestured to chairs set round a low table.

'I tried to avoid saying anything,' he said. 'It will serve no purpose. Roland was in Brussels when my wife was killed.'

'Anything you can tell them will help, even if it's only for elimination purposes,' said Fran.

Carl turned to the other man. 'Edward, tell them why you don't want to antagonise Roland.'

All eyes turned to the black man, now leaning forward eagerly with the elbows on his knees.

'My name is Edward Hall,' he began. 'I've known Ramani since university. I'm a historian, particularly interested in the English civil wars.'

'Wars?' said Libby. 'I thought there was only one?'

'It was more or less in three phases,' continued Edward, 'and in what is now called the second, there was an uprising in Kent, not just of Royalists, although they joined in of course. It culminated in the Battle of Maidstone on June 1st 1648.'

'Just after our house was extended,' said Adelaide.

'In 1643.' Edward nodded.

'I've never heard of the Battle of Maidstone,' said Libby. 'Have you, Fran?'

Fran shook her head.

'Unless you're a student of the period you probably wouldn't have. It's hardly as famous as Naseby or Edgehill.' Edward smiled at them both. 'Sorry, I'm not being very clear. You see, Ramani got in touch with me and told me that Mr Watson knew of a secret treasure at his house, which had been extended in 1643.' He looked from one to another of them waiting for a reaction.

'I'm sorry,' said Fran. 'I'm afraid I don't see ...'

'War between the King and Parliament was officially enjoined in 1642. Country squires, who would have mainly supported the King, knew there could be trouble.'

'Oh, I see! So whoever owned Dark House at that time extended the house and built what – a secret room?'

'I believe that's what Mr Watson thought.' Edward looked at Adelaide. 'Has he never told you, Mrs Watson?'

'No.' Adelaide looked down at her lap.

'Wait a bit,' said Libby. 'This is all very well, but what's it got to do with telling the police about Roland and Ramani?'

'Then Mr Watson would never let me investigate his house,' said Edward simply.

Libby and Fran looked at each other, taken aback.

'That's rather selfish, if you ask me,' said Fran.

'Look.' Adelaide gave a tired sigh. ' It was because of this that Carl found out about Roland and Ramani. She was excited about it, and told Carl she'd told Edward.'

'And I wondered how she knew.' Carl suddenly leant forward and put his head in his hands. 'God, I can't stand all this.'

'You have no idea why your wife should have been killed, Dr Oxenford?' said Fran suddenly. 'Why she had taken the car?'

He looked up. 'Burglary gone wrong, the police think. They found the car, you know.'

'They did?' said Libby. 'Where?'

'Somewhere in the woods. They've taken it in for – well, forensics, I suppose. She must have surprised a burglar.'

'During the night?' Libby frowned. 'She died during the night, didn't she?'

'I – I don't know.' Carl looked bewildered.

'But she wasn't in her nightclothes – she was dressed,' said Fran, cottoning on.

Carl shook his head. Adelaide and Edward Hall just looked confused.

Libby and Fran both stood up.

'We shouldn't be here,' said Fran. 'We'll leave you to it, but Adelaide, don't forget – tell DCI Connell. If you don't, we'll have to.'

They left silence in the room, but just as they were crossing to the car, Adelaide appeared on the steps.

'Look, I'm sorry I didn't tell you, but I couldn't think what it all had to do with Ramani's murder.'

'And didn't it occur to you that you could authorise Edward's search just as well as Roland?'

This time the colour fairly flooded Adelaide's cheeks.

'I couldn't. Roland wouldn't have him in the house.'

'Are you saying – racist?' began Libby.

Adelaide bit her lip.

'But he was having an affair with Ramani,' said Fran.

'I know.' Adelaide now looked thoroughly miserable. 'It doesn't make sense, does it?'

'You say Roland never told you any of this?' said Fran.

'How would he have got round looking through the house without you knowing about it?' said Libby.

'I don't know.'

'Well, *I* know,' said Libby briskly. 'We can do it. And Lewis will help. He's good on old buildings.'

'Not with Roland there,' said Adelaide, the hunted look coming back.

'Why ever not?'

'He wouldn't allow it.'

'Oh, for goodness' sake! He'd told Ramani, and she'd told Edward – and Carl, for that matter, so he must have intended to go through with a search.'

'What did he mean to do with me, though?' muttered Adelaide.

'He would have just told you when it was happening and

55

probably told you not to interfere, wouldn't he?' said Fran.

Adelaide nodded.

'Right. Now, are you going to call DCI Connell, or shall we do it?'

'Will you do it? Just tell them everything.' Adelaide turned to go through the door and then said, 'Why do you think he told Ramani and not me?'

'That was exactly what I was wondering,' said Libby, as Fran found a place to turn the car and they left Dark Lane.

'He told her to impress her, I expect,' said Fran. 'If she knew Edward Hall at university, it seems likely that she was a history student, too.'

Chapter Nine

'Time to recap,' said Libby, back at number 17. 'We now have Ramani Oxenford telling her old mate Edward Hall – who's quite a dish, don't you think? – about Dark House's history, which she got from Roland Watson, with whom she's having an affair.'

'And both Adelaide and Carl suspected it.' Fran sighed. 'Ian's not going to be pleased, is he?'

'He will be with us,' said Libby smugly. 'But he won't be very pleased with Adelaide or Carl. And I wonder why the police pulled Edward in?'

'No idea. Go on, you're supposed to be calling Ian.'

When Libby had finished telling him what she and Fran had discovered, Ian sighed.

'I don't know how you managed that, and I don't think I want to. What did you think of Edward Hall?'

'Apart from the fact that he's a bit of all right, you mean?'

'Libby!'

'Oh, OK. Well, he seemed quite nice, but a bit selfish. Very focussed on his subject.'

'It didn't seem odd to you?'

'Odd?' repeated Libby, frowning across at Fran. 'He's a historian with a special interest in the civil wars. Did you know there were three? I thought there was –'

'Yes, yes, Libby, I meant that he should come looking for Ramani just because of what she'd told him?'

'I think he probably would. He'd have been trying to get hold of her on her mobile, dying to get inside the house. They're obsessive, you know, these historical and archaeological types.'

'And you would know – how?' asked Ian.

'All right, all right. So, anything else we can do for you?'

Ian laughed. 'I'll let you know if there is. And if the Watsons do start a search in the house, I want you to go with them.'

'Oh, we'd already decided that,' said Libby. 'We're going to ask Lewis to come with us.'

'Oh, God,' groaned Ian. 'The whole Sarjeant chorus.'

'With bells on,' said Libby.

When Ben and Libby returned from rehearsal that evening, there was a message on the landline.

'Who was it?' asked Ben, coming in from the kitchen with two glasses.

'Adelaide, sounding very peeved that I wasn't here, and demanding that I ring her as soon as I came in.'

Ben laughed. 'And will you?'

'No, I bloody won't,' said Libby, plonking herself down on the sofa. 'Even though I am dying of curiosity.'

'Here,' said Ben handing her one of the glasses. 'So when will you ring her?'

'In the morning.' Libby curled her feet up under her. 'Isn't it funny? We've got Ian *and* one of the suspects both asking for our help.'

'Ian's asking you to spy for him.'

'I know he is, but let's face it, I don't owe the Watsons anything, and it's very interesting.'

'Born nosy, that's you,' said Ben.

Libby deliberately waited until late morning before ringing Adelaide Watson, ignoring the landline when it rang twice.

'Where have you been?' Adelaide's voice rose in a petulant shriek.

'I beg your pardon?' said Libby coldly.

'I've been trying to get hold of you since last night.'

'I know. I've been busy.'

'How? What have you been doing?'

'Is it any business of yours?' said Libby, ice seeping in to the airwaves. There was a short silence.

'I'm sorry. I've just been so – so –'

'Wound up?' suggested Libby. 'Yes, I can hear that. So what was so urgent?'

'It's Edward. Well, Edward and Roland. You see, Edward came round last night.'

'To Dark House?'

'Yes. And Roland tried to throw him out.'

'Ah. What did you think I could do?'

'I don't know!' wailed Adelaide. 'I didn't know who to turn to.'

'What happened in the end?'

'Edward left. But that inspector had been here talking to Roland in private and when they went he was furious.'

'He thought you'd told about the affair?'

'Well, of course he did, and I'd told you, so I couldn't deny it. I tried to tell him Carl knew, too, but he pooh-poohed the idea. Said I'd been spying on him.'

'What did you say?' asked Libby.

'I – I – nothing.' Something in Adelaide's tone told Libby this wasn't all there was to it.

'Adelaide, did he hit you?'

Silence.

'Right, that means he did. You really should leave, you know. You said you were going to.'

'I know,' said Adelaide in a small voice, 'but where could I go?'

Libby hardened her heart. 'What about one of your sons?'

'Oh, I couldn't! Besides, they wouldn't have room for me.'

Libby suppressed the thought of how her own children would react in this situation. Adelaide wasn't Libby, and her sons were not like Adam, Belinda and Dominic.

'Anyway,' said Adelaide, her voice sounding stronger, 'Carl and Edward said if I leave the house, he could try and maintain that I abandoned him and decide I couldn't have half the value.'

'I don't think he could do that,' said Libby, 'but he might try and prevent you going back to it. When did you speak to Carl and Edward about it?'

'After you left Carl's yesterday afternoon. And Edward

59

called me this morning.'

'Where's Roland now?'

Adelaide sighed. 'He had to go back to the station to give an amended statement. I think they're trying to break his alibi.'

'I'm not surprised,' said Libby.

'You didn't like him,' stated Adelaide.

'No,' said Libby. 'Do you?'

There was a pause. Then 'No,' said Adelaide in a surprised voice. 'I don't. I thought I loved him still, but even that's not true any more.'

'I should start making plans,' said Libby. 'You have every reason to leave him. Have you got a solicitor?'

'Only the one who did the conveyancing on this house. I could ask her.'

'More to the point, what about this treasure Roland said he knew about? Has he said any more?'

'No. That was what Edward wanted to ask, but Roland said he wasn't going to let a – well – a black man in to the house.'

'You could,' said Libby slowly, 'tell him to leave. You'd be entitled to, I should think. Is the house in joint names?'

'Oh, yes. The solicitor made sure we knew all about tenants in common and joint tenants. She got quite firm with Roland.'

'I bet.' Libby grinned. 'She sounds like the one for you, then. See what the legal position is. It might be that he will refuse to leave his own house, and of course, who could blame him, but you could always insist that you ask whoever you like into it.'

Adelaide sighed. 'I'll try, but I've never been good at standing up to him.'

'Meanwhile, do you think Edward would talk to me? I'm really interested in his research, and if we're going to help look for this treasure, or whatever it is – if Roland lets us, of course – I need to know more about it.'

'I'm sure he would. May I give him your phone number?'

'Good idea. And listen Adelaide, ring me if you need to, just be aware I can't always come immediately.'

'I know.' Adelaide sounded defeated. 'You have a life.'

'So do you, so chin up. I'll speak to you soon, and keep me

up to date.'

Libby relayed this conversation to Fran immediately she stopped speaking to Adelaide.

'If Edward agrees to meet you, I want to be there, too,' said Fran. 'I've got a feeling I might be of use in this search, if there is one.'

'I wasn't thinking of meeting him, just a phone call.'

'No, we must meet him. We need to know if he's a suspect as well as everything else.'

'We–ell,' said Libby, 'I might slobber all over him, but you know best. And he is a suspect, we know that.'

'I mean a suspect to us, not the police. And you will *not* slobber.'

Libby decided she'd better do a supermarket run to stock up on things not for sale in the village. As the nearest supermarket was either the small one in Nethergate or a choice of larger ones in Canterbury, this was not something done regularly and usually ended up in confusion, Libby being unable to resist a bargain.

Coming home laden with bulk buy toilet rolls and several packets of cereal on the buy one get one free basis, Libby saw the red light flashing on the answerphone.

'Give us a chance,' she grumbled, as Sidney streaked through her legs and out the front door.

Finally unloaded, and having found places for most of her purchases, Libby made herself a cup of tea and listened to the message.

'It's Edward Hall, here, Mrs Sarjeant. I'd like to talk to you – and your friend. Mrs Wolfe, is it? Would you ring me back?'

Libby punched in the number he gave.

'We'd like to talk to you, too, Mr Hall,' she said, after pleasantries had been exchanged. 'When would suit you?'

'I'm staying in the area, so anytime. This afternoon? Tomorrow?'

'Not tomorrow, Mrs Wolfe is busy on Saturdays. I could probably get her to come here this afternoon.'

'Could you? I'm in Canterbury, so how long would it take

me to get to you?'

'Half an hour or less. I'll call you back when I've spoken to Fran.'

Five minutes later the meeting was set up and Libby did a quick tidy of the sitting room, Sidney sitting on the table in the window with his ears back in disapproval. Fran arrived minutes before Edward Hall and made Libby go into the kitchen and stop flapping while she remained as the welcoming committee.

'What was it you wanted to talk to me about?' Edward Hall sat in the armchair on one side of the fire, while Libby and Fran sat side by side on the sofa.

'The whole situation, really,' said Fran. 'Ramani, and how much she told you of what she knew about Dark House. Whether she had any enemies.'

'She had a trail of ex-lovers, if that's what you mean.' Edward Hall looked amused.

'Ah,' said Libby. 'So did she tell you about the affair with Roland Watson?'

'No, I knew nothing about that. She just said it was a house belonging to a friend.'

'Mr Hall, why do you think it's important?' asked Fran.

'Please call me Edward.' He smiled at them both. 'Then I won't feel as though I'm in the headmaster's office.'

'Then I'm Libby, and this is Fran.' Libby stood up. 'Would you like tea? Or coffee?'

When all three were supplied with tea, Libby began again.

'So Ramani rang you and told you – what exactly?'

'She said a friend of hers and her husband's had an old house which dated back to the mid seventeenth century, and that in an old document held at the local church there was reference to a treasure hidden in the house.'

'And you got excited about it,' said Fran with a smile.

'Well, the dates fitted. I told you about the Battle of Maidstone, didn't I? You see, it was quite a ragbag of people who tried to stand against Parliament and the trained army under General Fairfax. Country squires, some of the landed gentry and some of the labourers and farm workers. Completely unfitted for warfare, and it wasn't like previous battles, it was man against man, up and down the streets of Maidstone. It's thought that many of the men left hidden gold to look after their families if they didn't return.' He looked solemn. 'And of course, many of them didn't.'

'How do you know it was Dark House?' asked Libby.

'She told me,' said Edward, looking surprised. 'Dark House, Dark Lane. I asked her exactly where it was, you see, to see if it could be linked to my research. I checked it out on the British Listed Buildings website, and as it happens, it's not far off the route that General Rich took to recapture the castle at Dover – '

'Hang on,' said Libby. 'General Rich? Don't forget neither Fran nor I are history scholars.'

'Sorry.' Edward looked sheepish. 'I tend to get carried away.' He sipped gingerly at his tea. 'Oh, that's good. I usually get dusty teabag stuff.'

Libby grinned. 'You go to the wrong places. Well, go on. Who was General Rich?'

'He was a Parliamentarian under General Fairfax, but I'm not really interested in him. You see, there is very little known about the people involved in the battle, and I'm trying to put some flesh on their bones. Archaeology hasn't helped much so far, and we don't know where to look except for the few obvious places. We have some names: Sir William Brockman, Sir John Mayney and Sir Gamaliel Dudley, but that's about all.'

'And you think Dark House could have been owned by one of the rebels?' said Fran.

'That's what Ramani thought.'

'I wonder which church holds the document?' mused Libby.

'Is there one at Steeple Cross?' asked Edward.

'I've not seen one, but that doesn't mean to say there isn't,' said Libby, and went to fetch her laptop. 'Here, look.' She turned the screen towards Edward. 'St Mary's.'

'Where exactly?' asked Fran.

'Well!' Libby looked triumphant. 'About five minutes from Carl Oxenford's house. No wonder Ramani found out about it!'

Chapter Ten

'How do you make that out?' asked Fran.

'Well, she was bored, wasn't she? I bet she just wandered in and ...' Libby stopped.

'And just happened across a document about Roland's house?' Fran shook her head.

'What religion was she, Edward?' Libby turned to her guest.

'She was an atheist,' said Edward. 'She broke with her family in Birmingham and more or less ran away to go to university. When I met her, she was determined to throw off all the shackles, as she put it. And she did.' He smiled with reminiscent fondness.

'Might she have gone to St Mary's with Carl?' asked Fran.

'I've no idea, but I don't think it's so silly to think she would have gone to St Mary's to see if she could find any trace of Dark House or its owners. She was a historian, and she'd been a researcher for a firm of heir hunters at one time, so she knew the value of church records.'

'So, can we go?' asked Libby.

'What, now?' Fran's eyebrows rose.

'No, not now. But can we go – perhaps Monday? Not a good idea to go at the weekend is it, with weddings on Saturdays and services on Sundays.'

'I'm sure we could,' said Edward. 'Are you sure you want to be involved in this?'

'Adelaide has asked us,' said Libby, conveniently forgetting to mention that so had the police. 'Anyway, before we go any further along that route, you said you wanted to see us. What about?'

Edward looked uncomfortable. 'This is going to sound weird,' he said. 'Adelaide said you were friendly with the police in charge of the investigation.'

'Yes?' Libby was wary.

'I wonder if you could find out if I'm a serious suspect?'

Fran and Libby looked at each other.

'I'm not sure the police would divulge that sort of information,' said Fran. 'It's not as if we're involved in the case, we simply came in to it by accident.'

'But Adelaide told us she'd asked you to tell the police something – after we'd seen you at Carl's house.'

'Yes, because she couldn't face it,' said Libby, 'and because the DCI will accept what we say even if it is hearsay. That's all. Why are you worried?'

Edward sighed and sat back in his chair. 'It's difficult.' He looked down at his hands. 'It's being black, you see.'

Libby and Fran exchanged looks.

'Go on,' said Fran. 'Are you talking about discrimination?'

'Yes.' Edward looked up. 'I know it sounds ridiculous, but I got so used to the stop and search routine when I was younger, and even now, occasionally, I will be pulled over by traffic cops who don't believe that a black man would be driving an expensive car.'

Libby gasped. 'That can't be true!'

Edward gave a wry smile. 'Oh, it is, believe me. And I'm afraid I was convinced that was why I was pulled in so quickly when I arrived on Carl's doorstep. I didn't even know Ramani was dead.'

Libby was pink with outrage. 'Ian would never behave like that!'

'Who's Ian?' asked Edward.

'DCI Connell,' said Fran. 'No I'm sure he wouldn't. At least not for a racially-motivated reason.'

'It was a uniformed sergeant and a detective constable who took me in,' said Edward. 'I was questioned by the DC – Robinson, I think he said.'

'Robertson,' said Libby. 'Surely he didn't bring you in off

his own bat?'

'The sergeant did, but the DC called someone.'

'So what happened when he questioned you?'

Edward shrugged. 'Not a lot. He just asked me what I was doing there, how I knew Ramani, where I'd been for the last week and asked me to sign a statement. Oh, and to inform the police of any change of address.'

'And where had you been?' asked Fran.

'At home.' He grinned suddenly, teeth startlingly white against the dark skin. 'And I have plenty of people to vouch for me – even overnight.'

'Oh, good,' said Libby, clearing her throat.

'So why do you think you might be a suspect?' asked Fran.

Edward shrugged again. 'Because I'm used to it. I would have sworn that the sergeant wanted to get at me, and I'd bet anything that my face is up there on their incident room white board.'

'It sounds ridiculous to me,' said Libby, 'but I suppose we could ask, Fran?'

Fran, remembering that Ian had already asked if they didn't think Edward turning up was "odd", slowly nodded. 'We could.'

'There,' said Libby. 'We'll ask Ian – carefully – and we'll pay a visit to St Mary's on Monday.' She turned to Fran. 'Shall we ask Patti if she's got an in with the vicar?'

'Who's Patti?' Edward looked from one to the other.

'A vicar friend of ours. The thing is, most village churches round here are served by one vicar to three or four churches, so sometimes access is dificult. There are usually churchwardens one can apply to, but Patti might guarantee us entry, and a look at any documents there might be.'

'Did Ramani actually say "document"?' asked Fran. 'Might it be something else?'

Edward frowned. 'Come to think of it, I'm not sure she said. She'd found something in the church, so I suppose I assumed it was a document.'

'It could be something else, then,' said Fran. 'I think asking Patti's a good idea, Lib.' She turned back to Edward. 'We'll

66

give her a ring and let you know what happens.' She smiled. 'And try not to worry.'

'What do you think?' asked Libby as soon as their guest had taken his leave.

'I don't think he's guilty,' said Fran. 'Selfish, yes, but not guilty. I'd love to know exactly what Ramani told him, though.'

'And I'd like to know exactly what it was Roland told Ramani,' said Libby.

'Quite. And he isn't likely to tell us, is he?'

'No, but he might tell the police. We ought to tell Ian what Edward's told us anyway, and they may be able to persuade Roland to let Edward search the house.'

'If Adelaide doesn't,' said Fran.

'I don't think she's that brave yet,' said Libby. 'Come on, who's calling who?'

'I'll call Ian and you call Patti. Friday afternoon – is she busy?'

'Oh, I can't remember. I'll risk it anyway.'

To Fran's surprise, Ian answered his official mobile immediately and listened carefully to Fran's story.

'That's more or less what he told us in brief. He didn't say anything about the string of lovers, though.'

'Will you ask Roland Watson if Edward can search the house? With us, preferably? We're going to see if we can find this document Ramani told Edward about.'

'I already have. I think I told you I wanted you to be there if the search went ahead, didn't I? Well, very reluctantly, he agreed. We laid on thick that we had to find out if this story had anything to do with Ramani's death.'

'Well,' said Fran, 'that's true, isn't it?'

'Yes,' said Ian, 'but I'm damned if I can see why.'

'So do we make an appointment with him?'

'I will,' said Ian. 'Or rather, I'll get Robertson to liaise between you, Libby, Hall, and Watson. Anytime that isn't convenient?'

'Not Saturdays. I help in the gallery. And we were going to try and look at the church on Monday, but that isn't certain yet.'

'Right. Robertson or I will come back to you as soon as possible.'

Libby had finished her own call to Patti and was waiting eagerly for news.

'So, Ian's setting up the search,' Fran concluded, 'but he didn't say anything about Edward except that his story tallied with the one he told the police. What about Patti?'

'She only knows the vicar of St Mary's vaguely, and we were right, it is a shared parish, but she's agreed to look up the churchwardens and give one of them a ring to see if we can go along and have a look. She also said that the churchwardens might know what we're looking for, to save us a journey.'

'Oh, we'd have to go ourselves, wouldn't we?'

Libby laughed. 'I knew you'd say that. Patti said she'll ring as soon as she's got any news.'

Neither DC Robertson nor Patti called back that day, nor did they on Saturday. Libby restlessly and erratically cleaned number 17 from top to bottom and began to make Christmas lists. Ben escaped to visit the timber yard on the estate and collect fresh eggs from one of the tenant farmers.

On Saturday evening they went to The Pink Geranium for dinner and found Adam in his long white apron being head waiter and watching a nervous young woman with a benevolent eye.

'New girl?' murmured Libby, as he presented her with a menu.

'PhD student,' he muttered back. 'Very nice girl.'

Libby grinned. 'I'll have the quesadillas de hongos, please.'

'And a bottle of red?'

'Of course. Is Pete coming in?'

'No, apparently he's gone to Canterbury to see James.'

Peter's younger brother James lived and worked in Canterbury and was rarely seen in Steeple Martin other than for occasional Sunday lunches at The Manor.

At the end of their meal, Harry joined them bringing another bottle of red wine with him.

'I had your pollo verde all ready,' he told Libby accusingly.

'Now it'll have to go in Adam's freezer upstairs.'

Harry cooked mainly Mexican vegetarian food, but he made an exception in order to cook Libby's favourite chicken dish, for which he kept separate utensils, chopping boards and pans.

'Sorry, Hal, but it'll keep, won't it?'

'Not for too long. Now tell me how Ad's case is going?'

'It isn't Ad's case,' said Libby. 'Or ours, really.'

'But Ian's asked you to help.' Harry grinned. 'I have little birds all over the place keeping me informed.'

'I think Ian's stuck. They've talked to the owner of the house who was having an affair with the victim, his wife and an ex-lover. All of them have watertight alibis.'

'They're the best sort of alibis,' said Harry. 'One of them will be the murderer.'

'I don't see how,' said Libby. 'One of them was in France – or Brussels or something – one of them in Hertfordshire and the other at home somewhere. All alibied up.'

'No other leads?'

'Not unless you count the historical aspect.' Libby explained about the "treasure".

'There you are then,' said Harry. 'Somebody thought this woman knew where it was and after getting it out of her, killed her to keep her quiet. Simple.'

Libby and Ben looked at him with wide eyes.

'Bloody hell, Harry! You could be right!' said Libby.

'I often am.' Harry preened.

'Now you know why Ian wanted you to be on the search team,' said Ben.

'To keep an eye out for someone who looks as though they know what they're looking for?' said Libby. 'But that wouldn't be Edward.'

'No?' said Harry and Ben together.

'He's a historian and accomplished researcher. What's the betting he already knows what he's looking for?' said Ben.

'But not because he murdered Ramani,' objected Libby.

'Just watch him when you go to visit that church on Monday,' said Ben.

'If we go,' said Libby. 'I haven't heard yet.'

'If you do,' said Harry, 'remember Monday's my day off. I'll come and provide the escort.'

'I remember what happened last time you provided me with an escort on a Monday,' said Libby darkly.

Ben laughed. 'The girls'll be fine, Hal. They're going to visit a church in broad daylight. Don't worry. Patti might not even be able to set it up.'

But she did. And on Monday morning, Libby, Fran, Edward Hall and Patti herself met at the lychgate of St Mary's, Steeple Cross to inspect the memorial tablet of Sir Godfrey Wyghtham.

Chapter Eleven

'A tablet?' exclaimed Libby.

'Yes.' The Reverend Toby Morley looked surprised. Patti grinned.

'Sorry, Mr Morley,' she said. 'Mrs Sarjeant was expecting something more spectacular, I think.'

The Reverend took off his glasses and smiled at Patti. 'Please call me Toby. And there is the Parish Register, even though the date was problematic.' He looked round at the puzzled circle of faces. 'Civil War, you see. All the upheaval within the church – there were gaps between 1642 and 1660.'

'How did you know who we were looking for?' asked Fran. 'We didn't.'

'Patti, here – may I call you Patti? – told me why you were looking, and I remembered the young lady immediately. Very striking.'

'Ramani?' Libby looked questioningly at Patti.

'It would appear so. She came asking for information about previous owners of Dark House,' said the Reverend Toby. 'Of course it wasn't Dark House then, but Wyghtham Hall. That was how I knew what I was looking for. And of course she had a date – 1648.'

'May we see?' Edward Hall spoke for the first time. 'I'm the historian of the party, Edward Hall.' He held out a hand, which the Reverend Toby shook warmly.

'I'll show you the tablet first,' he said, leading the way down the central aisle, and to a dark corner beside the door to the vestry. 'There.'

It was a stone tablet, with very little decoration, unlike

several they had passed on the way. A coat of arms, very worn, headed the inscription.

"In Memorie of Godfrey Wyghtham, late of Wyghtham Hall in this parish, who departed this life April 3rd 1664 and Rebecca, wife of above died September 15th 1665".

'But that's 1664,' said Libby, 'not 1648.'

Reverend Toby smiled again. 'But that meant he must have been living at the Hall in 1648, or at least to have had a connection to it, even if his father was still alive and living there, do you see?'

'He survived the war, then,' murmured Edward, 'and so did she. But there's no reference to hidden treasure. What was Ramani thinking of?'

'Come and see the parish register. Not that it mentions treasure, either. But there's a gift to the parish.'

The relevant book was already laid out for them in the vestry.

'This is very unusual, but there is a note under the entry for Rebecca's death that "her portion" is given to the parish.' The Reverend Toby pointed and Edward bent to peer at it.

'If found,' Edward said suddenly, looking up in triumph. 'That's it!'

'If found?' they all repeated. The Reverend Toby bent closer, then stood up with a puzzled expression on his face. 'You know I'd never noticed that! I suppose you're better at deciphering these things than I am.'

'So what does it mean?' asked Fran.

'I guess it means that there is money somewhere that, if found, will go to the church. I wonder if she had a will?'

'Oh, don't,' said Libby. 'We've done wills. And they were all lodged somewhere – Canterbury, was it? – before you could properly check them all.'

'We could check,' said Fran. 'What date did old Bartholomew die?'

'Who?' said Edward and Toby together.

'A man we looked into last summer,' said Libby. 'And he was seventeen hundreds, anyway. The wills of these people wouldn't be recorded, would they?'

'Not if they were made before 1660,' said Edward, 'and they probably were. So we're unlikely to be able to look it up. I just wondered if there's any other record in the church?'

'Not that I know of.' Toby shook his head. 'I wonder what it means?'

'Well,' said Libby slowly, 'we know that Ramani was told there was a treasure in the house. She came here to check out if there was any indication of the owner, like a good little historian, and obviously interpreted that text in the same way that Edward did.'

'Wild goose chase?' asked Patti.

'No, not at all,' said Fran. 'We're following Ramani's trail, which may well lead to finding out who murdered her.'

The Reverend Toby blenched. 'Oh, dear! I'd forgotten that.' He escorted them to the door and shook hands with them all. 'Will you keep me informed?' he asked Patti, who assured him she would.

'So what now?' asked Libby, as they walked back down the lane towards Carl's surgery.

'We need to find out what Roland told Ramani,' said Fran. 'She would never have gone to the church otherwise. She must have known Godfrey Wyghtham's name.'

'But will he tell us?' said Edward. 'He doesn't strike me as particularly forthcoming.'

'The police are going to ask him,' said Libby. 'It's relevant to Ramani's murder.'

'He could still refuse to tell them, or lie.' Patti dug her hands in her pockets and frowned. 'Murderers do lie to the police.'

'You think he's the murderer?' asked Libby.

'He seems to be the obvious suspect,' said Patti. 'Doesn't he?'

'I don't know,' said Fran doubtfully. 'After all, he was in Brussels at the time, and if they were having an affair …'

'I think,' said Edward suddenly, 'that he told her about the so-called treasure to keep her interest. And if he knew Godfrey's name that would add weight to it.'

'But there's the "if found" in the parish records,' objected

73

Libby.

'That might mean nothing,' said Edward. 'There are many odd notes in parish records. But Ramani would have taken it as confirmation of what she'd been told.'

'Let's just hope Ian gets Roland to set up our search,' said Libby. 'I was sure he'd come back to us over the weekend, but he hasn't.'

'Isn't that Adelaide Watson's car?' asked Fran, as they approached the Oxenford house.

'It's surgery time,' said Libby. 'Perhaps she's consulting him.'

'I don't think he's holding surgeries at the moment,' said Edward.

Libby and Fran looked at each other.

'They know one another far better than she admitted, don't they?' murmured Libby.

Back home in Steeple Martin, Libby did a little desultory housework, peered at the half finished painting on the easel in the conservatory and tried to decide what to cook for supper, all the while listening for the phone. By four o'clock in the afternoon, when it still hadn't rung, she called Fran.

'I can't understand it. Ian said he or Robertson would call us over the weekend. There's complete silence.'

'What do you want to do? You can't really call Ian to chivvy him up.'

'I could call Adelaide and ask her if Roland's heard anything from Ian. I want to know what she was doing with Carl Oxenford this morning, anyway.'

'I doubt if she'd tell you that,' said Fran. 'If she's concealed it up to now, she's not going to spill the beans just because you ask her.'

'I know!' said Libby. 'I could call Ian to tell him what we found in the church.'

'But it's not really relevant to his enquiry, is it?'

'It's not fair! Ian asked us to help, so did Adelaide, and now no one's telling us anything.'

'You'll just have to contain your soul in patience, won't

you?' said Fran, sounding amused. 'You're rehearsing tonight, aren't you? That'll take your mind off it.'

But when Libby walked up The Manor drive at a quarter to eight, her mind was still full of the Dark House murder, and it took a minute for her to realise that someone was waiting for her in the foyer of the theatre. Glancing up at the lighting and sound box at the top of the spiral staircase, she saw Peter making faces at her and pointing at the figure standing by the windows which faced on to the tiny garden, arms folded and legs apart. She approached warily.

'Yes, Reggie? Were you waiting for me?'

Reggie turned slowly, an expression of hauteur arranged on his face.

'I certainly was, my dear Libby. I need to tell you that I simply cannot carry on with this part the way you seem to want it.'

'The way *I* want it?' said Libby in surprise. 'I simply want the Dame played as a traditional Dame in a traditional pantomime.'

If anything, Reggie's nose rose even higher. 'It is lewd and vulgar. There is no sensitivity.'

Libby laughed. 'The traditional Dame is about as sensitive as a house brick, Reggie. Surely you've seen panto before?'

'Not since I was a child.' The nose descended a fraction. 'And I had to be removed from the theatre.'

'Were you scared of the villain?'

'No. I hated the Dame.' He had the grace to look slightly ashamed. 'I shouldn't have even tried to do this part.'

'Were you trying to exorcise the memory?'

'I think I was. I've disliked pantomime ever since, but as an actor I was convinced that I should be able to play all kinds of theatre.'

'Are you telling me that you don't want to continue?' Libby was conscious of conflicting feelings of relief and worry.

'Yes. I'm sorry to let you down, but I can't help but feel you'd be better off with someone less –' He stopped.

Libby grinned. 'I know exactly what you mean Reggie. We'll

be sorry to lose you, but I quite understand. I just hope you manage to get another job – preferably better paid than this.'

He bowed, then straightened up with a determined look and said, 'I shall forfeit the last two weeks of my salary in lieu of notice.'

'Don't be silly,' said Libby. 'It's already been paid into your bank. Now, off you go and better luck next time.'

'I knew that was coming,' said Peter, as the defeated Dame passed out of the glass doors.

'Did you? I didn't think we'd ever get rid of him.' Libby thoughtfully watched the retreating figure. 'But now we've got to find another Dame.'

'Ben,' said Peter.

Libby looked doubtful. 'Do you think he could?'

'He's done it before, remember? And he's always been brilliant in the comedy parts.'

'OK, I'll ask him.' Libby sighed. 'At least we'll be saving money. Perhaps we should give up having professionals in the company.'

'You're an old pro.' Peter grinned at her.

'Trouper, dear, trouper. But I'm not now. I'm not paid any more.'

'You're still a trained professional actor.' Peter turned to the auditorium doors. 'I'm going to put the workers on.'

'Who does he mean?' said a timid voice behind Libby's left shoulder. 'The workers?'

She turned to see one of the smallest dancers hovering in the doorway.

'Not people,' she said, wracking her brain to remember the dancer's name. 'Workers means the stage working lights.'

'Oh.' The dancer bobbed her head and followed Peter into the auditorium. Libby sighed. And that was one of the problems of having *non*-professionals in the company. She went to find Ben in the backstage workshop.

By the time the rest of the cast had assembled, including the two middle-aged ladies playing the Ugly Sisters – unusual, but Libby only had one Dame, so chose to make her Cinderella's

76

stepmother – she was able to tell them of the change in casting. She was amused to hear the murmurs of relief in her listeners, and, for Ben's benefit, decided to start with the boudoir scene, in which he made his first entrance, and sent the ensemble home, apologising for having wasted their time. She was also amused to see that several of them decided to stay, obviously to watch Ben put through his paces.

She found it rather odd to see her excessively masculine partner in the role of Dame, but had to admit he was going to be good at it. At the end of the rehearsal he smiled across triumphantly and she gave him a thumbs-up.

'Good,' said Harry, emerging from the darkness of the auditorium.

'When did you arrive?' Libby turned round.

'Ten minutes after Pete phoned to tell me what had happened.' Harry winked. 'My night off. I wanted a bit of amusement.'

Peter strolled up. 'Come back to ours and have a drink to celebrate.'

So it was almost half past eleven when Libby and Ben returned to number 17 and found the red light flashing on the answerphone.

'It's Edward Hall. I think I've found it,' it confided tinnily.

'You can't ring him back at this time of night,' said Ben.

'Wretched man,' said Libby, flinging off her coat. 'Found what? Why didn't he tell me?'

'I expect he thought you'd ring him back. Calm down. You can call him first thing in the morning.'

It was barely half past eight when Libby deemed it allowable to ring Edward.

'I'm having breakfast!' he complained.

'Sorry.' Libby sighed. 'Shall I ring you in half an hour?'

'No, hang on. I'll pour myself another cup of coffee and take it into the lounge.'

She heard the sounds of movement and finally, Edward's voice.

'I decided to go back and look for Wyghtham Hall! So far

we've been looking at Dark House.'

'I haven't even been looking for that,' said Libby, 'but I see what you mean. It makes sense.'

'Anyway, in some old documents dating from the early seventeenth century, before old Godfrey extended the house – '

'Oh, that was him, was it?'

'Yes, in 1643, the date on the front. It also has his initials entwined with the date. Anyway, before then, the cellars were in use and – get this – from one of them, a passage ran to Keeper's Cob!'

'Wow!' gasped Libby. 'That's incredible. When Fran and I went to Keeper's Cob we guessed that, despite all those tortuous lanes, it might be right behind Dark House.'

'It is. I've found an old map and the Wyghtham land extends right to the edge of the hamlet.'

'So they could just have wandered across the land to get there.'

'But they didn't. They obviously used this passage.'

'Was it a secret passage?'

'It doesn't seem to have been hidden, but it goes right up under another building.'

'Was brandy and tobacco being smuggled then? Or was that later?' asked Libby.

'It was actually after the Restoration that wool exports were forbidden, and in 1671 the King set up the Board of Customs. And of course, Kent was the centre of the trade.'

'So the passage could actually be one that was used in the old "Brandy for the Parson, Baccy for the Clerk" business?'

'It could. But what's more, there's no trace of it now.'

Libby frowned. 'But that doesn't help, does it? If it was there in the late seventeenth century, old Godfrey wouldn't have hidden anything in it, it would be too easy to find. And he died in 1664, anyway.'

'He might have hidden it somewhere inside the passage, and whoever had it bricked up didn't know.'

'What I don't understand is why he didn't get the treasure out and give it to Rebecca after he survived the war. She outlived him for a year, so there was plenty of time.'

'That is a puzzle, but then, as I said, those words in the parish records are open to interpretation, and we don't know exactly what Roland told Ramani.'

'And I still haven't heard when we can go and search the house,' said Libby. 'Do you think Roland's being reluctant?'

'I'm sure he is,' said Edward. 'He really is a most unpleasant man. I pity poor Adelaide.'

'Roland must have some documents, don't you think?' said Libby.

'Maybe, but maybe not, if we go with the idea that he simply told Ramani what she would like to hear.'

'Oh, he is a bugger!' said Libby. 'He's the key to all of this.'

Researching Wyghtham Hall on the internet wasn't as easy as Edward had made it sound. Libby assumed he had access to resources which were denied to her, and slammed the laptop shut in annoyance just as the phone began to ring.

'Ian!'

'Don't sound so surprised. Weren't you expecting a call from us?'

'I've been expecting it since Saturday,' said Libby.

'Sorry, Libby, but unavoidable circumstances. Have you spoken to Adelaide Watson?'

'Not since last week. Fran and I went with Edward Hall to see the church on Monday. Do you want to know what we found?'

'Later. Meanwhile, I think we might have to rethink the search of Dark House.'

'Oh, why? Is Roland being so difficult?'

'You could say that. Roland's dead.'

Chapter Twelve

Libby sat down suddenly on the stairs. 'Dead?'

'Yes, I'm sorry, Libby.'

'How's Adelaide? Is she all right?'

'Physically, she's fine. She's staying in a hotel at the moment. Do you have her mobile number?'

'I can't remember. You think I should call her?'

'She might need someone to talk to,' said Ian.

'Oh, no! I'm not spying on her under these circumstances. Anyway, won't her sons be there?'

'They may be, by now. Don't you want the details? I thought you'd be gagging for them.'

'Ian, that doesn't sound like you! But yes, of course I want to know – if you're able to tell me.'

'Neither Robertson nor I had been able to reach Watson by phone. Adelaide answered the landline, but always insisted he wasn't there. His mobile wasn't being answered. So on Saturday morning we went to the house. Mrs Watson wasn't keen on letting us have a look round, but we threatened her with a warrant. He wasn't there.'

'And you didn't find any secret passages or anything?'

'No, Libby, we did not. We decided to wait before raising a hue and cry, but yesterday Mrs Watson called us to say she was actually worried because he hadn't turned up. She seemed to feel it wouldn't be unusual in normal circumstances, but –'

'These aren't normal circumstances,' Libby finished for him.

'Quite. So we sent a team into the house again, yesterday afternoon, then put out a media call yesterday evening. You didn't see or hear it?'

'We were rehearsing yesterday evening and went for a drink with Pete and Harry afterwards. So, no.'

'Well, no joy there, except for the usual crackpot calls. So this morning we set up the usual procedures and sent a team to search the area.'

'And you found him?' said Libby, after a pause.

'We found him. In, of all places, the Victorian grotto.'

'Oh dear.'

'Robertson had the sense to instruct the team to start with that. The body was much better concealed than Mrs Oxenford's, but still …'

'How – ?'

'The same as Mrs Oxenford.'

'Oh.' Libby felt sick. 'Do you know when?'

'The doc wouldn't commit himself – a little wary after Ramani's murder, I think – and the post mortem isn't scheduled until tomorrow.'

'Do you mean because Ramani died later than he thought?'

Ian sighed. 'Apparently the signs were very confusing. We still haven't quite worked that one out.'

'Roland wasn't the murderer, then.' Libby thought for a moment. 'Pity. He was quite nasty enough. I wonder why he was murdered, though. Surely not by Carl as revenge?'

'We are, of course, questioning Mr Oxenford. I suppose, by rights, I should officially question you, too.'

'OK,' said Libby cheerfully. 'Your place or mine?'

Ian laughed. 'It's all right, Libby, I won't. Now tell me what you found yesterday in the church.'

Libby reported the visit to the church, seeing Adelaide Watson's car outside the Oxenford house, and Edward's subsequent discoveries.

'Is that why you asked me about secret passages?' asked Ian, when she'd finished.

'In a way, but that would have meant you going down into the cellar, and I bet you didn't.'

'We didn't even know there was one. Mrs Watson didn't say anything about it.'

'Maybe she doesn't know?'

'How,' said Ian testily, 'can you live in a house and not know there's a cellar?'

'She doesn't like the house. Never has. I don't suppose she's bothered to get to know much about it except for paying for constant updates and renovations.'

'Well, I think I'm going to suggest that she allows us to have a thorough search with a buildings expert. Lewis, perhaps, as he knows the house? You said he was going to be in on the original search.'

'Shall I ask? Or will you?' asked Libby. 'And will we still be allowed to join in?'

'I think so,' said Ian slowly. 'I think I want to hear if Fran senses anything.'

'Do you know she said herself she felt she might be of use. And she had that dream about being in the grotto.'

'Right. I'll make an official approach to Lewis – have I got his up-to-date contact details?' Libby recited them. 'Then you can make the follow-up call. Meanwhile, I'll get someone to call Adelaide to see if she wants to see you.'

'Not sure I want to see her,' grumbled Libby.

'Just for me, Libby, just for me,' said Ian with a smile in his voice, and rang off.

Adelaide did want to see her.

'I just don't know who to turn to,' she complained. 'None of my London friends want to come down here.'

'Have you asked them?'

'Well, no. But I know they wouldn't.'

What you mean is, thought Libby, you don't really know them that well. Fair-weather friends, probably.

'What about your sons?'

'Julian's here, staying in the hotel, but I can't really – well, I just can't. Not about Ramani and everything.'

'Well, I'll come over if you want me to,' said Libby reluctantly, 'but I can't stay too long.'

'That's fine. I felt so much better after talking to you and Fran the other day. Will she come too?'

'I can ask her,' said Libby. 'One or both of us will be with you this afternoon.'

Libby rang off and called Fran.

'Of course I'll come. How did she sound?'

'Petulant and irritated. How on earth those two stayed married I shall never know. I suppose we ought to ask her about the search. Ian will have been on to Lewis by now.'

They agreed to meet at the hotel in Canterbury at two o'clock and Libby rang Lewis.

'Yeah, I just got a message from your mate Ian. I'm free from tomorrow, so anytime after that. What about Adelaide?'

'Fran and I are going to see her this afternoon.'

'Give her my best and say all the right things, won't you?' Libby heard him sigh. 'Can't say he sounded like a great bloke to me. D'you know much about what's going on?'

'A bit. We'll tell you when we do the house search. Ian wants Fran's reactions.'

Just after two o'clock that afternoon, Fran and Libby found Adelaide in an anonymous room in a city centre hotel.

'I can't stand this,' she said. 'It's like being in prison.'

'It's not the nicest hotel,' said Libby. 'There are much nicer ones, and a couple of lovely ones just outside Canterbury. Wouldn't you prefer to be in one of those?'

Adelaide shuddered. 'No. I never want to live in the country again.'

Libby and Fran exchanged a look.

'What about the house?' asked Fran. 'Won't your boys want it?'

'No. They were away at school all the time we lived there. It was never home to them.'

'Where was home?' asked Libby. 'In the beginning?'

'Oh, London. South London.' Adelaide smiled sadly and reminiscently. 'I always dreamed of being able to live in one of the big houses on the edge of the common.' She brightened. 'I can now! Roland can't stop me selling the house, and I can live where I want. I'll stay in the flat until I find the right place.'

'Why can't you go back to the flat now?' asked Fran. 'Do the police need you to stay here?'

Adelaide shrugged. 'Well, of course they do. I'm a suspect now, aren't I? I was before, but now Roland's been – well, it stands to reason.'

'You don't mind?' Libby's voice rose in surprise.

'No, why should I? I didn't do it.'

'Why did you wait until yesterday before telling the police you were worried?' asked Fran.

'Oh, you know about that, do you?' said Adelaide. 'Well, I wasn't worried about Roland, exactly. I mean, over the last week I'd had my eyes opened, hadn't I? But I thought he'd done a runner, and I didn't want it to look as though I'd helped him.'

'I see.' Libby watched her thoughtfully. 'So is there any new information since we last saw you? We saw you were at Carl Oxenford's house Monday morning.'

Adelaide's mouth dropped slightly open.

'And we know he's not holding his surgeries at present,' put in Fran.

'If you must know,' said Adelaide, rallying, 'I was consulting him about Roland. He thought I should have told the police earlier that I was worried.'

'You didn't tell the police that when they came to search the house,' said Libby.

Adelaide turned from the window where she had been standing. 'Are you accusing me of something?'

'Of course not,' said Libby wearily. 'Look, you wanted to see us. Is there anything we can help with?'

Adelaide sat down. 'I want to know what's going on.' She plucked at the arm of the chair. 'I'm a bit scared, to tell the truth.'

Fran leant forward. 'I'm not surprised, so would I be.'

'Really?' Adelaide gave a half smile. 'I suppose you can't see anything? You know, like you have before?'

Fran shook her head. 'Sadly not. But the police want me on the search of the house to see if I can pick anything up. When is that to be, have you heard?'

'I've told your policeman friend he can do what he likes with the house now. I don't care.'

'So you won't want the swimming pool finished, then?' said Libby.

'I said before, if you remember, they can finish that because it'll add value. But I don't know when the police will let them back in.'

'Right,' said Libby. 'Oh, and you know Lewis is being consulted as a buildings expert? He asked me to send you his best wishes and condolences.'

Adelaide almost preened. 'How nice. Do thank him for me.'

Half an hour later, Fran and Libby were outside.

'Bloody star-struck about Lewis,' grumbled Libby. 'And what exactly were we there for? All she did was whinge. She's not even vaguely upset.'

'She wanted someone to whinge at,' said Fran. 'And she *is* scared. It was coming off her in waves.'

'Scared of what. though? If she doesn't know anything about Ramani's or Roland's murders she's not likely to be the next victim. And if she's the murderer, she definitely isn't.'

'But if she's the murderer, she'll be scared of being caught.' Fran looked into a shop window. 'Don't look now, but I think we're being followed.'

Libby obligingly peered into the window at an artfully arranged group of shoes. 'Who by? How do you know?'

'He came out of the hotel just behind us and has been hovering about ever since.' She pointed at the window, and Libby saw the reflection of a plump, dark young man in a suit looking into another window a few yards away.

'One of Adelaide's sons,' said Libby. 'Bet you. He looks just like his father. Why is he following us, do you suppose?'

'Because he wants to speak to us without his mother knowing, I expect,' said Fran. She turned round and walked over to the young man, who stood, irresolute, his face a mask of embarrassment.

'Are you Adelaide Watson's son?' she said pleasantly.

He nodded.

'And you want to speak to Mrs Sarjeant and me?'

He nodded again.

Libby joined them. 'Let's go and have a cup of coffee, then. There's a nice little place just down here.'

The coffee shop, still open but struggling a little against the might of the coffee chains, was warm and dim. The coffee was excellent, served by the owner and his wife, who scorned the pretentious title of "Barista".

'So, Mr Watson,' said Libby, when they'd ordered. 'What did you want to talk to us about?'

'Please call me Julian,' he said. 'I'm sorry if I alarmed you.'

'You didn't,' said Fran cheerfully. 'You didn't want your mother to know you wanted to talk to us, did you?'

'No.' Colour was seeping up his neck from under his tight, white collar. 'I know that sounds mad, but ...'

'What is it you want to know?' asked Libby, as their glass mugs in beautiful chrome holders were set before them.

'She said you'd been helping her since they found that woman's body. Are you private detectives?'

'No,' they said together.

He frowned. 'But you've been investigating?'

Fran sighed and Libby made a face.

'What happened was, we had a little local murder where I live and Mrs Wolfe here had a couple of psychic insights as to what was happening. It happened on another case and after that local people got to know and ask for advice, and sometimes, as in this case, the police themselves ask.'

'Psychic?' Julian's face registered scorn and disbelief. 'The police?'

Libby shrugged. 'Fine, if you don't believe me. No skin off our noses.'

Fran fixed him with a look. 'I'm sure your mother made you aware that we had connections with the police.'

Julian looked uncomfortable. 'Well, yes, she did. But I don't know how much of what she says to believe. That's why I wanted to talk to you.'

'OK,' said Libby. 'What do you know so far?'

'The first I knew about anything was when a couple of

constables came to my flat to ask if I knew who this dead body was.'

'Ramani Oxenford?' said Fran.

'I guess so. I was questioned twice, and Henry says he was, too.'

'Henry's your brother?'

'Yes. He's at uni in Leeds. I called Mum a few times after that during last week.'

'Not your father?'

'No. The next thing I knew was the police coming to tell me my father was dead.'

'We're very sorry,' said Libby.

Julian shook his head. 'I'm not. He was a bastard. I'm afraid Henry and I have both become suspects because it's obvious we hated him. He was foul to Mum, always having affairs. There must be hundreds of people who hated him.'

'Enough to kill him?' asked Fran.

'I don't know. I don't know what makes people kill.'

'And do you know anything about this supposed treasure?' asked Libby.

'No.' Julian now looked intrigued. 'Mum was trying to explain but I couldn't quite get it. There's something about this black man, as well.'

Libby held her tongue with difficulty, while Fran said peaceably 'Yes. Professor Edward Hall. He's a historian with a particular interest in the civil wars.'

'Oh? What has that got to do with us?'

'The date of your house? 1643?' said Libby.

'What about it?' said Julian, looking puzzled.

'That's in the middle of our civil wars,' explained Fran. 'We believe, from what your father told Mrs Oxenford, that something was hidden in your house at that time.'

'Treasure?' Julian's face lightened.

'It could be, but it may have been willed to someone, in which case it would pass to their descendants.' Libby watched as his face fell.

'I don't believe it anyway. He would have said anything to

87

impress a woman he was trying to sh– get into bed with.'

'We did rather wonder about that,' said Libby. 'We've found nothing, so far, but Professor Hall and a buildings expert are going to do a thorough search of the house within the next couple of days.'

Julian looked interested. 'Could I help?'

'I don't know,' said Libby. 'It's been ordered by the police, and they may not want the family there.'

'Oh. No, of course not.' Julian shifted in his seat and played with his coffee mug.

'Julian, did you ever meet Mrs Oxenford?'

'Didn't recognise the picture the police showed me. I knew him, though. He knew Mum and Dad, well, Mum, mostly.'

'Yes, he was their doctor, wasn't he?' said Libby innocently.

'I think so. But he was around when Dad went away. He'd only just moved, then. But Henry and I had both left home by then, so we didn't see much of him.'

'I don't think there's much more we can tell you, Julian,' said Fran. 'If either you or your brother have anything else to ask us, your mother has our numbers. Are you staying down here?'

'Yes, in that God-awful hotel. I'm going back to my flat as soon as I can. Mum says she's not going back to Dark House, anyway, so as soon as they let her off the hook she's going back to London, too.'

They parted outside the coffee shop.

'City trader, do you think?' Libby asked, as they watched Julian walk round the corner and disappear.

'Could be. But not a suspect,' said Fran.

'No?'

'Definitely not. Although he's as greedy as the next man. Would love there to be treasure for him to get his hands on. And you sounded quite convincing telling him it may be willed to someone.'

Libby grinned. 'And you sounded quite convincing when you called Edward "Professor". Racist little twit.'

'We don't know that he isn't a professor,' said Fran. 'Nor if

Julian is a racist little twit.'

'He's his father's son,' said Libby. 'Public school – minor, I guess – and just a little right-wing. Come on, let's go back and have an un-Julian-tainted coffee and find out when we're doing this search. Quite exciting, isn't it?'

Chapter Thirteen

Dark House looked charming in the bright sunlight of a crisp early December morning. Even the drive there had been pleasant, with views between the previously impenetrable trees.

'That was the fog,' said Fran, meeting Libby on the forecourt of the house. 'It turned everything into a sort of Birnam Wood.'

Edward and Lewis both arrived with Ian and DC Robertson.

''E wasn't takin' any chances of us not turning up,' said Lewis with a grin, coming to kiss Libby's cheek. ''Ow are yer, gal?'

'Simply didn't want to put you to any trouble,' said Ian, opening the huge front door with an equally huge key, before moving quickly to deactivate the burglar alarm. 'Now, where do we start?'

Lewis moved to the round table in the centre of the hall and spread out a plan.

'This is the architect's plan of the house when they moved in,' he placed another on top of the first, 'and this is when we did the alterations.'

'What about English Heritage? The listing?' asked Edward.

'Everything approved. Took 'em years.'

'I didn't think they'd been here that long,' said Libby.

'They come here when old Roland got his job down the road. Big step-up. The boys was at boarding school –'

'Told you,' whispered Libby.

'– and he and ever-lovin' Adelaide applied for permission almost immediately. It didn't come through until the eldest was at university. Then she commissions me and I gets the architect.'

'You, because of the TV programme?' asked Libby.

90

'Well, o'course!' Lewis sent her another grin. 'What else?'

'So you and the architect did a detailed search and survey of the house?' asked Edward.

'Sure we did. Proper architectural and archaeological survey, an' all.'

'And nothing out of the ordinary turned up?'

'The cellar.' Lewis pulled the top plan towards him and they all leant forward. 'See? It's blocked off. But in this plan –' he pulled the previous plan out '– you'll see a dotted line all the way under the back of the house into the garden. Although it was blocked up when we first saw it, it can't have been blocked up for that long.'

'Didn't the archaeological survey show anything up?' asked Edward.

'Said the bricks looked as though they was nineteenth-century, not seventeenth. Reckoned the passage went to the village behind.'

'That's what I found on the map,' said Edward. 'I believe the original passage, or tunnel, came up inside a building there. Probably a pub.'

'Or a church,' said Ian. 'Brandy for the Parson ...'

'That's what I said,' nodded Libby. 'But would it have been smuggling in the seventeenth century?'

'It doesn't really matter,' said Fran. 'What we're looking for is something Sir Godfrey could have hidden for his wife. Do we know how he died, yet?'

'Well, we know it wasn't in battle,' said Edward. 'He survived until after the Restoration.'

'And Rebecca outlived him.' Libby sighed. 'I still wonder if Roland wasn't just giving Ramani the run-around.'

'Even if he was,' said Ian, a trifle austerely, 'it could still be a powerful motive for murder.'

'Because someone believed him?' said Fran.

Ian nodded and Edward sighed.

'Well,' he said, 'we might as well look. There might even be a hidden room.'

'A priest's hole?' asked Fran.

'It's possible. Before the house was added to in 1643, the original building is said to date from around fifteen hundred.'

'I didn't come across anything like that when we was doin' up the house.' Lewis looked round at the panelled walls.

'Do you remember,' said Libby slowly, 'when we first met you we found something like that at Creekmarsh? And the outside didn't match up with the inside?'

'That's exactly the sort of thing to look for,' said Edward excitedly. 'And where was that? Creekmarsh? Where's that?'

Lewis grinned. 'Where I live. Come over one day. I'll show you round. Or me mum will.'

'Really?' Edwards eyes were shining. 'Where is it?'

'We'll come with you and show you the way,' said Libby, amused. 'I'd like to see Edie, anyway. Haven't seen her for ages.'

Ian cleared his throat. 'Can I remind you that we're doing the search *here*?'

'Sorry,' said Edward.

'So where shall we start?' asked Fran.

'I suggest the top and work down,' said Edward. 'If there's a secret room or hiding place, they'd want to be as far away from the hall as possible to avoid being heard or seen when getting into it.'

'I suppose so,' said Libby. 'If you heard the Roundheads coming you wouldn't want to be in the first place they'd look.'

'Worse, if it was earlier and they were looking for Catholic priests ...' Edward let the sentence hang.

'So, the attics,' said Lewis, and started up the stairs. 'We 'ad a great job with the attics. The dust! Cor, it was enough to put you off buildin' for ever.'

'Have they been restored?' asked Edward.

'Only tidied up. Couldn't touch 'em much, and they 'ad to be conserved, not restored.'

'Good.' Edward nodded his approval.

The house, Libby and Fran discovered, was a jumble of different staircases and passages. Meeting Edward, Lewis and Ian in the middle of a gallery which they had approached from a completely different direction – and staircase – Libby confessed herself thoroughly confused.

'It's fascinating,' said Edward. 'I've actually discovered a bricked-over medieval window, and when I check outside, I think I can trace a missing wing.'

'So whatever we're looking for may not even exist any more?' said Fran.

'That's quite possible,' said Edward, 'but let's not give up now.'

Ian, who was looking as disenchanted as Libby was feeling, sighed and nodded.

'Attics, then,' said Lewis. 'This way.'

He led them to a door set in the panelling at the end of the gallery, behind which he revealed a substantial ladder leading up through a large opening.

'No proper staircase?' Fran looked up in astonishment.

Lewis grinned. 'Not yet. There's more research to be done on where the original was, and what we might have to knock down to replace it. It's quite safe.'

Libby looked doubtfully at the ladder. 'You go first, then.'

Libby and Fran climbed carefully up the ladder with Lewis and Edward in front and Ian bringing up the rear. At the top, they found themselves facing an enormous Tudor brick chimney and a distinctly wavy wooden floor.

'They're all like that,' said Lewis. 'Haven't you noticed?'

'I suppose they are,' said Ian. 'Edward, where could you hide something up here?'

Edward went straight to the chimney and peered up inside it. Lewis began to go round the sloping walls and Ian started tapping the beams. Libby and Fran stood still in the middle of the room. Light came from small windows low down on the gable end walls, but Lewis switched on a working light on a stand in the corner which illuminated the dust which hovered in the air, disturbed by their presence.

'Here,' Edward called, his voice muffled.

Ian, Lewis, Libby and Fran crowded round the inglenook. Edward ducked and came out, dusty, but grinning, his eyes and

93

teeth white,

'See?' He pointed at a gap in the brickwork. 'It's a purpose-built hole. The brick is on a sort of swivel hinge.'

'What was in it?' asked Libby, as they all leant forward to see what Edward was holding.

'Sadly, nothing very exciting.' He displayed a roll of black cloth tied with what may have once been ribbon, both almost disintegrating.

'You don't know that,' said Ian. 'Anything could be inside it.'

'It doesn't feel like it,' said Edward. 'No one's got a newspaper or anything, I suppose?'

Ian, not surprisingly, in Libby's opinion, produced a snow-white handkerchief and spread it on the floor at Edward's direction. Edward then laid the roll of cloth on it and took out a pair of surgical gloves.

'Damn,' said Ian. 'I should have thought of that.'

'You haven't brought any?' Edward looked at him in surprise.

'Of course I have. I just didn't think to put them on.'

'Evidence bags, too, I hope?'

Ian's tone was as brittle as the roll of cloth. 'Of course.'

To Libby, the contents of the roll of cloth, which almost fell to dust as Edward unrolled it, were disappointing. What appeared to be a pewter, or possibly silver, chain with a rough Celtic cross hung from it, and a rather dull-looking ring.

'What are they?' asked Lewis, his head cocked to one side. 'Rubbish? Seen better down the Lane.'

Edward looked up. 'The Lane?'

'Petticoat Lane,' explained Libby. 'You must have heard of one of London's most famous rip-offs!'

'Certainly have.' Edward returned his attention to the jewellery. 'But this isn't rubbish. This,' he held up the cross, 'is enamel and diamonds set in gold.'

There was a collective gasp.

'Gold?' echoed Ian. 'How can it be?'

Edward looked up at him sideways and smiled. 'You just

wait until this is cleaned up.'

'What about that?' Libby pointed to the ring. 'It almost looks like a claddagh ring.'

'Well done, Libby.' Edward picked up the tiny object in surprisingly delicate fingers. 'It's the fore-runner of the claddagh, the gimmel ring. It turns into more than one ring, and the clasped hands are there to hold them together. I believe this one is black enamelled, and see this here?' he pointed to what could have been a stone set in the hands. 'That is, I think, a Vauxhall paste.'

'A what?' they repeated together.

'They were glass gems set on a mirrored back. A bit of a con, really, but now very rare.'

'I honestly don't know how you can see that.' Ian peered even closer. 'How would you know?'

'This era is my speciality,' said Edward, 'and I know as much about it, and all facets of it, as I possibly can. Jewellery is just part of it.' He straightened up. 'I can give you a learned discourse on the weaponry of the period if you like.'

They all smiled.

'So do we think this is what we were looking for?' asked Fran. 'I can't think it is, somehow.'

Ian shot a quick look at her.

'I don't know.' Edward shook his head. 'Nice though these are, they aren't worth a huge amount. They wouldn't make your fortune.'

'Not even for Rebecca?' asked Libby. 'Back then?'

'They might have helped. Bought her passage if she had to run away, for instance,' said Edward.

'This wouldn't have been enough to kill for,' said Ian, down on his haunches in front of the little items.

'I wouldn't have thought so,' said Edward. 'Nice enough if you picked them up in a burglary, but the average thief wouldn't know what they were. But, as you said, the impression may have been given that there was more. And perhaps there isn't.'

Ian stood up and walked away to the window, his hands in his pockets. 'Would Roland have known about this, that's the point. And how?' He swung round to look at Lewis. 'You didn't find it?'

'Course not. If we 'ad, we'd have notified somebody – you know how you have to?'

Ian nodded. 'Is it archaeology, though, hidden in a building? Who does it belong to?'

'Ah!' said Edward. 'Moot point. Pity so many records were lost at that period. If only we had Godfrey's will.'

'He may not have made one,' said Fran. 'A lot of people didn't.'

'Let's assume there was some kind of document,' said Ian, 'that was given to Roland with the deeds of the house. Where are they, do we know?'

'Solicitor?' suggested Libby. 'I understood that nothing was given to Roland though.'

'Don't you think it's possible that if there was a document, Roland wouldn't have shared it with his wife?' said Ian. 'And just as likely that he *did* share it with his lover.'

'Quite likely,' said Libby. 'He was a bastard.'

'So she has it and someone kills her for it?' said Lewis. 'But why kill Roland?'

'I think she was killed because she knew where it was but *didn't* have it. Once she'd passed on the knowledge, she had to be killed, and the killer then went to get it from Roland.' Libby looked round the group.

'It's the most likely scenario,' acknowledged Ian, 'but if so, has the killer now found the gold, or whatever it is, and gone for ever?'

'Oh, how depressing,' said Libby. 'Surely not?'

'Well,' Ian squatted down in front of the jewellery again, 'whatever the case, I've still got to find the killer, and it doesn't seem as though this search is going to help.'

'That's defeatist talk,' said Edward. 'Here,' he carefully rolled the jewellery back into the black cloth and handed it to Ian. 'Why don't you go back and report this to the coroner's office, or the Finds Liaison Officer, and we'll carry on here.'

'You said yourself the rumour of treasure might have been

enough to kill for,' said Libby. 'We can at least look for signs that there might be something else, or even that secret passage out of the cellars.'

Ian looked doubtful. 'I shouldn't really leave you here at a crime scene unattended.'

'Is there someone on duty at the grotto?' asked Libby.

'Of course. And the tent and forensics are there still.'

'Well, we're not unattended, are we?' said Fran. 'And I suggest you go and tell them we want to look at the grotto, too.'

Ian sighed. 'Anyone ever tell you you were bossy?'

Fran and Libby looked at one another and grinned. 'Yes, you,' said Fran.

Chapter Fourteen

'Where now?' Libby asked after Ian had left, taking with him the jewellery in an evidence bag.

'Cellar,' said Edward, 'but we can explore each level on the way down.'

'There are so many levels,' said Fran. 'And staircases.'

'Edward and I will go down one side of the house and you go the other,' said Lewis. 'Come on, down the ladder and I'll point you in the right direction.'

Libby and Fran's way lay along a heavily panelled corridor, with three bedrooms leading off to the left. Ahead, a tall stained glass window sent lozenges of colour on to the floorboards. To the right, a carved banister protected them from the equally heavily panelled stairwell.

'The steps are shallow,' said Libby, peering over the banister. 'Not much room to hide anything underneath one.'

'We need to look in the bedrooms,' said Fran, opening a door. 'Come on.'

The first bedroom was the master, and retained little impression of either Roland or Adelaide. A concealed door in the panelling led to a large en-suite bathroom.

'Nothing here,' said Libby, after they had tapped carefully on all the walls and opened all the cupboards and drawers. 'Not that I would have expected there to be.'

The other two bedrooms were the same as the first and obviously kept for the two sons' occasional visits home. The only difference was a shared bathroom between the rooms.

'Still nothing,' sighed Fran. 'I wonder why we thought there might be?'

'Because Roland said there was, Ramani thought there was, and because of the parish record.'

'Hmm,' said Fran, starting down the stairs, before coming to a halt halfway down.

'What?' said Libby, bathed in multicolours from the window.

Fran stood still, her head cocked to one side.

'Fran?' Libby took two more steps down, to stand beside her friend.

'There's something ...' Fran reached out a hand to the panelling on her left and swayed slightly.

'Fran!' said Libby again, grabbing hold of her friend's right arm. Fran straightened up.

'Sorry, Lib.' She cleared her throat and turned to smile at Libby. 'That was very odd.'

'I gathered it was some sort of –'

'Moment, yes,' said Fran with another smile. 'But I don't know exactly *what* it was. There was a feeling of darkness, but not suffocation. And a sort of claustrophobic feeling.'

'A secret passage?' suggested Libby. 'That's what it sounds like.'

'Honestly, I don't know.' Fran turned to look at the panelling beside the staircase. 'Perhaps there is one, behind here.'

They both began to tap the walls all the way down the staircase but heard nothing to indicate there was an empty space behind them. At the bottom, they went through another door and found themselves in the hall beside the kitchen, where Edward and Lewis had made themselves at home at the table with steaming mugs of coffee.

'I'm gonna get one of those,' said Lewis, indicating the coffee machine. 'Great coffee.'

'Have you found the cellar yet?' asked Fran, as Libby went to fetch more mugs.

'No, but we haven't looked. When we've had our coffee we will. Let's have a look at that plan again, Lewis.'

'I think there might be something behind the panelling.' Fran sat down at the table.

'Really?' Edward's eyebrows shot up.

Lewis squinted over the top of his mug. 'You been 'avin' one of your wotsits?'

'Yes.' Libby put the mugs on the table and poured coffee. She glanced at Edward. 'You know about Fran, don't you?'

'Do I?' Edward looked puzzled.

'I can't remember now if anyone's put you in the picture,' sighed Fran, 'so here goes. I have occasional – I suppose you would call them psychic insights – which have sometimes helped the police.'

'Is that why your DCI wanted you on this search?' Edward showed no particular surprise at Fran's revelation. Fran nodded.

'So what did you see?' asked Lewis.

'I didn't see anything,' said Fran. 'I just felt this awful darkness and sort of claustrophobia on the staircase.'

'A secret passage?' said Lewis and Edward together.

Libby laughed. 'Exactly what I said. But we've tapped every panel we could reach and there doesn't seem to be space behind them.'

Edward frowned. 'Some of the doors were built into the panelling to conceal them ...'

'Yes, like the door to what is now the en-suite in the master bedroom,' said Fran.

'But if they were bricked up behind the door you wouldn't know there had once been a room there,' said Edward.

'Like the bricked-up cellar?' asked Libby.

'I'm wondering if there was a reason for that,' murmured Edward.

'What, you mean nothing to do with our Godfrey?' said Libby.

'We've been assuming that it dates to the Battle of Maidstone – '

'No, you were,' said Fran. 'No one had thought about that until you came along.'

There was a shocked silence round the table. Then Lewis laughed.

'Way off the beam, then, mate!' He slapped Edward on the back. 'Much more likely that it's something to do with the nineteenth century, innit?'

'The Aldington gang,' murmured Libby.

'What?' said Lewis.

'Didn't we hear about them once before?' said Fran.

'Who were they?' asked Lewis.

'A famous band of smugglers who operated along the coast between Deal and Rye. There was activity right up to Felling,' said Libby.

'The Hawkhurst Gang,' put in Edward.

'They were earlier,' said Libby. 'Mid seventeen hundreds, but yes, much the same.'

'So this place could have been used for smuggling? Like mine was?' said Lewis.

'We thought that before,' said Libby. 'When we went to The Feathers pub in Keeper's Cob.'

'You went there?' Lewis's voice rose in disbelief. 'It's a hellhole.'

'We know,' said Fran grimly. 'But we did think it was probably a former smugglers' haunt.'

'Probably still is,' said Lewis. 'Don't go there again.'

'I think that may be where the tunnel comes out,' said Libby. 'Perhaps not now, but ...'

'Quite possible,' said Edward, frowning. 'What we need is a geophysics team.'

'That would cost a fortune, and wouldn't get your research any further,' said Libby.

'No, but wouldn't it be fascinating?' said Edward with a grin. 'Come on, let's find this cellar.' He pulled Lewis's plan towards him. 'According to this its entrance is in the inner hall.'

There were no obvious doors in the inner hall.

'There must be some other way of opening the door,' said Libby.

'If we had a vague idea of where it was,' said Fran. 'There aren't any handy carvings to pull or push.'

'Have a look, Lewis,' said Libby. 'You've got an eye for things.'

'Not sure about that,' said Lewis, but obligingly squinted

along the walls, feeling as he went, until he stopped almost next to the outside wall.

'Gives a bit,' he muttered. The other three crowded round.

Suddenly the panelling moved a little, scraping along the floor and groaning with the weight of years.

Edward and Lewis grinned at each other in triumph.

'Well, open it, then,' said Libby impatiently.

Lewis gave the door a shove inwards. It moved a few inches.

'Torch,' said Edward. 'Where did I put mine?'

'I bet you left it in the attic,' said Libby.

'Kitchen table,' said Fran. 'Hang on.' She retrieved the torch and handed it to Lewis, who shone it through the gap.

'Stuffy. Can't see anythin' except brick walls.' He tried pushing the door further in. 'Won't budge.'

'Could it open outwards?' Libby suggested diffidently.

Lewis and Edward exchanged amused glances.

'These sort of doors open inwards, Libby,' said Edward. 'Less noticeable.'

It was Fran and Libby's turn to exchange looks.

'Where are the hinges?' said Lewis. 'See? None out here. Must open inwards.'

'Oh. I didn't think of that.' Libby sighed.

'Ice House,' said Fran suddenly.

Edward frowned. 'Is there one?'

'I get it,' said Lewis. 'We had a tunnel that led to an ice house, and to the church, and a pub once. Built along under the ha-ha.'

'I fell into it,' said Libby gloomily.

'So could there be one here?' said Fran. 'Is there one shown on the plan?'

'Where would it be, though?' asked Libby. 'Lewis's was down by the creek so ice could be loaded straight into it.'

'And smuggled goods,' said Lewis.

'And,' remembered Fran, 'the parson drew the map!'

Edward gave an exasperated sigh. 'What does that have to do with this place?'

Libby turned him an innocent face. 'Brandy for the Parson,'

she said.

"'Baccy for the Clerk,'" added Fran.

"'Laces for a lady; letters for a spy, Watch the wall my darling while the Gentlemen go by!'" they finished together.

'That was about smuggling in the eighteenth century,' said Libby, 'but he wrote it in the nineteenth.'

'Anyway,' said Lewis, 'what about this ice house? Or do we think they didn't have one? Is it big enough?'

'This house is quite small compared to Creekmarsh,' said Libby, 'so it might not. Or a strong room.'

'I still think we should try the County Archive for any household accounts or other material,' said Fran. 'Have you had a look, Edward?'

'No. But I could. You think we might find something in there? But not as early as 1648, surely?'

'Can I just ask,' said Libby, frowning, 'whose idea it was that this so-called treasure was anything to do with the Battle of Maidstone?'

They all looked at each other.

'Well,' said Edward slowly, 'Ramani's, I suppose.'

'Just because Roland told her it was here,' said Libby.

'So we could be barking up the wrong bloody tree altogether,' said Lewis, giving the recalcitrant door a shove. Obligingly, it swung inwards with a groan and a scrape.

The little party was silent for a moment.

'Well,' said Edward eventually. 'We've found the cellar.'

No one wanted to go into it, Libby claiming she'd had enough of cellars and secret passages for a lifetime, and Lewis saying he was sure nice Inspector Connell would say they shouldn't.

'No, we shouldn't,' said Fran firmly. 'Whether there is anything down there or not, we ought to let the police look. And whether Roland was telling porkies or not, Ramani was still murdered and left here.'

'And then Roland himself was.' Libby sighed. 'And both murders might have nothing to do with any treasure.'

'But as Ian said, someone else might believe it and that

would be a reason in itself,' said Fran. 'Oh, come on. Let's just phone Ian and say we've found the cellar and get out of here.'

'What about your moment on the stairs,' murmured Libby, as they went back to the kitchen, leaving the cellar door open.

Fran shook her head. 'I don't know, and I'm not going to worry about it.'

'Well, what about the ice house, then?'

'I've had an idea about that,' said Lewis, turning back to them. 'I reckon it's inside the grotto.'

'And I've had another thought, too,' said Libby. 'I don't know why I didn't think of it before.'

'What?' said the other three together.

'Pope's grotto!' said Libby triumphantly.

Lewis and Fran shook their heads, but Edward beamed.

'Of course! Alexander Pope's house in Twickenham – he built a grotto in what was originally the cellars so he could reach his garden on the other side of the road.'

'So,' said Fran, 'our grotto here could be the entrance to the cellars.'

'And an ice house,' said Libby.

'Pope's grotto had a natural stream,' said Edward, 'if this one has it would be ideal for keeping ice cool.'

'I don't think Adelaide and Roland did anything to the grotto,' said Lewis. 'It was just something that made 'em look good.'

'That's the impression I got when I asked about it,' said Libby.

'So we've got a possible ice house and smugglers' tunnel leading from the grotto back to the house,' said Fran, 'and presumably onwards to The Feathers pub in Keeper's Cob. We've been jumping to a hell of a lot of conclusions.'

'Let's go out and look at it, anyway,' said Libby.

'They've still got a team there, Ian said,' Lewis reminded them. 'We won't be able to get near it.'

'Perhaps we can get Ian to get the team to investigate it,' said Libby. 'After all, if there is a tunnel leading from it, that could be how the bodies were dumped there.'

'It could, but it would have to have been from the other end,' said Fran. 'There was no one in this house when Ramani was dumped.'

Libby looked at her. 'How do we know that?' she said slowly. 'And Adelaide was certainly in the house when Roland was murdered.'

Chapter Fifteen

After a moment's silence, Edward shook his head. 'I don't believe it. How have you got to Adelaide being the murderer?' He sat down on the edge of the kitchen table. 'I wish I'd never got involved.'

Lewis patted his arm sympathetically. 'We all feel like that at some point.'

Libby looked affronted and Fran laughed.

'Come on,' she said. 'Let's go and see if they'll let us get near the grotto.'

'You know,' said Libby, as they left the house, 'we've never talked to that Johnny.'

'No.' Fran frowned at her feet. 'The police have, though. And Ian's said nothing about him to us.'

'No, but then, he wouldn't. He's not likely to tell us anything that isn't to do with our connection with the case. There might be all sorts we could find out.'

'There's the cleaner, too,' said Fran. 'Didn't someone say she lived in Keeper's Cob?'

'Yes. Adelaide said so. She drives here in her son's Land Rover. He farms there. Fairbrass, her name is. But she's not actually the cleaner. A sort of occasional housekeeper, from what Adelaide said.'

'Should we try and see them both?'

Libby looked at her in surprise. 'How could we? We've no introduction or anything.'

'Adam could get hold of Johnny – what was his name?'

'Templeton, I think. Why would he?'

'To find out what was going on. Johnny won't know Adam

has an inside source, so it would be perfectly believable.'

'I suppose it would,' said Libby, 'but where do we go from there? Ad can hardly suggest that his mum wants to talk to him.'

'Oh, I'm sure we could find some way round that,' said Fran, 'the difficulty will be the cleaner.'

Libby looked nervous. 'You're getting a bit into this, aren't you?'

'Yes. And I'm not going to give up on the passage or room or whatever it is inside the house, either.'

'You said you weren't going to worry about it,' said Libby.

'I'm not. But I'm not going to forget it. Here we are.'

Beyond the entrance to the grotto they could see the familiar white tent and two or three white-suited figures moving around.

''Scuse me, mate,' called Lewis.

One of the figures turned sharply, hesitated and then came forward, pulling his face mask down.

'You the people DCI Connell said was in the house?'

'That's us,' said Lewis. 'We were just wondering if you'd found the entrance to the passage yet.'

Libby opened her mouth to speak and Fran trod on her foot. Edward looked surprised but said nothing.

'Passage?' White Suit raised his eyebrows. 'We weren't told about no passage.'

Lewis gestured to Edward to take over. With commendable aplomb, he did.

'There's a passage which originally led from the house to Keeper's Cob. It's been partially bricked up.'

'No one said,' grumbled White Suit. 'Suppose we'll have to get down on our hands and knees under that bridge, now.'

'Suppose you will,' said Lewis, before anyone else could speak. 'That's where it is. We'll tell DCI Connell you're going down there.' He gave a half salute and turned away, leading the other three at a brisk pace.

'Before that bloke decides to call Ian and ask him what's going on, we need to be out of sight,' he said.

Edward laughed. 'Getting them to do the work for us? Clever.'

'You certainly sounded sure of yourself, especially about the entrance being under the bridge,' said Libby.

'He's right,' said Fran.

The other three turned towards her.

'Here we go again,' said Lewis.

'What?' Edward looked nervous and took a step backwards.

'Come on, you've already had Fran explained to you,' said Libby. 'This shouldn't faze you.'

Edward scowled. 'I should bow down and say "Yas, Massa" should I?'

'Oh, really, Edward.' Libby sighed with impatience. 'You must stop being so bloody sensitive. It isn't all about you.' She turned to Fran. 'I said he was selfish, didn't I? Well, he is.'

Edward turned his back. Lewis laughed.

'Come on,' said Fran. 'We can't do any more here.'

They walked back to the house, where Lewis locked the back door and ushered them out to the front.

'We'll have to come with you,' he said. 'Ian brought us.'

'Where to?' asked Fran and Libby together.

'Canterbury. My car's at the police station.'

'What about you, Edward?' asked Libby.

'My car's still in the hotel car park,' said Edward grumpily.

'Oh, snap out of it,' said Libby wearily. 'I'll take you both back to Canterbury, it's the wrong direction for Fran.'

'And if you're good,' said Lewis, climbing into the back of Libby's car, 'I'll take you to see Creekmarsh.'

Brightening visibly, Edward paused by the passenger door. 'Thank you, I'd love to come,' he said, and turned to Fran. 'Sorry if I was rude, Fran.'

Libby grinned at her friend. 'I'll ring you,' she said. 'Get in, Edward.'

'So,' said Lewis, as they set off back down Dark Lane, 'was that helpful at all?'

'I'm not sure,' said Libby. 'We think there's a passage under the house, we also think there's at least a hidden room inside. Whether it's any use to Ian, I don't know. Was it useful to you, Edward?'

Edward slid her a sideways look. 'I think so. Thank you.'

'What are you trying to establish?' asked Lewis. 'Bullet points.'

'OK, number one: were Ramani and Roland killed in the grotto or elsewhere? Number two: why were they killed? Was Roland killed as a result of Ramani's death, or for a different reason? Number three: was Roland's tale of a hidden treasure true? In fact, did he even spin that tale?'

Edward half turned in his seat. 'But she told me he had. Well, she actually said "they" had.'

'Oh, yes, that's true. But the fact remains, was it a true story?'

'As you keep reminding us, even if it wasn't true, someone could have believed it enough to kill for it.' Lewis leant in between the front seats.

'It's a puzzle, though,' said Libby, turning out on to the Canterbury Road. 'Ramani's murder looked planned. It doesn't fit.'

'Why does it look planned?' asked Edward.

'We know now that she died later than we thought, which looks like a deliberate attempt to divert suspicion or provide an alibi,' said Libby.

'How's that?' asked Lewis.

'Apparently, as far as I can make out – Ian wasn't at his most forthcoming when he told me this – her throat was cut and she was left to – to bleed out, if that's the right expression.'

'Ugh,' said Lewis.

'That's the right expression,' said Edward, 'but it also means she died where she was found. The murderer couldn't have slit her throat elsewhere and transported her there, he'd have risked her dying on the way, and the blood would be everywhere.'

'So it would,' said Libby. 'Well, then, she could have been transported there unconscious, couldn't she?'

'And, depending on the entrances to the tunnel, easier to do it underground than risk being seen,' said Edward.

'Yes, but if one entrance is inside Dark House and the other under some pub or church that would be almost impossible,' said Libby.

'The other thing is,' said Edward, 'it really doesn't look as though any of this relates to my areas of research, does it?'

'Will you explain that to me?' asked Lewis. 'I'm dead iggerant, you know.'

Edward enthusiastically explained the Battle of Maidstone and its putative relevance to Dark House, his discovery of Sir Godfrey Wyghtham and the note in the parish records. By the time Libby pulled up on the forecourt of the police station, Lewis was almost as enthusiastic as Edward himself.

'Go and get your car,' he said, as they climbed out, 'and meet me here. You can follow me back to my place.'

'Great,' said Edward. 'Your house has definite links with the smugglers, doesn't it? And it must have links to the seventeenth century, too.'

'It wasn't built until after the Restoration,' said Libby. 'We found that much out last time.'

'Oh.' Edward's face fell.

'But there's a reference to a house being there on the site in 1508, remember?' said Lewis. 'And wasn't there something about the owner signing Charles I's death warrant?'

'He was one of the twelve?' Edward's eyes were now nearly popping out of his head.

'It was only a rumour,' said Libby, 'and there's no actual mention of the hall until 1569.'

'I don't care!' said Edward. 'I'll go and get my car.' He turned away, then turned back and surprised Libby by giving her a kiss on the cheek. 'Thanks, Libby, and sorry if I was selfish.'

Libby shook her head as she watched him walk away. 'I don't know. Historians.'

Lewis laughed.

'Go on, gal, you love it. You coming back? Edie was asking after you.'

'I'd better get home, Lewis. I'll come over another day. I'm going to do a bit of digging of my own about the smuggling.'

'You're as bad as any of 'em,' said Lewis, giving her a quick hug. 'Go on, then. I'm just going to pop in to tell Ian what's going on.'

Libby drove home without really noticing where she was going. Things had changed now because of the blocking of the tunnel with nineteenth-century bricks, although, she thought, that merely meant it was blocked in the nineteenth century, it could have been there for much longer. But it did seem much more likely that if anything had been hidden there it was due to eighteenth- or early nineteenth-century smuggling.

But Roland had specifically mentioned the date to Ramani, apparently, which was why she'd got in touch with Edward. Libby sighed. Now it looked as if their theory that he was only trying to impress her was right.

'Easy for him,' muttered Libby, as she approached the village. 'The date's on the front of his house.'

Once inside number 17, she hunted round for something for lunch, and called Fran.

'Oh, good, you're there. Listen, I thought of asking Andrew to do a bit of research for us.'

'Again?' said Fran dubiously. 'Poor man's always being co-opted for something. He must wish he'd never met Rosie.'

'Come to think of it,' said Libby, 'we haven't heard anything from her for ages.'

'Since that business at St Aldeberge's really,' agreed Fran. 'Perhaps we should ask how she is.'

'I'll ask Andrew,' said Libby. 'But I really am going to ring him, whatever you say. He can always say no.'

But there was no reply from either Professor Andrew Wylie's landline or mobile phones, so Libby left messages on both, finished her lunch and turned to the laptop.

Smuggling in Kent threw up many references, including several mentions of linked cellars and tunnels, some of which had lain undiscovered until the twentieth century when unfortunate farmers and gardeners fell into them.

'Free traders,' muttered Libby. 'Owlers.'

But owlers didn't seem likely. This was not a marshland area, but a wooded one. Owlers were wool smugglers, and the main centre of their operations was the Romney Marsh, over to the west.

'Although,' said Libby to herself, getting up to put on the kettle, 'we do have our own marshes and saltings. Creekmarsh is on the edge of them, where we found the tunnels from the pub to the church, and the ice-house tunnel.'

'What was that?' Ben appeared at the back door. 'Talking to yourself again?'

'I give the best answers,' said Libby, with a grin. 'Tea?'

She told Ben about the discoveries of the morning and the beginnings of the research into smuggling.

'I'm going to ask Andrew again. He's good at County Archives and things. We might find something.'

'It doesn't look as though it would help to find Roland and Ramani's murderer,' said Ben, sipping tea thoughtfully.

'It might help find out why, though. If there really is some kind of treasure, isn't it more likely it was left there during the smuggling years, and someone knew about it?'

'It would have been found years before now,' said Ben. 'And what about this tunnel you think leads to the grotto? That must have been discovered, if it was there, when the grotto was built in – what? The Victorian era?'

'Adelaide doesn't seem to know much about it, but I bet Andrew could find something. And if the grotto *was* built in the Victorian era, the tunnel would have been blocked by then. The bricks in the cellar were nineteenth-century, Lewis said.'

'Could have been blocked at the same time, then,' suggested Ben.

'Oh, yes, so it could.' Libby gazed pensively into her mug. 'We need help.'

'You're getting hooked on all this research again,' said Ben. 'I don't know why you don't just join the local history society and be done with it.'

Libby grinned. 'Don't think I haven't thought about it! But I need history to have purpose, not simply for interest's sake.'

The landline rang.

'Andrew?' said Libby, snatching up the handset.

'No, Ian. I was ringing to let you know that a tunnel has been found under the Victorian grotto.'

Chapter Sixteen

'Really?'

'Apparently, my SOCOs were told they had to look for it. That would be you, would it?'

'No,' said Libby guiltily. 'It was Lewis. He said he was going into the police station to tell you.'

'I was told he'd been asking for me, but I wasn't available.'

'Oh, right. Well, Fran is sure there's a passage in the house, and there's definitely a passage leading from the cellar, but it's been blocked up with nineteenth-century bricks. Ben thought it might have been done when the grotto was built.'

'*Ben* did? You've dragged him into this?'

'No. I haven't,' said Libby indignantly. 'He's simply interested. And I have to remind you that it was your idea to go and search the house.'

'All right, all right. So, this passage. Ben suggested the search there?'

'No!' Libby was impatient. 'Lewis did. There's this suggestion of a passage linking Dark House and Keeper's Cob, and we thought …'

'And you were right, of course.' Ian sighed. 'Did Fran say so?'

'Yes,' said Libby unwillingly. 'What now? Will it be excavated?'

'It'll be searched to see if there's any trace of Ramani's body being down there. If the tunnel's blocked at the house end, I don't see how anyone there could be involved.'

'Apart from being murdered,' muttered Libby.

'Look, we'll instigate a more thorough search of the house if

Fran thinks there's a secret room or passage there. But I'm blowed if I know what relevance it has.'

'Something's hidden there,' said Libby. 'Something that Roland knew about and told Ramani, who told someone else, who then murdered her and finally murdered Roland.'

'It's that important? Why hadn't Roland already disposed of it, then?'

'I don't know, do I?' said Libby. 'Perhaps, as we said, he was telling porkies.'

'But well enough to convince Ramani and whoever she told.'

'Thing is,' said Libby, 'I doubt if it could be a fortune left by Godfrey Wyghtham for his wife. If all his silver or whatever it was had been buried he would have dug it all up after the war. It's more likely to be smuggled goods from the late eighteenth century, isn't it?'

Ian sighed heavily. 'I have no idea. We'll search, anyway. There may just be some evidence in the god-forsaken hole that will link to the murderer.'

'What about the Johnny person?' asked Libby. 'It seems very odd that he didn't hear or see anything, or know anything about the grotto, living so close to it, and having to go through it to get to the main house.'

'He's been questioned more than once, Libby,' said Ian, 'and believe me, it doesn't surprise me that he doesn't know anything.' He cut the line.

Almost immediately, the phone rang again.

'Andrew! Thank you for calling back.'

'And what do you want me to investigate this time, Libby?' asked Professor Wylie, sounding amused.

'Oh, dear,' said Libby. 'I'm so sorry. It looks as though that's the only reason I ever want to speak to you.'

'Well, it is, mostly,' said Andrew, with a laugh. 'Come on then. Tell all.'

'A job for the County Archives, methinks,' he said when Libby had finished.

'That's what I thought.'

'So, Dark House, Dark Lane, formerly Wyghtham Hall

115

owned by Godfrey Wyghtham who enlarged it in 1643 and died some twenty years later. And was he involved with the Battle of Maidstone?'

'Oh, you know about that?' said Libby. 'Oh, of course you do. Well, perhaps you could also talk to Edward Hall. He's involved, too.'

'Dr Hall?' Andrew sounded surprised. 'Where does he fit in? He's an expert on the seventeenth century of course, and in particular the civil wars.'

Libby explained.

'Right,' said Andrew. 'First I'll do a bit of digging at the County Archives, and when I've got a bit more you can introduce me to Dr Hall. What's he like?'

'Very good-looking, very well-dressed and very selfish. Thinks of his subject before everything else, and thinks everyone, including the police, is prejudiced against him because of his colour.'

'Oh. I didn't know that.'

'Well, now you're forewarned. Is there anything else you need to know?'

'I don't think so. If there is, I'll ring you.'

'Thanks, Andrew, you're a pal. Have you seen Rosie lately? Fran and I were saying we haven't heard anything since the Aldeberge business.'

Andrew sighed. 'She's gone off to the States. They love her books there, apparently, and she's doing the grand book tour.'

'What about Talbot?'

'He's with me, which is a bit rough on him, as he only has the balcony to go out on, but luckily he's so lazy I don't think he minds. Cats are adaptable.'

'You might as well take him on permanently,' said Libby, 'the amount of times Rosie leaves you to take care of him.'

'Oh, I'm thinking of it, don't worry. He and I get on well. Two old buggers together.'

Later in the evening, it being Wednesday, Ben, Libby and Peter joined Patti and Anne in the pub after rehearsal.

'So, I hear you've found out more about your murder?' said

Patti, after Ben had supplied them all with drinks.

'Not found out, but I'll update you,' said Libby and did so, starting from when they'd left the church on Monday morning.

'So it's two murders now?' said Anne. 'Same person?'

'The police assume so, but there's not much to go on so far.'

'You know,' said Peter, pushing a lank lock of hair off his forehead, 'it may be nothing to do with this so-called treasure.'

They all turned to look at him.

'It could simply be that they were having an affair.' He leant back and looked down his aristocratic nose at them. 'Simplest is often best.'

'Quite right,' said Ian, appearing like a genie from the bottle.

Libby made room for him at the table while he refused offers of a drink.

'They're making me coffee,' he said. 'I guessed I'd find you here.'

'Are you on or off duty?' asked Ben.

'Off, of course,' said Ian with a grin. 'I always am when I come here. Ah, thank you.' He accepted his tall white cup of coffee from an indifferent waitress.

'I can't think why you want to socialise with us when I cause you so much trouble,' said Libby, eyeing him over the rim of her glass.

'Because I can thrash out ideas and listen to fantasies here, and I can't at the office.'

'What do you want to thrash out?' asked Patti.

'And what fantasies?' asked Peter, looking pointedly at Libby.

'Your point about the victims having an affair. It's become the single most important factor, and therefore we're looking very closely at Carl Oxenford and Adelaide Watson. It's become clear that they were both aware of the affair, even though at first they denied it.'

'Because they thought they'd come under suspicion,' said Patti.

'They did anyway,' said Libby, 'but I must say I'm impressed with Adelaide as an actress. When I was with her that

Monday night I'd never have known.'

'Watson himself wasn't as impressive,' said Ian.

'Thoroughly unpleasant,' agreed Libby.

'So what about the treasure?' asked Ben. 'Does it or doesn't it exist?'

'We've no idea. The reason we're trying to track it down, or find a reference to it, is simply to see if it could be a motive for murder. But no one's seen it and no one knows anything about it.'

'Or professes to,' added Libby. 'We've just said Adelaide's a good actress.'

'And you said her son was keen to help with the search,' said Ben.

Ian turned to Libby. 'You didn't tell me that.'

'I told him he couldn't, so there didn't seem to be any need.'

'Which son?'

'Julian. Works in the city, I believe. He didn't seem to know about the supposed treasure, but his eyes lit up at the thought.'

'If there was anything there,' said Anne, 'who would it belong to?'

Everyone looked at her.

'Good question.' Ian nodded. 'It would depend on the traceability.'

'If it was eighteenth-century contraband I don't suppose it could be proved who it belonged to,' said Peter.

'But if it was family silver it could possibly be traced to the Wyghtham family,' said Libby.

'It wouldn't be reported to the Crown or whoever, then?' Anne turned to Ian.

'It's the Finds Liaison Officer now,' he said, 'but depending on where it was found, yes, it would be. And the coroner would still have to look into it. If it's in the house, it could be said to legitimately belong to the current owners, but if it's in the grounds it's a difficult one.'

'If Roland had been alive he'd have said it was his regardless,' Libby said. 'Or just not told anyone.'

'Then his problem would have been getting rid of it,' said

Ben. 'He doesn't sound to me like a collector, and if he'd tried to sell anything obviously old or valuable it would have set off alerts, unless he knew exactly who to go to.'

Ian looked at him with interest. 'Indeed. And he worked in Brussels. And spent a lot of time in Amsterdam.'

Patti looked from one to the other. 'And?'

'Illegal art and antiquities routes,' explained Libby. 'At least, I think that's what they're talking about. And talking about illegal routes, are we going to look into the eighteenth-century smuggling aspect of those tunnels?'

'You can,' said Ian, 'but I'm actually more concerned in catching a double murderer.'

'But if there are tunnels, that could also be a motive for murder, like the Wyghtham connection. Smuggled stuff left behind.'

'Brandy? After two hundred years? Tobacco? Not worth it,' said Ian.

Libby frowned. 'But wasn't money involved somewhere?'

'The customers paid the smugglers, the smugglers paid the French,' said Ben.

'I thought ...' Libby tailed off, staring at the table.

'Thought what?' asked Patti.

'I've got this vague memory of money being involved with the smugglers. Being smuggled. I don't know where it came from.'

'They exchanged wool for goods at one point,' said Peter.

'The owlers, yes,' said Libby. 'Mainly on Romney Marsh, which isn't that far away, after all, but then there was some act or other and it stopped. I shall look it up.'

'Or get Andrew to do so?' asked Ian.

'I've already asked him,' said Libby sheepishly.

'Why am I not surprised?' asked Ian of the table in general.

'There are lots of smuggling stories in the area,' said Patti. 'Kent and Sussex were almost the worst in the country because they were closest to the French coast.'

'There were families controlling huge bands of free traders,' said Peter. 'I did a certain amount of research once, thinking I

119

might base a play on it.'

'Oh, that would have been good,' said Libby. 'Audiences love anything with local references.'

'Not with my record they don't,' said Peter, and got up to go to the bar.

'Tact, Libby,' said Ben. Anne looked puzzled. 'Both his last plays have culminated in murder, even though it wasn't his fault.'

'Oh, I see. The Monastery ...' Anne shifted in her wheelchair and cast a hesitant look at Peter's back.

'Would he let me look at the research, do you think?' said Libby in an undertone.

'If he's still got it,' said Ben.

'Still got what?' Harry draped himself over Libby's shoulder. 'Come on, I'm behind in this conversation.'

Peter looked over, grinned and turned back to the bar.

'I shall go and help my helpmeet,' said Harry, uncoiling himself. 'Hold the thought.'

'What thought?' asked Libby, smiling in spite of herself.

'The one about what you were going to tell me.'

Patti and Anne were laughing and even Ian looked amused.

'I don't know why he doesn't go on the stage like the rest of you,' said Ian.

'I think he'd clam up,' said Libby, watching Harry and Peter at the bar. 'He clowns around with us, but put him on a stage and he'd stop being himself.'

Peter and Harry returned carrying the drinks between them.

'Now,' said Harry, squeezing a chair between Peter and Ben. 'Fill me in.'

Between them, Libby, Ben and Peter repeated the conversations.

'You've still got all that smugglers stuff,' said Harry, flinging an arm round his beloved's shoulders. 'It's all in the bureau.'

Peter shrugged. 'You can have a look at it. There's a couple of books there, too.'

'Thanks, Pete.' Libby turned to Ian. 'If I find anything useful

I'll tell you, shall I?'

Ian laughed. 'You usually do.'

Later, walking home through the frosty high street, Ben said 'What did you mean about money earlier? Money laundering?'

'I don't know,' sighed Libby. 'I've just got this feeling that there was something going on to do with money and the smugglers. I can't remember whether I found out about it when we were looking into those tunnels at Creekmarsh, or it's just a memory of reading Dr Syn.'

'The Rudyard Kipling poem,' said Ben slowly, 'does that mention people being paid for allowing their homes to be used to store the goods?'

'No, it only says the little girl may be given a doll if she keeps quiet, with a cap of Valenciennes, remember?'

'So it isn't that,' said Ben.

'Maybe Andrew will turn something up,' said Libby.

'And will it help find the murderer?' Ben glanced sideways with a grin.

'Gawd knows,' said Libby.

Chapter Seventeen

Thursday passed with no word from the police or Andrew Wylie, but when Libby returned from a supermarket run on Friday, she found a message on the answerphone.

'Libby, I've found something interesting, I think,' said Andrew. 'Are you free? Would you like to come here, or shall I come to you? And will I be able to have a look at Dark House sometime?'

Libby rang Fran.

'Shall we both go to Andrew's? Easier for you.'

'If you like, but I'm quite happy to come over to you. Guy wants to see Ben, anyway, so we could combine the trip.'

'Oh, lovely! Shall I see if Harry can squeeze us in?'

At three o'clock, Fran arrived closely followed by Andrew, brandishing a brand new tablet.

'Much better for research,' he explained, swiping the screen and demonstrating a page of ancient text. 'Look, I can make it much bigger. So much easier to decipher.'

'So it is,' said Libby, amused. 'Sit down, and I'll bring the tea. And a lovely piece of apple cake I bought from that vegetarian stall in Canterbury.'

When they were settled, and Libby had put more wood on the fire, Andrew began.

'I decided to look up Wyghtham Hall, rather than Dark House. Your Godfrey inherited it from his uncle, and believe it or not, it began life as a hunting lodge for someone close to the court of the day. The Wyghthams seem to have acquired it in around 1536, which accounts for its mostly Tudor appearance, but successive owners have always added to it – or improved it, as they would say.'

'When was the name changed, and who by?' asked Fran, as Andrew took a sip of tea.

'I'm coming to that. Godfrey, as you know, fought on the Royalist side in the civil wars, although it was very much a Hobson's Choice. But he kept his little manor, and it passed to his eldest son on his death.'

'April 1664,' remembered Libby.

'Right.' Andrew nodded. 'There seems to be a gap in the records after that, but in the mid-seventeen hundreds it pops up again as the property of one William Goodman. Now, Goodman turns out to be a name that is synonymous with smuggling in the area.'

'Ah!' Libby breathed a sigh of satisfaction.

'There isn't anything to say he was a smuggler himself, but he was definitely one of those who not only turned a blind eye, but actively encouraged it. He was a local magistrate, and even though, after the Smuggling Acts of 1736 and 1746, the regulations and punishments were tightened up, there is considerable evidence of him turning a blind eye, if not, as I say, actively encouraging smuggling.'

'So would he have been storing goods?' asked Fran.

'It's certainly possible. He was allowing contraband through the area and as a person in authority had influence in the right places. I would think he received his fair share of brandy and tobacco.'

'That wouldn't be treasure, though.' Libby frowned and Andrew twinkled.

'Ah, but what happened later! Do you know much about the Napoleonic Wars?'

Libby looked up nervously. 'N–no. Should I?'

'Well, you know the basics, surely?' Andrew looked from Fran to Libby, eyebrows raised.

'Waterloo and Trafalgar?' said Fran.

'Elba and Saint Helena?' said Libby.

'Wellington and Nelson?' they said together.

'Yes, all of those.' Andrew sipped his tea. 'One thing that

isn't generally known, or studied, at least, is the subject of the French Prisoners of War.'

'Oh, yes!' Libby sat up straight. 'Now, hang on, I do know a bit about this. Weren't they held in the prison hulks in the Medway?'

'Yes, they were, among other places, including the Thames estuary and just off Sheerness. Terrible places, even worse than the prisons of the day, which were bad enough. And have you heard about the escapes?'

'No.' Libby shook her head. 'Were there any? I thought it was impossible.'

'Oh, yes, there were escapes. And do you know who helped them escape?'

'No?'

'The smugglers.'

'Wow!' said Libby.

'Good Lord!' said Fran.

'In this area? But we're not near the sea here,' said Libby.

'We're not that far, as the crow flies,' said Andrew. 'And the route those French prisoners were sent on was purposely devious. A lot of them were landed at Whitstable – '

'Whitstable?' echoed Libby. 'But if they were landed there, why did they come here? Couldn't they have been transported back to France direct from Whitstable?'

'There were various reasons, not all of them fathomable. But you must know – in fact you *do* know – that the whole area is peppered with smugglers' haunts. You told me that you suspect a tunnel leading from Dark House to a pub in Keeper's Cob, and you've told me about other tunnels you've discovered in the past. Anyway, it's a fascinating subject, and I'll give you some of the sources I found.'

'How did they do it, though?' asked Fran. 'I thought French ships stayed off the coast and smaller boats went to and fro with the contraband. Is that what they did with the prisoners?'

'Sometimes. But they also got transported direct to France.'

'How could they do that? Surely they'd be spotted by the French in the channel? We were at war,' said Libby.

'But not entirely,' said Andrew.

Libby sighed. 'I don't understand. We either *were* at war, or we weren't.'

'Oh, we were. But although trade had been blocked, both the French and the English realised that a certain amount of trade had to take place between the two countries and a limited number of licences were issued. And then Napoleon allowed smugglers entry, providing further outlets. And this was where the prisoners were landed. And something else was being smuggled in.'

'Into France?' asked Fran.

Andrew nodded.

'Well, what?' said Libby.

'Bullion,' said Andrew.

Both Fran and Libby gasped.

'Bullion?' repeated Libby. 'Gold?'

'Mainly gold in the form of guineas,' said Andrew. 'And they built special, fast boats to do it.'

'Let me get this straight,' said Libby. 'English smugglers were smuggling gold into France. What for?'

'Because Napoleon needed gold to pay his troops.'

'So who was giving it to him?' asked Fran.

'British merchants.'

'British?' squeaked Libby. 'No! That would be treason.'

'But it was happening. It was such big business that special boats, known as "guinea boats" were built in Deal and could be rowed across the Channel in five hours. When they were forbidden in England, they simply went to France and built them there, under the protection of the French government.'

'Unbelievable,' said Libby.

'So are you saying,' said Fran, 'that these guineas might have been smuggled through here?'

'There is some evidence that this was a house on the smuggling route even after William Goodman. It was tenanted by a Reverend Mostyn, for whom there seem to be no records, so I expect it's not a real name or a real person, but the estate stretches quite a long way, and includes most of Keeper's Cob, so it would have been a protected smugglers' area, from the owling trade through to Victorian times.'

'That could definitely be the treasure Roland told Ramani about,' said Libby, turning to Fran. 'Blimey! Suppose it's true?'

'It would belong to the Crown,' said Andrew with a smile. 'Don't go getting excited.'

'Oh, I know, but if it was true, Roland would never have given it up.'

'Black market?' said Andrew. 'Very difficult.'

'Yes, but as Ian and Ben reminded us, Roland spent a lot of time on the continent in exactly the right area for the illegal arts and antiquities smuggling routes.' Libby shook her head. 'I don't know. We don't even know if his story of treasure was true.'

'It's a reasonable assumption,' said Fran, 'that if somehow he knew this house was used for bullion smuggling, he would have made it into a story to impress Ramani Oxenford.'

'Even though it wasn't her era?'

'She was a historian. It wouldn't matter,' said Fran.

'That doesn't work.' Libby shook her head. 'She told Edward, and he's a Civil War authority.'

'True, and he was – or is – certainly looking for that connection.'

'This is all very interesting,' said Andrew. 'Will you explain? And can I have more tea?'

Between them, Libby and Fran went into slightly more detail, including the story of their own investigations so far.

'It seems to me,' said Andrew, leaning back and sipping his fresh cup of tea, 'that you're chasing moonbeams.'

Libby looked gloomy. 'I know. It looked so perfect at first. Godfrey Wyghtham left some silver behind for his wife when he went off to Maidstone in 1648 and it's still here.'

'But except for that tiny notation in the parish records, there's nothing,' said Fran. 'And he came safely back here and died some years later. If he had left something here, it would have been retrieved.'

'Unless he forgot where he'd put it,' said Andrew, laughing.

126

'I doubt that,' said Fran. 'Would you?'

'I wouldn't, but I know people who might.'

'Rosie,' nodded Libby. 'She even forgets where she's put Talbot.'

'So, has this got you any further?' asked Andrew, changing the subject.

'Well, yes.' Libby looked at Fran. 'We know there must be tunnels, and possibly secret passages in the house itself.'

'Think of when it was first built,' said Andrew. 'Catholic persecution.'

'Priest holes,' said Libby.

'Quite probable.'

'Roland found it, perhaps?' suggested Fran.

'And there was something in it?' Libby looked at Andrew.

'Oh, I doubt that, unless they left a rosary behind when they were escaping. No, if there is any sort of treasure, I think the best bet is gold from a guinea run.'

'So where were these smuggling runs, then? Are they still traceable?' Libby leant forward, elbows on knees.

'Some are, and a lot of the old names are still there.' Andrew reached down into his briefcase and brought out a small pamphlet. 'Here. This is all about the smuggling routes and the Prisoners of War.' He opened it and pointed to a picture – very fuzzy and in black and white. 'See?'

Libby and Fran both leant to see it and gasped.

'It's Dark House!' said Libby.

Andrew smiled triumphantly. 'It certainly is. And this booklet gives the route on which it stood.'

'Why didn't you tell us that in the first place?' said Libby indignantly.

'I'd only have had to backtrack to the beginning, wouldn't I?' said Andrew, still grinning. 'This way, you'd already absorbed the background information, so the picture makes sense.'

'I can see you were a good lecturer,' said an amused Fran.

'I'm going to make more tea, and then we can have a look at that route,' said Libby, getting to her feet and collecting mugs.

'Don't worry,' said Andrew, once more brandishing his tablet. 'I've done it all on here.'

Libby stood with her mouth open for a moment, then retreated to the kitchen.

Ten minutes later, the three of them were seated at the small table in the sitting room window, Andrew's tablet between them.

'Now look,' he said, swiping the screen. 'This is the map of the route in that booklet.' Up came a rather amateurish hand-drawn map. 'And this is the modern Ordnance Survey map overlaying it.'

Andrew had highlighted the old route in thick black lines in order to show up against the multi-coloured OS map.

'I still don't understand why, if the prisoners were landed at Whitstable, they had to go up to London and back out again,' said Libby.

'They didn't always,' said Andrew. 'As far as I can make out, some of them came this way, and were then taken down another route to go with the guineas. But the only boats that were supposed to go to France, not the guinea boats, left from places like Tilbury, so the prisoners had to be taken there and smuggled aboard.'

Libby shook her head. 'It's so complicated.'

'It is, but interesting, isn't it?' said Fran. 'I think we should investigate the Dark House tunnels and see where they go.'

'According to this booklet, they go to Keeper's Cob, which you know, and down to a church –' Andrew peered at the map '– here.'

'Good lord, that's St Mary's, the Rev. Toby's church!' said Libby.

'That's where the notification in the parish records is,' said Fran.

Yes.' Andrew nodded. 'I found a reference to his memorial tablet.' He smiled at them both. 'So there you have it. All your ends neatly tying together.'

'And adding up to nothing,' sighed Libby. 'Oh, I'm sorry, Andrew – what you've done is brilliant, but it probably doesn't do anything to catch a murderer, does it?'

Chapter Eighteen

'You're lucky Andrew wasn't offended,' said Fran later, when the professor had gone.

'I know. He found it funny.' Libby was washing mugs in the kitchen. 'And it is interesting. Fascinating, in fact, but I honestly don't see Roland bothering to do all that detailed research, do you? Just to get Ramani into bed?'

'Was it Peter or Harry who said the whole reason for the murder could be as simple as the affair? Either Adelaide or Carl bumping off the two of them because of that?'

'Or both of them in cahoots,' said Libby. 'Yes, it's possible, except that they're both alibied up to the hilt. Carl was miles away at a conference or something and Adelaide was in London.'

Fran perched on the kitchen table. 'So if we wash out the treasure motive – sadly – we need to find another reason for the murders. Because I really don't think we have two separate murderers. Too far-fetched altogether.'

'OK.' Libby sat on the other side of the table. 'What are the usual motives for murder?'

'Money, fear, revenge – '

'Revenge is a very unlikely motive.'

'All right, but money and fear are strong.'

'Sex? Love?'

Libby shook her head. 'Only if someone is in between you and the object of desire. In this case both partners in the affair were killed and there isn't anyone else in the equation.'

'We don't know that,' said Fran, slowly.

Libby looked interested. 'So Adelaide might have killed

129

Ramani in order to get Carl? But then why kill Roland?'

'To get him out of the way so the road was clear?' Fran put her head on one side and considered. 'Too far-fetched again.'

'There could have been someone else,' said Libby. 'Someone who wanted Carl, so killed Ramani, then Roland found out so he had to be killed, too.'

'Well, that fits Adelaide,' said Fran. 'And we do know now that she and Carl knew one another better than anyone thought.'

'Still doesn't feel right, though, does it?' Libby stood up. 'Come on, let's forget all about it and go and watch an old film or something until it's time to go out.'

Later, in The Pink Geranium, they found Peter waiting for them on the sofa in the window, with Adam and the pretty PhD student in attendance. Harry popped a dishevelled head out of the kitchen and shouted.

'I took your pollo verde out of the freezer, so you'd better eat it!'

Libby blushed as the other customers regarded her with amusement.

'So where are you with the case of the murders in the dark?' asked Peter, when wine had been brought and poured.

'Nowhere,' said Libby. 'We've begun to think your theory of a wronged wife or husband may be the true one, despite the fact that we've found out all sorts of fascinating historical things from Andrew.'

'Such as?'

'Did you know that the English were selling gold to Napoleon –'

'To pay his troops, yes,' said Peter.

'Oh, bum. You know everything,' said Libby.

'But I don't,' said Guy. 'What's that all about?'

'Me neither,' said Ben. 'You weren't very forthcoming when we arrived earlier.'

'Because we hadn't got anywhere, that's why,' said Libby.

'But we'll tell you now, because it's fascinating,' said Fran.

Between them, with occasional interjections from Peter, who obviously knew all about it, they told Ben and Guy of the guinea

130

boats, the French prisoners of war, the prison hulks and the smuggling routes.

'I've got a lot of that in the notes I made,' said Peter when they'd finished. 'Harry did say.'

'But you didn't give them to me,' said Libby. 'And anyway, you wouldn't have had those lovely overlaid maps that Andrew had.'

Peter looked amused. 'I expect I could have worked it out.'

'Andrew enjoyed doing it,' said Fran, soothingly. 'It gives him something to do.'

'But we're no nearer catching a murderer,' said Libby, peering gloomily into her glass of red wine.

'To be fair, it isn't your job,' said Guy.

'What might be a good idea,' said Ben, topping up glasses, 'is to go for a day out and try and get as far as possible along one of those smuggling routes. I do like the sound of the Bogshole Brook.'

'Bogshole Lane is still there,' said Libby. 'And so is Convicts' Wood. It was on Andrew's map.'

'So you could walk it?' said Guy, looking interested.

'Well, you might,' said Libby doubtfully. 'I don't see me doing it.'

'Not even in the interests of research?' grinned Ben.

'You ought to know our old trout doesn't do exercise,' said Peter. 'Ah, here's Adam to take our order. Saved by the bell.'

As they lingered over coffee at the end of the meal, Fran turned to Libby.

'Would it be a good idea, though? To investigate the smuggling routes?'

'I can't see why. They're hardly likely to be in use today, are they?'

'Not for their original purpose, no. But it might be interesting.'

Libby shrugged. 'You and Guy go off on a hike then.'

Fran looked at her closely. 'What's up?'

'Oh, I'm just fed-up that we've got nowhere after trying so hard,' sighed Libby. 'Even though I didn't want to get involved in the first place.'

'But we've found out some really interesting facts,' said Fran. 'And we can still have a look at the Dark House tunnels.'

'If Ian allows us to,' said Libby. 'Let's face it, there's nothing we can do that the police can't. And Edward can be just as useful to them as he was to us, and so can Lewis. And even Andrew – Ian knows him, too, if he wants to consult any more expert witnesses.'

Fran sat back in her chair. 'In that case, we might just as well forget all about it and go back to normal. After all, you've still got the panto to occupy you.'

'That's true,' said Libby, looking mournful. 'I'll have to be content with that.'

Exasperated, Fran turned to Ben. 'For God's sake, cheer this woman up. She's going into a decline.'

Harry appeared at the table.

'She'll have to lose some weight first,' he said, dragging over a chair. Libby hit him.

'I suppose you could always ask the vicar of the church at Steeple Cross if he knows where the entrance to the tunnel was,' said Peter, gazing thoughtfully out of the darkened window.

All eyes turned towards him.

'Why?' asked Libby, suddenly looking a little brighter.

'Didn't you say the woman went there? Looked at the parish records? Must have seen that message or whatever it was?'

'Yes?' Fran looked puzzled.

'Suppose she was also looking for the tunnel. Suppose her inamorata had found out something about it and told her?'

'I don't see what difference that would make,' said Libby. 'If she knew ...'

'Then someone also knew about it and wanted to keep it quiet?' asked Ben.

'And that someone found out Watson knew –' began Guy.

'Or he *told* that person he knew,' said Libby, getting excited.

'So it must be someone Watson and Ramani knew,' finished Harry.

'Well, of course it was.' Libby was scornful. 'Whatever the

reason, it always had to be someone who knew them both.'

'There's no way we have the resources to find out about the people they knew,' said Fran. 'We only know about the people immediately concerned. Carl, Ramani and Roland will have hundreds of social and family contacts between them, and the only people who can look into that are the police. But we can ask the Rev. Toby about a tunnel to his church, or ask Patti to ask him.'

'We could ask Adelaide,' said Libby.

Everyone looked at her.

'I thought you were going to give up and be an ostrich?' said Fran.

Libby felt the colour creeping up her neck. 'I was.'

'Give up? Our Lib?' Harry let out a crowing laugh. 'Never!'

'I was,' said Libby. 'But perhaps it wouldn't hurt to talk to Adelaide.' She glanced at Fran. 'We could tell her about the smugglers' tunnels. And the Prisoners of War.'

'The what?' Harry topped up Peter's glass and took a healthy sip. 'In the last war?'

'No, the Napoleonic,' said Fran, and turned back to Libby. 'We could, of course, if you think it would get anywhere.'

'I don't know, do I? But it's better than sitting doing nothing.'

'Or completing that Christmas order for me?' asked Guy.

'Or looking after me?' said Ben.

'Or directing the pantomime?' said Peter.

'Oh, all right,' said Libby over their laughter. 'I'll do all that too.'

Tomorrow being Saturday, Ben didn't go into the estate office, so Libby didn't feel she should go off investigating while he was at home, and instead worked in the conservatory on Guy's painting, "Christmas in Nethergate", in the morning, took him for a drink at lunchtime and spent time preparing a special meal for Saturday night. Ben watched with amusement until, after a very good boeuf bourgignon and a bottle of Shiraz, he leant across the kitchen table and took her hand.

'You don't have to go overboard, love. I don't feel

neglected – not at the moment, anyway – and I much prefer you to be doing something that you're interested in, stopping short of getting hurt, of course.'

Libby lifted his hand to her cheek. 'I don't know what I did to deserve you,' she said.

'Nor do I,' said Ben. 'Now, are we going to do all this washing up, or are we going to sit on the sofa and pretend we're teenagers?'

Sunday dawned cold and frosty again.

'It's the beginning of December,' said Libby, turning the central heating thermostat up a notch. 'Should I go up to Joe and Nella's and see about a tree?'

'Already?' Ben leant back against the Rayburn rail.

'Otherwise the best ones will have gone.'

'Are they open on a Sunday?'

'Yes. We could go and find a tree and get some flowers for your Ma.'

'We could,' said Ben. 'But let's have breakfast first.'

Joe and Nella's Cattlegreen Nursery was just outside Steeple Martin on the Canterbury Road. The "boy" Owen, came out to meet the car.

'You come to tag a tree, then, Libby?' he said, with an enormous grin.

'We can take it away today, Owen,' said Ben. 'See? I've got the big car.'

Owen nodded wisely. 'I'll get a spade then.'

When Libby found the right tree for the window of number 17, Ben dug it up and Owen loaded it onto a trolley.

'Made some hot chocolate,' he said over his shoulder as he wheeled the tree to the car.

Ben raised an eyebrow.

'He's very proud of his hot chocolate,' whispered Libby. 'We must have some.'

Inside the nursery shed, Joe took Libby's payment while Owen fetched the hot chocolate.

'And we want some flowers for Mum,' said Ben.

'Sunday lunch, then, is it?' said Joe. 'Bet she don't want

chrysanths, your mum.'

'No, thanks, Joe. What have you got?'

'Oh, I don't know,' said Libby. 'Look at these lovely white ones. And you could put some of those berries with them. What are they, Joe?'

'Hypericum.' Joe put his head on one side. 'Yeah – that'd look pretty. Shame my Nella's not here. She knows.'

Owen re-appeared with the chocolate.

'Oh, that's lovely, Owen.' Libby beamed at him.

'Yes, it is,' said Ben, taking a lava-hot sip. 'Thanks, Owen.'

'So you chasin' any murderers, these days, Libby? You and that Fran?' Joe handed Libby her card and receipt.

'Of course she is, Joe,' said Ben with a grin. 'And smugglers.'

'Smugglers?' said Owen, round-eyed.

'Old smugglers,' explained Libby. 'Like the ones you see in books, like pirates.'

'Ooo-argh!' intoned Owen solemnly.

'Exactly,' said Libby.

'They old owlers and such?' said Joe.

'Yes, and the brandy and tobacco runners,' said Ben. 'Libby's found a house with a tunnel.'

'All the old houses had a tunnel back in them days,' said Joe. 'Old Hall had one goin' to the church here. I bet your Manor's got one tucked away somewhere.'

Libby caught Ben's eye. 'All right, I promise we'll look for it. Do you know anything else about the smugglers, Joe?'

'Oh, it were common knowledge. Everywhere between here and Whitstable, here and Nethergate, down to the Wytch at that there Creekmarsh, and o' course Deal. They was all routes. Every big 'ouse stored something for the Gentlemen.'

'Even after all the acts of Parliament?'

'No one took no notice, did they? Gentlemen were more powerful than them Ridin' Officers.'

'What about the French prisoners?'

'Oh, yeah. They was brought through, too. And that gold, an' all.'

Libby and Ben stared at Joe in amazement.

'How do you know all this?' asked Libby eventually. 'We've only just found it out from the County Archives.'

Joe shrugged and grinned. 'Local family, see. All the stories get passed down. Bet you didn't know that.'

'So you know about the guinea boats,' said Libby. 'Did any of that gold come this way?'

'Don't know all about it. My old great-great-great grandfather or summat, he got paid for takin' it down to Whitstable with the prisoners.'

'What?' yelped Libby.

'Calm down, Lib,' said Ben, patting her shoulder and laughing.

Joe was laughing, too. 'I told you afore, Libby, you got to go and talk to the old locals. Better than all those old papers.'

'So you haven't got any papers, then?' asked Ben.

'No, but we got a couple of old pictures. You come up the house sometime and we'll show you.'

'After all our research,' said Libby, as they fastened their seat belts and prepared to drive back to the village, 'and Joe knew all about it.'

'But you wouldn't have known what to ask him about if you hadn't done all your research,' said Ben reasonably. 'And he's talking about this area, not Steeple Cross or Keeper's Cob.'

'Oh, hang on! Draw a line from Steeple Martin to Keeper's Cob and it goes right through Steeple Cross. It's a straight run.'

'And straight inland from Whitstable,' said Ben, thoughtfully. 'Although you do have to go through Canterbury.'

'But Canterbury wouldn't have been as big as it is now. You could have skirted it.'

'Anyway, I thought you'd given up on the tunnels and the smugglers?' Ben gave her a sideways grin.

'I know.' Libby sighed. 'It was just such a coincidence.'

Ben drove the car to the end of Allhallow's Lane, took the tree out of the boot and dragged it down the back alley to the back garden of number 17, where Libby had a bucket of water waiting.

'Now let's go and see your mum and tell her all about it,' she said.

Chapter Nineteen

Monday morning, and two weeks since Ramani Oxenford's body was found, one week since Roland Watson was found in the same state, in the same place. Libby decided to call Adelaide Watson.

'Hello?' said a cautious voice.

'Adelaide? It's Libby Sarjeant. I was just wondering how you were.'

'Oh, Libby! Hello. Nice of you to call. I'm bored bloody stiff.'

'Have they let you go back to London yet?'

'No! I'm still in Canterbury. I've moved to a better hotel, though. Do you want to come over? We could have lunch.'

'Love to,' said Libby, thinking quickly, 'but I was supposed to be meeting Fran.'

'Can't you both come?'

'I'm sure we could.' Libby awarded herself a pat on the back. 'What time?'

'Twelve thirty? Do you know the hotel in the High Street?'

'Ah. What used to be the County?'

'Did it? Well, I'll meet you in reception.'

Libby called Fran.

'Can you make it? She obviously wants to see us.'

'And she's gone up in the world, by the sound of it,' said Fran.

'Well, she can afford it, especially now.'

Adelaide, looking less mousey than usual, was waiting for them in the expensive-looking reception area of the hotel.

'Very nice,' murmured Libby, looking up at the beams.

'Oh, the rooms are really modern and tasteful,' said Adelaide. 'if I never see another wooden beam in my life, I shan't be sorry.'

Embarrassed, Libby hustled them out in to the high street. 'Is your son Julian still with you?'

'No, he's gone back to London. They've been asking questions about him, you know.'

'Who have? The police?' asked Fran.

'Yes.' Adelaide made a face. 'They keep ringing up and saying "Just a few more questions, Mrs Watson." Honestly – why didn't they ask them all at the time?'

'Are they asking about Ramani or Roland?' asked Libby.

'Both. And now they're saying Julian possibly knew Ramani before we did.'

'How? He hasn't lived with you since you moved here, has he?'

'No, but I get the feeling they think he might have met her in London before she and Carl moved here.'

'Is that where they moved from?' said Fran.

'No. Carl's practice was up north somewhere.'

'So why –' began Libby.

'Oh, I'm sick of talking about it,' said Adelaide. 'Where are we going for lunch?'

But she obviously couldn't stop herself, because by the time they were halfway through their main courses, she was complaining again.

'And I don't want to go back there to live, obviously. But they won't even let me go back to collect clothes! They want me to tell an officer what I want and let her go through my things.' She sounded indignant.

'Adelaide,' said Libby gently, 'they'll already have gone through your things.'

Adelaide gasped, went red and then white again.

'They hadn't before Roland died, but once he was dead, and his body having been found in the grounds of Dark House, they would have searched every inch.' She forebore to mention that she and Fran had been searching, too.

'Don't they need a search warrant?' Adelaide found her voice.

'In those circumstances, I very much doubt it, but one would have been issued as a matter of course,' said Fran, sounding sure of her ground.

'I know it's not nice thinking of people going through your personal things,' said Libby, 'and I know I'd be dreadfully embarrassed about it. You should see the state of my wardrobe! But there's nothing to be worried about. They aren't judgemental, you know. They won't imprison you for untidy drawers or an unemptied bin.'

'But it's not –' Adelaide stopped abruptly. After a moment, she went on. 'Not untidy,' she finished, unconvincingly.

'That's all right then, isn't it?' said Libby brightly, trying not to look at Fran.

Adelaide bent to her plate once more.

'Have you seen Carl?' asked Fran. 'How's he holding up?'

Adelaide's head shot up again. 'How should I know?'

'You haven't seen him?' said Libby.

'No.' Adelaide almost spat the word. Then, with an obvious effort, she sat back in her chair and re-settled her shoulders. 'So. Did the police search the house for that treasure? You said they'd asked Lewis Osbourne-Walker to help.'

'Didn't they tell you?' said Fran in surprise. 'Yes, they did, but they didn't find anything.' She looked at Libby. 'Except the tunnel, of course.'

Adelaide became very still. 'The tunnel? What tunnel?'

'From the grotto. It seems to be blocked, but apparently it once went to a pub in Keeper's Cob and back into your house.'

'Really. Well, that makes me even more glad I'm not going back there.' She gave an artistic shudder.

'What will you do about packing up when the time comes, though?' said Libby. 'You'll have to go back then.'

'But not overnight.' This time Adelaide looked genuinely sick. 'I couldn't bear it.'

'Well, if you need someone to go with you, give me a ring,' said Libby. 'I'm not far away.'

140

After lunch, Fran had to get back to Nethergate, but Libby found herself wandering round Canterbury's shops with Adelaide.

'You must be bored rigid,' she said, as they strolled into Waterstones. 'Have you been reading a lot?'

'Yes. I've got a new tablet, and I've been downloading books on there. And films and box sets. It's great.' Adelaide picked up a best-seller placed prominently on the table in the front of the shop. 'Don't waste my money on print books any more.'

'Oh,' said Libby, who did? They eventually found their way to Westgate gardens and found a bench to sit on in the weak winter sun.

'You'll be back in London in time for Christmas I expect,' said Libby, struggling to find topics of conversation now that the murders seemed to be off the agenda.

'Oh, yes – they wouldn't be so heartless as to keep me here then. I've been doing my present shopping online and having it delivered to Julian.' She shrugged. 'He says he doesn't mind.'

'That's good,' said Libby, and looked at her watch. 'Well, I have to be going now. If I hear anything, I'll let you know, and as I said, if you want me to help you pack up at the house, give me a ring.'

And what have I let myself in for there? she thought as she dashed across to the car park.

As soon as she got home, she rang Fran, who was minding the shop while Guy was out on a buying trip.

'She knew about the tunnel,' Fran said straight away.

'I thought so, too. And she's worried about something the police might find in her things. And what about Carl?'

'She's either annoyed because he hasn't got in touch, or she's frightened of saying he has.'

'But which?'

'Well,' said Fran, 'I think we can take it that they are a *lot* closer than anyone thought at first.'

'When she said they hardly knew one another.'

'And neither she nor her husband knew Ramani.'

'And,' said Libby, 'what about Julian knowing Ramani?'

'Yes, that was a surprise. The police must have found something. And she wasn't very clear about that, either. Carl's practice was somewhere up north, but Julian met Ramani in London.'

'Perhaps before she married Carl?' suggested Libby. 'We need to find out if Ramani *was* in London. We can ask Edward.'

'Back on the trail again, then, are we?' Fran sounded amused. 'That didn't take long.'

'I'm not saying that we'll find anything out that the police won't, I'm just interested. And it might be worth telling Ian that Madam thinks there might be something of interest hidden in her things. What do you suppose she means by her "things"?'

'Clothes? The stuff she brought down with her, or that she left in the house permanently.'

'Toiletries? Toilet bag? Oh, no, she'd have taken that to the hotel, wouldn't she?' Libby frowned at the floor. 'So it must be something left in the house all the time.

'Or just hidden in the house. But in that case, why haven't they found it?' said Fran.

'Perhaps they have. Why would we know?'

'If they found something incriminating, or interesting in some way, they'd have questioned her about it, and they obviously haven't.'

'Oh, yes, of course.' Libby chewed her lip. 'How can we find out?'

Fran sighed. 'Look, against all my inclinations, I'll get hold of Ian on his official phone and tell him what we think, while you get on to Edward and ask about Ramani's London connection.'

Before she called Edward in his rather less swanky Canterbury hotel, Libby made herself a cup of tea, then sat down with Sidney on her lap.

'Edward, it's Libby. Are you busy?'

'Not at all, Libby. I'm pleased you called, I've just got back from lunch with Andrew Wylie. Isn't he delightful?'

'Oh, he did ring you? Good. He was terribly impressed when I mentioned you.'

Edward's rich laugh rang out. 'I was impressed by him. And the research he's done for you.'

'Oh, the smugglers and the guinea boats? But do you know, all the old local families round here know the stories, too, even though they haven't got them written down. I was gutted.'

'That's often the way,' said Edward. 'All historians know the value of oral history.'

'I suppose so,' said Libby. 'Look Edward, I wanted to ask you something. Funnily enough, Fran and I were in Canterbury today, too. We went for lunch with Adelaide Watson.'

'Did you? That was brave. But Andrew and I went to some country restaurant he knew, not in Canterbury.'

'Oh, right. Anyway, Adelaide told us that the police have been asking about her son Julian, and she seems to think – well, the police think – that Julian knew Ramani in London. Yet she says Carl's practice was up north before they moved to Steeple Cross.'

'Leicester,' said Edward. 'Where they met. Then she moved to London and he followed her.'

'Really? How long ago was that?'

'Let me see … Ramani wasn't brilliant at keeping in touch, but we'd meet up if I had to go to London, and the last time was – oh, must have been four, five years ago.'

'They weren't married then? I assumed they'd been married longer than that.'

'They were about to get married. I assumed she wouldn't want to see me without Carl, but –. Well, let's just say I was wrong.'

'Why did she marry him? Although I never met her, it seems such an unlikely partnership.'

'She was a chameleon. When Carl met her, she was being a serious PhD student, with a serious part-time job. He never saw the other side of her, which was a little wild, to say the least. And when she realised how wealthy he was – '

'Wealthy? I didn't know that.'

'Oh, yes. Apart from a GP's salary, which is comfortable, he had money behind him. Beautiful house, up-to-the-minute surgery. We used to tease her about him. You know, the upright, uptight Doctor Oxenford.'

'So why did she leave him and go to London?'

'As far as I can tell,' said Edward slowly, 'to have a bit of fun and to test him. See if he really wanted to marry her. Which he did. But he wouldn't move the practice to London, I think because, although she never showed her other side to him, he was probably aware of it, and wanted to get her away from temptation. So he set up down here.'

'Right.' Libby was frowning. 'So you think she might have met Julian in London?'

'It's entirely possible. She was very much into the wine bar culture, if that's what he's into, too.'

'He's in the city,' said Libby, 'so yes, he would be. So is he a suspect, do you think?'

'Obviously, he is, if the police think so.'

'He said he didn't recognise the photograph.'

'Which was of a dead woman in her doctor's wife persona.'

'That's true.' Libby thought for a moment. 'I wonder if he knew about her and his father?'

'And if his father knew about him?'

'Blimey, yes! Well, I suppose that's a more credible motive than some mythical buried treasure.'

'So you don't think there is any?'

Libby sighed. 'Oh, I don't know. I'm still rather inclined to think Roland invented it to grab Ramani's attention. After all, she was a young woman and he was – well, certainly middle-aged, despite thinking himself irresistible to women.'

It was Edward's turn to sigh. 'A wild goose chase, then?'

'My favourite sort,' said Libby. 'I've chased more wild geese than you've had hot dinners.'

Edward laughed. 'Talking about dinner, can I take you dinner tonight? You and your – Ben, isn't it?'

'Sadly not, Edward. Tonight's a rehearsal night. Panto, you know.'

'Did you say "panto"? I love panto.'

'Really? You don't strike me as a panto type.'

'I'll have you know I was the best baddie in our uni drama society. I was a loathsome King Rat.'

'Would you like to come and sit in on our rehearsal? It's a bit rough and ready at the moment, but you'd be welcome if you're still getting bored in Canterbury.'

'I'd love to! Shall I come to you first?'

'No!' said Libby in alarm. 'Let me warn them they've got a visitor first. Anyway, there's more parking at the theatre.'

She gave directions, rang off and then called Fran to tell her about the conversation.

'So Julian's in the running after all,' said Fran. 'He didn't strike me as the murderous type.'

'No, but if the police found out he had known Ramani and then lied about it – which he did – he's bound to be a suspect.'

'But why would he kill her? She'd already married someone else.'

'Because he was disgusted about her affair with his father? And then killed his father?'

'I suppose it's possible.' Fran sounded doubtful. 'And slightly more feasible than buried treasure.'

'That's exactly what I said to Edward. Who, by the way, turns out to be a panto fan. He's coming to watch rehearsal tonight.'

Fran laughed. 'That I'd like to see!'

'Well, you can come, if you want.'

'No, I can't leave poor Guy on his own yet again. Tell me about it tomorrow.'

The pantomime cast weren't noticeably enthusiastic about having a guest in the auditorium, especially on hearing he was a top-flight academic, which automatically made him the enemy of some of the younger members.

However, he slipped in so quietly that no one saw or heard him until his spontaneous applause at the end of one the comedy set pieces. Libby turned and gave him a thumbs-up, then waved at her performers to carry on.

'It's excellent,' he said when they broke for coffee. 'Even now. How many of them are professional?'

'Lots of ex-pros,' said Libby, 'including me. The dancers aren't in yet. They're senior students from a local stage school.'

'And I love your theatre. Is it council-owned?'

Libby grinned. 'No, it's ours.'

'Yours?'

'It's owned by Ben and his mother. Ben is – or was – an architect, so he turned it into a theatre, and Peter – that's Peter, over there – is his cousin, so he and I became directors of the company. We put on what we like, but have to keep it solvent, so we hire out to other companies. We're lucky that we have a good deal of local talent to draw on, and our sound and lighting people are all professional.'

'I'm impressed, for the second time today,' said Edward, turning on the spot to look up at the sound and lighting box at the top of its spiral staircase.

'Well, while you're in a good mood,' said Libby, 'can I ask you something?'

Edward looked down at her, his white smile splitting his face.

'Yes, you can, yes, I know what it is, and yes.'

Libby smiled doubtfully. 'You really know what I was going to say?'

'Our conversation earlier surely gave you the answer?'

'In a way,' said Libby in confusion. 'But I didn't want to speculate ...'

'At university, I was one of Ramani's sexual partners. When she moved to London it continued when I visited. But it was always very casual, because Ramani was like that. Nothing serious.'

'Except for Carl.'

'Even that wasn't serious for her. Yes, she married him, but that was for his money. She had no intention, as far as I could see, of being faithful to him. In fact, I'd be very surprised if there weren't more men to crawl out of the woodwork.'

'Really?' Libby's eyes widened. 'So there could be loads of new suspects?'

'I don't know about loads.' Edward put his coffee mug down. 'Or any that would have killed Roland Watson, too.'

Edward was introduced to Peter and Harry in the pub, and Harry flirted outrageously.

'Don't take any notice,' said Libby, 'he only does it to draw attention to himself.'

'I must say, I like your friends.' Edward leant back in his chair and stretched long legs out in front of him, looking a little like a black Peter. 'I wish I'd stayed here instead of Canterbury.'

'You could always move from the hotel into the pub,' said Harry.

'No,' said Edward with a sigh. 'I've got to get back home. There's no reason for me to stay down here any more, unless the police really have got me on their radar.'

'They've not come near you apart from to ask your advice,' said Libby, 'so I don't think they have. Must you go?'

'I must. Life goes on, although it's now the Christmas vacation, I still have work to do. And then, there's Christmas.'

'Don't remind me,' groaned Libby.

'But you will keep in touch and let me know what happens, won't you? I'm still going to look into Godfrey Wyghtham. He's going into the book.'

'The book?' several voices echoed in surprise.

'Didn't I tell you? That was why Ramani told me about the house. I'm writing a book on the lesser known figures and aspects of the civil wars.'

'So you see,' said Libby, on the phone to Fran the following morning, 'there's every reason to keep in touch with Edward, and every reason to look into Ramani's private life to see if any more men creep out, as Edward put it, of the woodwork.'

'I rather suspect the police are already doing that,' said Fran, 'especially since they've turned up Julian Watson.'

'Oh, dear, poor old Carl.'

'Unless he killed her.'

'Oh, well, that, of course. But it must be hell, having your dead wife's lovers dragged out in front of you.'

'It must, yes. But I think we've gone as far as we can at the moment, don't you? There's no one else we can talk to – or no one who would talk to us, anyway.'

'S'pose so. Pity though.'

'I know, you'll be bored. I bet you, though, that something will turn up and set you off again.'

'Is that a feeling in your water?'

'You could say that,' said Fran, and rang off.

In fact, two things turned up that very afternoon, while Libby was making a first effort with the Christmas cards, helped at intervals by Sidney.

Libby snatched up the phone as soon as it began to ring.

'Libby, you said you'd help me pack up some things at the house?' said Adelaide.

'Yes,' said Libby cautiously.

'Well, they're letting me go back in tomorrow. Could you come with me?'

'Does that mean it's no longer a crime scene?'

'I don't know, do I? They just said I could go back and collect stuff, and they're letting me go back to London.'

'Oh, you will be relieved,' said Libby. 'And can you put the house on the market yet?'

'I don't know that, either, all I know is I can get out. Will you come?'

'Yes, of course. What time?'

They settled on meeting at Dark House at ten thirty. Libby had just gone to put on the kettle to aid concentration on the Christmas cards, when the phone rang again.

'Libby? It's Edward.'

'You sound excited. Have you left yet?'

'No, I haven't, and yes, I'm excited. I checked out of the hotel this morning, and decided as a courtesy I ought to let the police know I was going, and where. And your Inspector Connell asked to see me.'

'Golly, did he? Did he clap on the irons?'

'What? No, of course not! No, he invited me to go and see the tunnel under the grotto!'

'He did what?' said Libby, stunned.

'The tunnel! Under the grotto. He's asking Lewis, too, and he also said he supposed you and Fran would have to come along.'

'Oh, nice! But it's great news. Did you get anything out of him about the actual investigation?'

'No, but I guess the tunnel's been cleared, or they wouldn't let us down there.'

'True. So when is this supposed to be happening?'

'Tomorrow.'

'Ah.' Libby thought for a moment. 'Well, I shall be there from half past ten anyway, as Adelaide wants me to help her pack up her things. I don't actually think that will take that long, as she doesn't seem to want much out of the house, just her clothes and personal belongings. All this sounds as though they've cleared the whole place, doesn't it?'

'It does, but that's a bit odd, isn't it? After all, the grotto was where both the bodies were found.'

'But perhaps not where they were killed,' said Libby.

Leaving Edward to make arrangements about the tunnel tour, she booked him a room , at his request, at the pub, and a table at The Pink Geranium.

'So he hasn't gone after all,' said Harry. 'I knew my charms would have an effect.'

'You leave him alone. He's as straight as – well, a straight thing. And very sexy.'

'Ooh, I know dear.' Libby heard Harry's artistic shudder. 'Shall you allow him to eat here alone at my mercy, or are you going to join him?'

'No, I can't do Pink Geranium twice in a few days.'

'I don't see why not. I have to.'

Libby laughed. 'I'll see what Ben says.'

Fran rang a little later.

'So we're all going back to Dark House tomorrow, then? See, I told you something would turn up.'

'I think they're going to need your particular expertise,' said Libby.

'In the grotto? I agree,' said Fran. 'In fact, I'm almost sure that's why Ian's suggested this trip.'

'Are you? You mean, sure, sure? As in you absolutely know?'

'I think Ian wants to know where they were killed. And it wasn't in the grotto.'

Chapter Twenty

Ben was only too happy to eat at The Pink Geranium again, and at eight o'clock he and Libby joined Edward on the sofa in the window.

'Fran says she thinks Ian – Chief Inspector Connell – is hoping she'll come up with something tomorrow.' Libby helped herself to wine.

'What – you mean using her – um ...' Edward trailed off.

'Yes,' said Libby bending on him a minatory look.

'It's absolutely true,' said Ben, looking amused. 'I first met her when she was actually employed by a company of prestigious estate agents –'

'Goodall and Smythe,' put in Libby, and saw Edward's eyebrows go up.

'– to scope out properties for anything that might have occurred in the past that would affect a sale.'

'I've never heard of that,' said Edward.

'I hadn't, either, but in fact, Fran nosed out a body for them in one place. And there were a couple of other instances where she was successful.'

'So now she helps the police as an expert witness,' said Libby. 'And you can scoff all you like, but it's worked several times. I mean, she's even discovered murder where a natural death had occurred.'

'The trouble is,' said Ben, 'she can't do it to order. And she's out of practice. When she worked for Goodall and Smythe it was routine to go into properties with an open mind regularly, but she's not required to do that now, so that part of her brain stays switched off.'

'Except when it breaks through with something startling, like it did with the St Aldeberge murders,' said Libby.

'The – what?' Edward was looking, horrified, between the two of them.

Libby grinned and patted his hand. 'Don't worry about it. We're used to it. I ought to write all the cases up one day, I suppose. People might want to read about them.'

Edward took a large gulp of wine. 'I know I said I liked your friends, but if you keep getting mixed up in murders, I'm not sure any more!'

'But that's why we're involved this time,' said Libby. 'It's because it's happened before that we get asked to look into things. Adelaide asked us, although I'm not sure she's pleased about that, now.'

'To be fair, you were already on the periphery,' said Ben, 'with Adam being on the spot when the first body was found.'

'Adam?' said Edward.

'That's Adam,' said Libby.

'Hello,' said Adam. 'I'm Libby's son. How do you do?'

Edward, bemused, reached out to shake Adam's hand. 'And how –?'

'Was he on the spot? Come on, order your meal and I'll explain,' said Libby. Which she did while they waited for Adam to bring their food.

'Well,' said Edward when she'd finished. He looked at Ben. 'Did you know all this would happen when you first met Libby?

Ben laughed. 'Oh, we met years and years ago when we were both married to other people. We hadn't seen one another for a long time until the theatre brought us together. With a murder, of course.'

Edward shook his head. 'I'm not sure it's safe being friends with you.'

'Oh, you're safe enough,' said Libby. 'It's when we *don't* like you that the problems start.'

Harry and Peter joined them at the end of the meal and Harry offered brandies on the house.

'I can see that you're well on the way to becoming one of our happy band,' he said, handing Edward a brandy balloon. 'Waifs, strays and misfits, the lot of us.'

'And what, exactly, does that mean?' asked Libby.

'Libby's Loonies,' grinned Harry. 'Think about it. Pete and me, your mate Patti and her Anne, Fran, all Ben and Pete's mad family …'

'Don't take any notice, Edward,' said Libby. 'I told you yesterday, he's just trying to attract attention.'

Edward laughed. 'I don't think I'd mind being one of Libby's Loonies. In fact, I might be honoured.'

'We'll see about that,' said Libby darkly. 'We haven't seen the end of this investigation. You'll probably be glad to scuttle off back to – actually, I don't know where you'll scuttle off to.'

'Oh, I'm still in Leicester at the moment, but I'm a visiting lecturer. I need to find a proper home.'

'Aren't you a proper professor, then?' asked Libby. 'Sorry, I'm a bit ignorant about academia.'

'I'm an assistant professor. I need tenure – that is, as I said, a proper home. I've already published a fair body of work, and this book – if it ever gets published – should be the finishing touch, and I can apply for full professorships.'

'Just like an ordinary job, then?' said Libby.

'Except that it takes rather longer to qualify,' said Edward.

'Well,' said Libby, 'here's to you finding a full professorship in Kent. Then we could borrow you whenever we like.'

'You've already got Andrew doing your historical donkey work,' said Ben. 'Leave the poor man alone.'

'Oh, I wouldn't mind,' said Edward. 'Even if I don't get a post in Kent.'

'And meanwhile, you've got an exciting little adventure tomorrow,' said Harry. 'So, cheers.'

Wednesday morning was back to misty and frosty. Libby drove carefully along Dark Lane, trying to ignore the trees pressing in on her left and the wavering shapes looming on her right. She turned on to the forecourt of Dark House with a sigh of relief.

Adelaide opened the door before she'd got out of the car.

'Did you know all your friends are coming to look at the tunnel?' she asked without preamble.

'Yes,' said Libby. 'I'm going, too.'

'But you're here to help me.' Adelaide's chin went up.

'Adelaide, did you ever wonder about the reason for your rather unpleasant assumption of superiority?' asked Libby conversationally, as she pushed past Adelaide into the main hall.

'What do you mean?' Adelaide's voice went up an octave and Libby turned to face her.

'I mean – you have taken advantage of me from the moment I came over here – at your request, I may add – when Ramani's body was found. I have offered to help, you have asked for help and help both Fran and I have tried to give. In return, you've lied to us and treated us, particularly me, like servants. So why is it? You came across when I first met you as rather a mousy woman, intimidated by her husband.'

'I was.' Adelaide now adopted a mulish expression.

'I know, anyone would have been. But since then, presumably because he is no more and you found out more about him anyway, you've become seriously arrogant and complaining. So you can get on with packing your things on your own. I'm going outside to wait for the grotto party.'

Adelaide stepped forward, her expression now anxious.

'Oh, Libby, I'm sorry, I didn't mean to be like that. I really don't want to do this on my own, and you've been so kind.'

Libby looked at her thoughtfully. 'I'm not sure. If you tell me why you lied, and what about ...'

Adelaide looked away, and Libby watched a tide of pink wash up her neck. 'It doesn't matter.'

'Well, it does, obviously. I mean, was I there on that first night as a witness to your conversation with Carl, to see that you didn't know him or his wife well?' This had only just occurred to Libby, and she was rather proud of it.

Adelaide opened her mouth, but no sound came out. Libby realised she'd been right. She nodded.

'That was why you switched to speakerphone, wasn't it? I thought that was rather an odd thing to do.' She waited for a

154

reply, which didn't come. 'So, where are your clothes? Come on, if I'm going to help, I'd rather get on with it.'

Adelaide looked back in surprise, but without saying a word, turned and went up the stairs to the main bedroom, where Libby and Fran had been last week.

'The police have been in here,' she said. 'You were right. All I want is the stuff from the drawers and the wardrobe.'

Libby picked up a black plastic sack. 'In these?'

Adelaide shrugged. 'I couldn't go back and get cases.'

'Right, I'll start on the wardrobe, and you can tell me all about just how well you really knew Carl and Ramani.'

Adelaide stared at her, then slowly opened a drawer in the dressing table and began taking things out before throwing them on to the bed.

'I told you before. I saw Roland and Ramani together.'

'Yes, you told me eventually. What you haven't told anybody is how well you knew Carl. Julian said he was around when Roland went away.'

Adelaide gasped, her hand going to her throat. 'That's not true!'

'Unethical, certainly,' said Libby with a grin. 'You were his patient, weren't you? Still are, I expect.'

'We were friends,' muttered Adelaide. 'That's all. Ramani used to go off to London and Roland to Brussels. And neither of us knew anyone else.'

'And when Roland and Ramani were at home?'

'Then we didn't see much of them. Well, Ramani not at all. I told you that.'

'Was Carl disappointed that she wouldn't stay down here?'

'I think so. He wanted to get her away from London, I know that.'

'Yes, I heard that.'

'How?' Now Adelaide sat on the bed and just stared.

'Edward Hall, of course. He's known her longer than anyone else.'

'I wonder why he isn't the chief suspect, then,' said Adelaide venomously.

155

'The little matter of an unbreakable alibi.'

'They can always be broken.'

'Not when it's a live television programme.' Libby crossed her fingers behind her back.

'Oh. But when? They say they don't know exactly when she – Ramani – died.'

'On the Sunday night, live from somewhere up north.' Bugger, why had she started this lie?

'He could have flown down.'

'Not at night.'

'Hmm.' Adelaide stood up and went back to the dressing table.

'So when did you start to spend so much time in London?' Libby started pulling things off hangers.

'When Roland spent more and more time abroad. And – ' Adelaide stopped abruptly.

'And Ramani began spending more time in Steeple Cross?'

Adelaide turned her back and Libby grinned. Right again, Mrs Sarjeant.

So Carl was using Adelaide to keep him warm at night when Ramani went off on her own. Was that before Roland started seeing Ramani? And was Roland the reason Ramani began to spend more time in Steeple Cross? And was any of this a motive for double murder? Libby sighed and stuffed another coat into her sack.

After another half an hour most of the drawers and all the wardrobe had been cleared.

'You start taking the bags downstairs,' said Libby, breaking the half-hour-long silence. 'I'll finish the shelves.'

Adelaide shot her a look, but picked up two bags and left the room. Libby began methodically to check the shelves and drawers, finding odd buttons, safety pins and a grubby cotton bud. And the corner of a brown envelope.

She was just about to throw it into the bin that they'd been using for rubbish, when something caught her eye.

'Oh, this is just too ridiculously like a detective story,' she muttered to herself, nevertheless going to the window and holding the paper closer.

Printed in the corner of the envelope were the words "Institute of Napoleonic Studies".

Chapter Twenty-one

Libby stood still, staring at the envelope. There was no printed address beneath the words, just a jagged tear. She heard Adelaide returning and tucked it up her sleeve.

'Finished?' said Adelaide, sounding tired.

'I think so,' said Libby. 'I haven't checked the top of the wardrobe.'

Adelaide paused, looking at her quizzically, before picking up a hanger and sweeping it across the top of the wardrobe, releasing a cloud of dust.

'That's it, then. Thank you so much for your help.'

Libby handed her a black bag and took the other herself, before preceding her down the stairs.

'Shall I help you get these into the car?'

'Would you?' Adelaide's manner had definitely changed. 'Then I'll get straight off.'

Eyeing the other woman's rather dusty appearance, Libby said 'Back to the hotel?'

'No, thank God. Back to the flat. That inspector knows where to find me. And Julian.'

'Right.' Libby clicked open the boot, which was already fairly full of bags and cases. 'Shall I put these on the back seat, then?'

'Oh, yes, please.' Adelaide opened the door and pushed her own bag inside. When all the bags were loaded, she held out the keys to Libby. 'Would you give these to the police, please? I don't want to come back here.'

Libby took them gingerly. 'I don't really think I ought to.'

'There'll be police at the grotto, won't there? You can give

158

them to them. I don't want to get involved.'

'All right.' Libby stood back as Adelaide climbed into the car. 'Are you sure you'll be all right? Does Carl know you're going?'

Adelaide's face tightened. 'He does. And I'll be fine. You've got my mobile number if you need me. Thanks again.'

The window glided up and Adelaide drove neatly out on to the lane. Libby watched her go with mixed feelings.

'Oh, you're here.' Fran came up behind her.

'Yes, I've just seen Adelaide off the premises.' Libby turned to her friend. 'I've just found something peculiar.'

'Tell me about it as we go,' said Fran. 'Edward and Andrew are waiting at the grotto.'

'Andrew? Who asked him?'

'Edward, apparently.'

'Has he told you what he told me about Ramani in London?'

'No. What?'

Libby told Fran of all she had learnt from Edward and Adelaide in the last twenty-four hours.

'So what do we get from all that?' asked Fran, as they approached the grotto. 'Carl and Adelaide were having an affair, either as a result of Roland and Ramani having an affair, or because they were both lonely. And they both lied about it. And Ramani probably did know Julian Watson, and carried on seeing other men in London even after she was married to Carl?'

'That's what it sounds like. I expect Ian knows all that by now, but I found something else.' Libby stopped and pulled the piece of paper from hr sleeve. 'Look.'

'Is this the something peculiar?' Fran took the piece of paper. 'Good God.'

'Yes.'

'Where was it?'

'Caught in the back of a drawer.'

'So we don't know if it belonged to Adelaide or Roland?'

'I somehow doubt it was Roland's. He wouldn't have left anything around for Adelaide to find while he was away, and he was never here when she wasn't.'

159

'Do we know that?' asked Fran.

'Well, no. I assumed, because he always wanted Adelaide to pick him up.'

'At least it proves that one or other of them knew something about the smugglers and the guinea boats.'

'Is that a leap of the imagination, though?' asked Libby with a frown.

'Perhaps we should give it to the police?'

'Oh, that reminds me.' Libby looked over her shoulder to where the police tape stretched across the entrance to the grotto. 'Are there any police there?'

'Just one poor constable to keep an eye on us.'

'Only Adelaide gave me the keys to the house. She said to give them to the police.'

They stood looking at one another for a moment.

'Dare we?' said Libby.

'Adelaide gave you the keys. I think you'd be perfectly within your rights to pop in and check on things.'

'Shall we tell Edward and Andrew?'

'About the piece of paper? They probably have more knowledge about it than we have.'

'Come on, then.' Edward and Andrew were standing looking down into the hole under the stone bridge in the grotto.

'We waited for you,' said Edward, his white smile splitting his face. 'It's a bit of a climb down.'

'What have they actually found?' asked Libby, as Edward started down the ladder.

'Tunnels going back towards the house and forward to Keeper's Cob,' said Andrew, 'not news, exactly, but confirmation.'

Standing at the bottom of the hole, they could see the brick built tunnels leading away in both directions.

'There's a fall of rock in the Keeper's Cob tunnel,' said Edward, 'but the one leading back to the house has been properly bricked up.'

'So there's no way the bodies could have been brought here that way?' said Fran.

'None.' Edward shook his head. 'Do you want to have a look?'

The tunnel towards Keeper's Cob was low and dank. Andrew and Edward both had powerful torches, but it didn't stop it feeling claustrophobic.

'Creepy,' said Libby, and shivered, as they came upon the fall of rock that blocked the tunnel.

Edward clambered over the lowest rocks and shone his torch into crevices.

'Nothing,' he said coming back down, 'but there wouldn't be. The police have been all over this place.'

'Let's go back and look at the other tunnel,' said Fran.

The tunnel towards the house was wider and taller and appeared to be better built. It ended abruptly in a brick wall.

'There's nothing to see,' said Libby. 'Why did Ian say we could come and see it?'

'He wanted an opinion on the date of construction. Lewis couldn't come, so Edward asked me,' said Andrew. 'It's quite exciting.'

'And what's your opinion?' asked Fran.

Andrew looked at Edward. 'Difficult, isn't it?'

Edward was peering at the walls and tapping the ceiling, which was also brick. 'Nineteenth-century?'

'That's what we thought when we were here before,' said Libby.

'It is,' said Fran.

Libby looked at her. 'That's what Ian wanted from you, isn't it?'

Fran was frowning. 'There have been deaths here.' She looked up at Libby. 'I don't know.'

'Shall we go into the house and see if we can find the passages and the tunnels from there?' asked Libby.

'The house?' Edward turned to look at her. 'Is that woman still there?'

'No. She gave me the keys.'

'What?' Edward looked over his shoulder towards the opening to the grotto. 'Does he know?'

'No, so keep it quiet.'

Edward turned without another word and led them back to the entrance. Once at the top of the ladder, he turned to the police officer. 'That's it, we're done,' he said. 'Have you got to stay here?'

'No, sir. I'm off back to the station.' He moved a large wooden pallet over the hole. 'You can see yourselves out?'

'Yes, thanks,' said Libby. 'We'll just go and check on my son's tools before we go?'

'Tools?' The officer raised an eyebrow.

'My son and his colleague were landscaping the new swimming pool when the first body was found, and everything's been left here,' Libby explained.

'Swimming pool, blimey. Fine, you go and have a look.' He sketched a vague salute and went off to his car on the forecourt. Libby led the way through the arch in the hedge to where Mog's tarpaulin covered all the tools, and where the carefully-dug earth round the perimeter of the empty pool had been spread all over the garden.

'I hope she pays them overtime after this,' muttered Libby.

'I hope she pays them, period,' said Fran. 'I bet she tries to get out of it. Come on, let's go in through the kitchen.'

'Now,' said Edward, as they grouped round the kitchen table, 'how do we go about this?'

'The door we found before,' said Libby. 'Have the police checked it out?'

'We told them about it, so I should think so,' said Fran. 'Let's go and look.'

'Before we do,' said Libby, 'I want to show Edward and Andrew this.' She pulled out the piece of paper and put it on the table.

'Well!' said Andrew.

'I've never heard of this Institute,' said Edward.

'It's a proper printed envelope, though,' said Libby. 'Not a mocked-up one, as far as I can tell.'

'One way to find out,' said Edward, bringing out his phone.

'Wish I'd brought my tablet, now,' said Andrew, gazing

162

enviously at Edward's phone.

'Well, it doesn't show up in searches, although there is a French Foundation, the *Fondation Napoléon* and an Institute on Napoleon and The French Revolution at Florida University, of all things. But no British Institute.' Edward scrolled through a few more searches.

'Or at least, not one with an online presence,' said Fran.

'Even if it didn't have its own website, it would be mentioned on others,' said Edward. 'So what do we think about that?'

They all looked at each other.

Libby shrugged. 'It can't be coincidence,' she said. 'If either Roland or Adelaide – or even Ramani – was following the same trail we have, they would have found out about the links with the French prisoners of war and the guinea boats. And tried to find out something about it.'

'Paper analysis,' said Andrew suddenly. 'Your detective chief inspector should be able to find out which paper that scrap is.'

'It'll be standard manila,' said Libby. 'You can buy it in packs from every supermarket, apart from stationers.'

'You said it isn't a home mock-up,' said Fran, pulling the paper towards her. 'So it could be a proper printer.'

Libby shook her head. 'No, I know what it is. One of those online companies where you can order anything with anything printed on it. We got the leaflets for The Manor done by one of them.'

'Of course. All Ian would have to do was find out which one.' Fran sighed and leant back. 'Do we think it is a mock-up? And if so, how did it happen?'

'Goodness knows. Perhaps Ian can ask Adelaide.'

'But would she tell him?' asked Edward. 'No, I think we need to find out ourselves.'

Libby regarded him with some amusement. 'Oh, we do, do we? And what happened to poor old Sir Godfrey?'

He grinned across the table at her. 'Oh, I'm hooked, now. Fully paid-up member of Libby's Loonies.'

'Libby's what?' said Andrew and Fran together.

'Harry being silly,' said Libby.

'That's the boy with the restaurant?' said Andrew.

'He'll thank you for the "boy",' said Libby. 'Yes, that's him. He's decided that everyone who makes friends with me is slightly odd.'

'I'm not sure he's not right,' said Fran with a sigh.

'Come on, then,' said Edward, standing up. 'Let's go and look at the cellar.'

The police had obviously investigated, because the cellar door now opened fully and smoothly.

'I thought Lewis said the cellar had been bricked up,' said Libby, peering nervously into the darkness, where a flight of steep steps led downwards.

'He did.' Edward was standing on the top step. 'But it isn't.'

He shone his torch round, showing them brick walls.

'These are much earlier than the bricks blocking the grotto tunnel. And the police have been down here – no cobwebs.'

'I am *not* going down there,' said Libby firmly.

'I am,' said Fran suddenly. 'Libby, you remember where I was on the stairs? Can you go back there?'

'Yes. Now?'

'Please.' Fran stepped on to the top step beside Edward, who, along with Andrew, was looking bewildered. 'Come on, Edward, let's go down.'

Libby watched them descend. 'You'd better stay at the top, Andrew, so they don't accidentally get shut in. I'm going up the stairs.'

Libby found the right staircase below Adelaide's room and sat on the third step down. After a few minutes, she heard a muffled shout and Andrew's answering call. And then, with stomach-dropping suddenness, Fran's voice spoke almost in her ear.

Chapter Twenty-two

'Libby? Are you there?'

Libby shot to her feet and slipped. Grabbing hold of the banister rail, she hauled herself upright.

'Wh-where ...?' she managed.

'Oh, good,' came Fran's slightly muffled voice. 'I thought I was right. Go back to the half landing.'

On slightly shaky legs Libby climbed back to the half landing, where the tall stained glass window looked out over the side of the house.

'Can you see this?' asked Fran, sounding nearer.

'See what?' said Libby, and then saw. Part of the panelled wall was shaking. She went across to it and gingerly gave it a push. It gave way and she almost fell through, straight into Fran's arms.

'Bloody hell!'

Fran steadied her and stood back. 'Look,' she said.

Libby saw that she was standing in a small, stone-walled room. Fran was shining a torch into the corners.

'Did you borrow Andrew's torch?' asked Libby.

'No, this is Edward's. He went back and got Andrew's.'

'So how did you find it? And how did the police miss it?'

'At the bottom of the cellar steps you can see where the tunnel goes towards the grotto, and eventually, where it's bricked-up. And the police had obviously been there. But something took me back to the cellar steps. And there's a door underneath them.'

'But surely,' said Libby, 'the police would have found that when they were investigating?'

'Oh, they did,' said Fran. The hinges had been oiled and the door opened really easily.'

'So how did they miss – er, what *did* they miss?'

'It was a classic understairs cupboard. I don't know what it was used for when the cellars were in use, if they ever were used for anything legitimate. That's when I borrowed the torch.'

'And?'

'At the back was a panelled wall. I thought that was a bit odd in a cellar cupboard.'

'So would I.'

'So I went and pushed. But it didn't work, so I called Edward and he came and we levered it open. This one opened outwards. It had to, because of the stairs behind.'

Libby gasped. 'A hidden staircase after all! And it led here?'

'It's actually built underneath the main staircase, so there's not much head room, but it leads here, look.' Fran pointed the torch to the nearest corner of the room, where the steps could just be seen. 'No one very big could have gone up and down, but people were smaller a couple of centuries ago, weren't they?'

'What date are we talking, though?' asked Libby. 'Could this have been constructed after the house was built?'

Edward's head appeared at the top of the steps. 'It's a bit of a squeeze,' he said, with a grin, 'but I've made it. I sent Andrew up the main stairs.'

'And here I am,' said Andrew stepping into the little room behind Libby and going straight to the walls.

'Prop that door with something, Libby, so we don't get shut in and we've got some light.' Edward squeezed himself through the gap and stood up, brushing himself down. Libby ran up to Adelaide's room and fetched a small chair which she used as a doorstop.

'What do we think?' she asked. 'Priest's hole? What we were looking for last week?'

'It certainly looks like it,' said Andrew. 'And it goes right down into the cellar and then away to Keeper's Cob. The grotto wouldn't have been there, then.'

'Do you suppose the Victorians who built the grotto found it and they were the ones who bricked up the tunnel?' asked Fran.

'Do we know when the grotto was built?' asked Andrew.

'Yes, there's an inscription on the underside of that fake bridge,' said Edward. '1883. But I would have thought the bricking up was done earlier.'

'Can I have that torch, Fran?' asked Andrew. He took it and peered at the wall. 'Look, here.'

The other three came to peer over his shoulder. Very faintly, they could see, scratched into the stone, "1647".

'The date it was made?' asked Libby.

'No.' Edward stood back. 'The last date it was used, maybe.' He swung his torch round the room, revealing cobwebs. 'This was made earlier. By Nicholas Owen, do you think, Andrew?'

'A bit crude for Owen, perhaps?' Andrew turned a full circle looking at the little room.

'Excuse me,' said Libby. 'Who is Nicholas Owen?'

'Saint Nicholas Owen,' said Andrew, 'according to the Catholics, anyway. He was a Jesuit lay brother who was an expert at constructing priest's holes. He died in 1606.'

'So if he built it, it was before Godfrey Wyghtham made the alterations in 1643,' said Fran.

'And that's when he would have found it!' said Libby. 'And where he would have hidden his treasure for Rebecca.'

'It isn't here now,' said Edward, giving the room another sweep with his torch, 'but I really want to examine this place thoroughly. Andrew?'

'It's all very well keeping the keys to have a quick look round,' said Libby, 'but suppose Adelaide checks with the police that we've handed them in?'

Edward looked at his watch. 'Could we stay here for a couple of hours now?'

'We-ell,' Libby looked at Fran.

'We were given permission to be here, today,' she said.

'But only at the grotto under police guard,' said Libby.

'And you had Adelaide's permission to be here in the house,' said Fran.

Libby fidgeted.

167

'It's not like you to be squeamish about doing something without the benefit of police blessing.' Fran eyed her friend quizzically.

'I know, but …'

'I'll call the chief inspector,' said Edward suddenly, stepping out on to the half landing and taking out his phone.

'No need. I'm here.'

Four people swung round to face Chief Detective Inspector Connell, looking up at them from the foot of the stairs.

'And for once,' he said, starting to climb towards them, 'I was very pleased to hear Mrs Sarjeant upholding the law.'

Libby went pink.

'I suppose you were going to tell me eventually what you were doing?' Ian joined them and peered into the priest's hole. 'What have we here?'

'That's what you wanted us to find, isn't it?' said Fran. 'Why you asked me, specifically? You let us have a look at the grotto, hoping for dating evidence of the tunnel and that I might have a revealing flash of inspiration. Well, this was it.'

Andrew, Edward and Libby looked relieved.

Ian smiled. 'Well done. I knew I could rely on you.' He went inside the priest's hole and looked round. 'No sign of anything relevant?'

'Not yet,' said Edward, 'but Andrew found a date scratched on the wall.'

Andrew took his torch and showed Ian the marking.

'And the steps?' asked Ian, going down on his haunches in front of them.

'If we go downstairs, we'll show you,' said Fran.

Leaving the door to the little room open, they trooped down the stairs to the inner hall, where Edward and Fran led Ian into the cellar. Andrew and Libby retired to the kitchen, where Libby rooted round and found tea, coffee and sugar, and even a container of dried milk.

Whe Ian, Fran and Edward appeared, divesting themselves of even more cobwebs, Libby offered tea or coffee.

'I'm sure Adelaide wouldn't mind,' she said. 'After all, she did ask me to come and help her pack this morning.'

'And you did, obviously,' said Ian, pulling out a chair and sitting at the table.

'That's why I've got the keys,' said Libby, omitting the fact that she was supposed to be handing them over. 'And there's something else.'

Edward frowned at her, but she nevertheless produced the scrap of paper.

'We think it must be all connected. If any of them was looking for so-called treasure, they would have come across the guinea boat story as we did. But there is no Institute.'

Ian took the paper and squinted at it. 'So this is –? What?'

'A fake. But who by?'

'Edward? Andrew?' Ian turned to the two men. 'No idea?'

'Neither of us have ever heard of the Institute,' said Andrew. 'What interests me is why someone should have bothered to set it up, and how they knew to get in touch with someone in this house.'

'That's not necessarily so,' said Fran. 'It could have been someone here who set it up.'

They all looked at her.

'We've said all along Roland could have been trying to impress Ramani,' Fran went on. 'What better than to set something like this up?'

Edward shook his head. 'She wouldn't have been fooled. She was a historian, remember.'

'The other way round, then?' suggested Libby. 'Ramani invented it to – to – well, to do something.'

Ian turned to Fran. 'Do you think those steps and the priest hole are connected to either of the murders?'

'I don't know. But when we went into the tunnel under the grotto, I knew there'd been deaths there.'

'But not whose?'

'No, sorry.'

Ian sighed. 'We'll get forensics to go over the priest's hole and the steps to the cellar. It's a perfect escape route.'

'Roland couldn't have got down there,' said Libby. 'Edward

169

only just managed it, and Roland was twice his size.'

'We'll still look at it,' said Ian, and took a small evidence bag from his pocket. 'I think this is closing the stable door, considering you've all probably handled it, but better safe than sorry.' He dropped the piece of envelope into the bag. 'Where did you find it, Libby?'

Libby told him. 'I didn't tell Adelaide.'

'Was it one of her drawers?'

'I assume so. We discussed it, and we don't think Roland would have left it behind, and it was a drawer we'd emptied. It didn't occur to me, but she would only have emptied her own drawers. His stuff will still be there.'

Ian sighed. 'And we've let her go back to London.'

'Can't you go up there?' asked Andrew. 'Surely it's enough of a – a – what do I mean?'

'Clue?' suggested Libby.

'I'll send someone to ask her,' said Ian.

'But unannounced. Don't give her a chance to think up an answer,' said Libby.

Ian laughed. 'Yes, Libby. I think we know enough to do that.'

'Sorry.' Libby made a face.

'Well, if that's all, I think we might lock up and go home.' Ian held out his hand. 'I'll take the keys, thank you, Libby.'

Libby handed them over. 'We did find something out for you.'

'You did.' He turned to Fran. 'Thank you, Fran.'

Fran cleared her throat and gazed at her feet.

Libby collected mugs and rinsed them in the sink, then, in silence, they all trooped out of the house.

'Is the back door locked?' asked Ian.

'We didn't lock it,' said Fran.

Ian sighed and went inside.

'That's it, then,' said Libby. 'We can't do any more searching.'

'We've still got a lot to look for,' said Edward. 'I'm determined to find out about that Napoleonic Institute, and as much as I can about Godfrey Wyghtham.'

'You're getting worse than me,' said Libby.

Ian came out of the front door and locked it behind him. 'I've set the burglar alarm,' he said, 'so don't try getting back in.'

'As if we would,' said Libby indignantly.

'I wouldn't put anything past you, Libby.' Ian smiled and patted her shoulder. 'Will you be in the usual place this evening after rehearsal?'

Edward's eyebrows went up.

'Yes, I expect so. Will you be popping by? Edward's staying in the pub for the time being, by the way.'

'I know,' said Ian. 'Don't forget I was the one who told him he could come over here today.'

He turned to Edward and Andrew.

'Will you give me a brief report on your thoughts, both of you? In writing?'

'I'll email it later,' said Edward.

'So will I,' said Andrew. 'When you've given me your email address.'

Ian nodded. 'See you later then. And Libby, please don't go poking round the garden or the grotto.'

'Who am I? The naughtiest girl in the school?' grumbled Libby, as they watched Ian drive away.

'Meet you behind the bike sheds,' said Fran.

Chapter Twenty-three

'Do you really think Edward will carry on on his own?' said Ben later, when Libby had relayed the day's doings.

'I really think he might, but he's got to get back home at some point,' said Libby. 'I expect he'll be in the pub tonight to see what Ian has to say.'

Sure enough, when Ben, Libby and Peter followed other cast members down to the pub at just after ten o'clock, Edward was there, nursing a drink at the bar.

'Come and meet the gang,' said Libby, leading him to the table where Patti and Anne sat. 'You know our friend Patti, and this is her friend Anne.'

'I thought it was you, but I didn't like to intrude,' said Edward, sitting down next to Anne's wheelchair.

By the time drinks had been fetched, Ian had joined them and asked for his customary coffee. He fixed Edward with a stern eye.

'Now don't tell anyone anything that's said tonight. I've got into the habit of coming and talking things over here whenever Libby's involved in something, which,' he said, turning the stern eye on Libby, 'is far too often. You'll have already seen how helpful she and Fran –'

'Mostly Fran,' Libby put in.

'– mostly Fran,' amended Ian, 'can be. And as long as it doesn't hamper the police investigation, I'm happy with the situation. However, my superiors, not to mention some of my junior officers, wouldn't be.'

'That's fair,' said Edward. 'But haven't you ever let out something in front of someone who turned out to be – well – the wrong person?'

'I don't think so,' said Ian. 'Unless you're confessing to something?'

It was difficult to tell, but Libby was sure Edward flushed.

'No, of course not.'

'Good.' Ian looked at him for a moment longer. 'So, anyone come to any startling conclusions since this morning?'

Patti, Anne and Peter all demanded to be told what had happened that morning, and after Libby and Ian between them had filled in the details, Patti said, 'What about that jewellery you found last week?'

'I'd forgotten about that!' said Libby.

'It's gone to some experts,' said Ian. 'We haven't had the results back yet.'

'It strikes me,' said Anne, leaning forward in her chair, 'That this whole thing is an elaborate set-up.'

Everyone looked at her earnest, pixie face, with its lively brown eyes.

'Set-up?' repeated Ian.

'Everyone's said at one time or another, if I've got it right – Patti tells me things I don't know, you see – that they think that this Roland made up the treasure story to capture the woman's interest. The envelope and fake Institute would be part of the same thing.'

'But why on earth go to such lengths?' said Peter. 'The other woman – what's her name – Adelaide – said he was always having affairs. Why did this one matter so much?'

'He'd really fallen in love?' suggested Patti, to be met by scornful snorts from all the men. 'Obviously not, then.'

'You know,' said Libby, 'the one thing we haven't thought of. At least, I haven't. What did Roland want from Ramani if it wasn't just sex? If Anne's right, and the fake Institute is part of the hoax?'

'We talked about that this morning,' said Edward. 'I said, if you remember, it wouldn't have taken her in.'

'But you're right,' said Ian. 'Roland wanted more than just sex from Ramani. And I don't think it was love, either.

'But then he was killed too.' Anne looked round at them all. 'Why?'

Libby leant back in her chair and looked at the ceiling. 'I think we've been looking at this upside down.'

All attention turned to her.

'What if,' she said, returning her gaze to the company, 'Roland wanted Ramani to help him in some kind of scam?'

Silence met the remark.

'Good Lord,' said Ian eventually. 'I think you might have done it again.'

Ben grinned and patted Libby's hand. 'Classic, love.'

'You see,' Ian looked round the table, finishing up with Edward. 'This is where the leaps of faith come in. As police officers, we can't speculate and we're not supposed to go on blind hunches, so blind hunches get trained out of us. And occasionally, Libby or Fran come up with something that wouldn't have even occurred to us. Oh, we might get there in the end after pursuing a lot of tortuous leads, but this way we might be able to work backwards to prove it.'

'I'm not entirely sure I understood that,' said Edward, with his large white grin, 'but well done, Libby, anyway. I think.'

'It makes perfect sense,' said Ben. 'Think of the jewellery. The clues that you have all followed up. Suppose people were *supposed* to follow those clues. Or suppose Roland and Ramani were going to lay them out for people. Then the fake Institute *would* be part of the scam.'

'Exactly,' nodded Libby. 'Roland, for some reasons of his own, probably financial, wants to prove that the house is of some historical importance. Edward, would that make sense?'

'It's already Grade II listed,' said Edward. 'It attracts any funding that might be going from English Heritage, but it's not of huge importance.'

'So would faking a connection with historical events make a difference?' asked Ian.

'It might, if they were going to go public, say, with a book?' said Patti.

'It's an awful lot of trouble to go to,' said Libby dubiously, 'but I still think it's a possibility.'

'And they were both killed because of it?' asked Peter, nursing his glass of pale lager.

'Well, it's about the only thing that's made sense so far,' said Libby.

'And it does make sense,' said Ian. 'Thanks Libby. You've done well today. What with Fran's secret stairs and priest hole, and you with the envelope and inspiration.'

'Thank you.' Libby beamed at him. 'Oh – I know what I wanted to ask you. Did you get anyone to speak to Adelaide?'

'Not yet. Local officers have called twice and there's been no answer. Tomorrow, Robertson and a female DC are going up to try again, and they'll try Julian Watson, too.'

On the way home, Libby linked her arm with Ben's and sighed.

'It was a brilliant theory, but I actually can't make it fit anything.'

'No,' admitted Ben, 'neither can I.'

'I like the idea of Roland and Ramani being in cahoots, though. It makes more sense than just the sex thing.'

'I wonder if Ramani's husband had any idea what was going on?' said Ben.

'He lied about the affair, so he might have done. And I still wonder about his relationship with Adelaide. She's been very tight-lipped about it.'

'Perhaps it was those two who were in cahoots,' suggested Ben.

'Oh, don't,' groaned Libby.

The following morning, after a brisk flurry of housework and washing, Libby, settled herself down at the laptop. Sidney sat down beside it and butted her fingers with a wet nose.

'You are not helping,' said Libby reprovingly, and tried to move him aside. He put his ears down and closed his eyes. Libby sighed and began her internet search. But whatever search terms she used, she couldn't find anything which would relate to a historic house scam.

'Had this brilliant idea,' she emailed Fran, 'but I think I was on the wrong track.' She went on to describe the brilliant idea, but the more she wrote it down, the more ridiculous it sounded. In the end, she pressed send and shut the laptop.

'OK,' she said to Sidney, 'what shall I do now?'

If it was summer, or spring at least, she could go exploring, round the lanes near Steeple Cross and Keeper's Cob perhaps. But her experiences of the lanes on her own and with Fran had put her off. And now that Adelaide had gone back to London there was no point of contact with the investigation. Carl Oxenford was an unknown quantity; she couldn't go bothering him.

Brainwave: what was the name of Adelaide's housekeeper? And Johnny Whoever who looked after the grounds. Why hadn't they seen him yesterday? Libby called Adam.

'Marilyn Fairbrass is the housekeeper. She comes over from Keeper's Cob in her son's Land Rover. And Johnny – I've forgotten his surname – he's still living in his cottage, or hut, or whatever you'd call it, but keeping strictly out of the way. Mog spoke to him the other day.'

'You don't know the Fairbrass son's name, or the name of his farm?'

'Of course not, Ma.' Adam sounded exasperated. 'What are you planning, anyway? You can't go barging in asking questions when you've never met people.'

'No, I suppose not. You don't fancy taking me over to see Johnny?'

'No, I do not!' Adam exploded. 'Honestly, Ma. Grow up and leave this to the police.'

'A fine way to talk to your mother,' said Libby huffily and switched off the call. 'Phone book,' she said to Sidney, and went to find it. Sometimes, old technology beat new.

But although there were three Fairbrass entries in the phone book, one was in Dover, one was in Felling and one was in Canterbury.

'Which,' Libby told Sidney, 'means only that they no longer have landlines, Marilyn and her son. Would have thought the farm needed a landline, though.' She sighed, and opened the laptop to see if Fran had replied. She had.

'It's a very good theory,' she wrote, 'but I can't see the point of it. There would have to be a pay-off, and just faking the Napoleon site as a connection wouldn't be enough. There has to be gain somewhere.'

'Exactly,' Libby wrote back. 'And that doesn't seem possible.'

Unless, she thought a little later while making toast for lunch, they were planning something else.

'I've had another idea,' she told Fran over the phone. 'I think I need either Andrew or Edward to look at the county archives again.'

'How about,' said Fran, 'we don't bother with them, but we go into Canterbury and find Anne in her library. I bet she's got access to stuff there.'

'I never thought of that!' said Libby. 'How clever. Do we know which library she's in?'

So it was that Fran arrived at half past one, collected Libby and drove into Canterbury.

'We could go to Waitrose while we're here,' said Libby, as they emerged from the car park.

'Have you come in to money?' asked Fran.

'Just to have a look,' said Libby. 'Where are we going?'

They found Anne in the beautifully modernised library where she was working at a computer.

'Hello!' she said, surprised.

Libby explained what she was looking for.

'Items connected to the Napoleonic Wars?' Anne looked doubtful. 'Yes, there are some, but there are more in Maidstone.'

'What about smuggling?'

'Oh, yes, we've got some of that, but then, so has Whitstable. What are you looking for specifically.'

'You know those guinea boats we were talking about?'

'Yes?'

'What about guineas? Or gold?'

Anne laughed. 'You don't imagine any of that would have survived! No one would have left any gold lying around for

177

nearly two hundred years.'

'No,' said Libby, strangely triumphant.

'What's this all about?' asked Anne. 'What aren't you telling me?'

'Libby's told me about her great idea last night,' said Fran, 'which she then decided was a non-starter.'

'Until,' said Libby, 'I suddenly realised that could be what Roland and Ramani were planning to create. Fake guineas. A fake French prisoner of war hide out. Think how famous that would make Dark House!'

Chapter Twenty-four

Anne frowned. 'It might, I suppose, but I can't see that there would be any money in it.'

'If they could prove the link to the prisoners of war and the smugglers' runs, what they found would be of huge interest,' said Libby. 'Look, they'd report the stuff to whom? The local Finds Liaison Officer. Then the coroner would decide if it was treasure trove. Meanwhile, some kind of provenance would be needed, so the fake Napoleonic Institute provides information that proves Dark House's connection to the whole business. As long as there's enough there, once it had been authenticated, it would be bought by a museum and Roland would have got the spoils.'

'But not a lot,' objected Anne. 'Not like a Saxon hoard. And surely he'd be better keeping the guineas if he'd got any.'

'That is a bit of a stumbling block,' said Libby, 'but he could never get rid of them unless he sold them on the black market, anyway.'

'So we're back to the arts and antiquities smuggling game,' said Fran.

Libby turned and looked at her in awe. 'Bloody hell, Fran! Of *course*!'

'Eh?' said Anne, bringing her chair a bit nearer. 'And keep your voice down.'

'Oh, sorry. But they haven't got the silence rule any more, have they?' Libby obligingly moved nearer the desk. 'That's it, don't you see? I'd got it a bit wrong. Roland was trying to smuggle stuff and the fake Institute was to provide provenance for fake antiquities.'

179

Fran looked smug. Libby squinted at her. 'I bet you didn't actually think of that, but never mind – it works.'

'It does,' said Anne. 'More sense than faked guineas or whatever going to the FLO.'

'Well, there! So what antiquities have you got that might be worth money?'

'None. Not of that period. Hang on, I'll look up Maidstone.' Anne slid her chair back to behind her computer and tapped at the keyboard. 'Napoleon's chair from St Helena at the Maidstone Museum,' she said. 'I don't know if I can access the new Kent History and Library Centre. I think you might have to go there and ask. But it won't have artefacts.'

'That's a help, though,' said Libby. 'What do you think, Fran?'

'Apart from the fact that you're off on another wild goose chase?'

Libby was indignant. 'You said it was a good idea, too. You wanted to come.'

'Yes, to see if there was anything in it. By accident, we – or you – think it might be to do with an antiques faking enterprise. So not entirely wasted.'

Anne laughed. 'Damned with faint praise,' she said. 'Anything else I can do for you?'

Libby went to Waitrose after all.

When they arrived back at number 17, the local free paper had been delivered. Fran picked it up while Libby went through to the kitchen to unpack and put the kettle on.

'That pub on the corner of Dark Lane,' said Fran coming in to the kitchen with the open paper. 'Is it The Dragon?'

Libby thought for a moment. 'Yes, I think so. Why?'

'They've got a special on tonight.'

'A special what?'

'A Middle Eastern night, three courses for the price of two.'

'With belly-dancing?'

Fran looked up. 'I could do without that.'

'What are you suggesting?' Libby put the last item in the fridge and brought out the milk. 'That we go there tonight?

Why?'

'I don't know. I thought it might be interesting. And Carl Oxenford lives right behind.'

'I somehow doubt he'll be there,' said Libby, pouring boiling water into the teapot.

'He might come out if we took Edward with us.'

Libby laughed. 'Fran! You're getting even more devious than I am.'

'Well? What do you think? You're not rehearsing tonight, are you?'

Libby put mugs on the table and sat down. 'Are you suggesting we go without Ben and Guy and ask Edward and Doctor Oxenford to escort us?'

'No, of course not. Well, not quite. Just us and Edward. And he could call in on Carl to see how he was.'

'How would our menfolk react, do you think?'

'I'll ask Guy.' Fran found her phone. 'Hello, darling. Oh, I'm at Libby's. No, no, I was just wondering if you minded if we went out for dinner tonight? No, Libby and me.' She rolled her eyes at Libby. 'Yes, of course it is. The pub at Steeple Cross. Yes, we will. Of course. See you later.'

She put the phone away. 'There. Guy doesn't mind. He did ask if it was to do with "the case" and told us to be careful.'

'Are you going home first? Only we'll have to take both cars …'

'Yes, yes. Now call Ben.'

'No need, I'm here.' Ben appeared in the kitchen doorway. 'What about?'

Fran explained while Libby got out another mug. 'Guy's all right about it,' she finished.

'Neither of us would stop you going out together,' said Ben, 'but we might be concerned about your safety.'

'We're hoping Edward will come with us,' said Libby.

'Oh, nice! You don't want us, but you do want Edward!'

'We wouldn't mind at all if you wanted to come with us,' said Libby. 'It's just you don't usually want to get involved.'

'I think it would make a change,' said Ben, grinning at Fran.

'Go on, we'd love to come. I'll phone Guy and ask – er – tell him!'

Fran shrugged and laughed, Ben got out his phone and Libby got hers to call Edward.

Edward volunteered to drive, grateful, as he said, to have something to do.

'Not that I don't have plenty of things to do at home,' he said, negotiating the turn into the car park of The Dragon, 'but I can't seem to drag myself away.'

'Libby's now decided the whole thing is an arts and antiquities scam,' said Ben, unfastening his seat belt.

Edward came round to help Libby out of the back seat. 'So nothing for me at all?'

'Well,' said Libby, 'no treasure, maybe, but you do know about Sir Godfrey. He's worth researching in his own right, isn't he? He'll fit into your book.'

'You're right, of course.' Edward ushered them both into the pub. 'Table for five for Hall,' he told the waiter.

'Oh, you booked?' said Libby in surprise.

'Look,' said Edward indicating both sides of the bar. It was almost completely full.

'I didn't even think about it,' said Ben. 'Thanks, Edward.'

They were led to a table at the far end of the right hand room, where Fran and Guy were already seated.

'Look!' said Libby. 'Proper tagines!'

The main course was, in fact, a choice between chicken, lamb or vegetarian tagine served with couscous. There were various desserts, a lot of which featured semolina, and starters including Dolmades, hummous and meze. After they'd ordered, Edward sat back and regarded them quizzically across the table.

'Why here?' he said. 'Right in front of Ramani's husband's house?'

'It was Fran's idea,' said Libby defensively. 'She saw the ad in the paper for the Middle Eastern night.'

'To be fair, I liked the sound of the evening,' said Ben. 'I persuaded Guy we should come.'

'So no ulterior motive, then?' said Edward.

'Would you have minded if there was?' asked Fran.

'No.' Edward chuckled. 'I'm obviously as mad as you are, now.'

'I did wonder if anyone knew anything about either who owned Carl's practice or Dark House before Carl and the Watsons,' said Libby. 'It's the only thing we don't know.'

'Would they know in here?' said Guy.

'Not if the people I met the first time I came here are anything to go by,' said Libby. 'I came in to ask the way. They weren't friendly.'

'But didn't they think you might be press?' said Fran. 'That made a difference.'

'Yes, I suppose so. And there was no one except the three of them in here. It doesn't seem like a proper local.'

'Obviously this is what they rely on.' Edward waved a large hand.

'Doesn't hurt to ask,' said Guy. 'They didn't take a drinks order, did they? I'll go to the bar.'

'I'll come with you,' said Ben, and they left the table to squeeze between the other diners.

'Not like them to get involved,' said Libby, following their progress.

'Oh, I don't know. There have been times.' Fran sat back and watched her husband complacently.

The men came back with a bottle of wine and two and a half pints of bitter, Edward limiting himself to the half.

'I'm having just the one pint,' said Guy. 'I think the tagine will soak it up.'

'So did you ask?' said Libby.

'We did,' said Ben. 'Very casually. You'd have been proud of us.'

'And?' prompted Fran.

'Carl set up the practice. There hadn't been a doctor here for some time. People were surprised.' Guy poured wine for Fran and Libby.

'I asked about Dark House, but the barman was very cagey about that,' said Ben. 'Said they'd had enough of reporters and didn't want to get involved.'

'I expect the police have asked Adelaide,' said Fran.

'Adelaide didn't think there was anything in the documents when they bought the house,' said Libby. 'But then he probably didn't show her everything.'

'Surely if they bought it between them –' began Ben.

'With mainly her money,' said Libby.

'She would have had to see all the documentation?'

'She was so cowed by him, I imagine he did the "don't bother your pretty little head about it, just sign here" thing,' said Libby.

'I can see that,' agreed Fran, 'but she's changed a lot since he died.'

'She was beginning to change after Ramani died,' said Libby. 'A lot stronger.'

'And we still don't know if she and Carl were having an affair,' said Fran.

Just then, the waiter brought their starters, and conversation stopped. When it resumed, Edward had obviously been thinking over what had been said.

'I don't know about an affair,' he said, pushing his plate away, 'but there was certainly some kind of relationship between them. Remember that first day we met?'

'Yes.' Libby and Fran nodded.

'They were very uncomfortable around one another. I got the feeling they didn't want me there.'

'Well, it was a difficult time,' said Guy.

'But it was as though they didn't want me to see something. I don't mean something like a book, I mean something intangible.'

'You were being a bit pushy,' said Libby.

'Was I? Oh. My obsession again, was it?'

'Your subject means a lot to you,' said Fran peaceably.

'So, if no one in here will talk about Dark House,' said Guy, 'how are you going to find out who Roland bought it from?'

'Ask Adelaide?' suggested Libby. 'I can always call her tomorrow to see if she got home all right.'

'She might not tell you, she's got out and wiped our dust off her feet,' said Fran. 'I think that's it as far as Adelaide goes.'

'I suppose so. So, nowhere to go, then?'

'I might pop over to check on Carl after we've eaten,' said Edward, his familiar white grin breaking out. 'That's what you were hoping, weren't you?'

Libby felt the heat coming into her cheeks.

'I did wonder,' said Fran, calmly. 'We know so little about him.'

'Then you all have a final drink at the bar when we've finished, and I'll go and see him.'

The tagines were all pronounced delicious. Libby decided she would have to persuade Harry to include a vegetarian version in his repertoire.

When they assembled at the bar, Edward left to go and see Carl, and Ben ordered drinks all round. A different barman served him.

'Heard you was asking about the Middleton place earlier,' he said conversationally, pouring wine.

'Middleton?' repeated Ben with a frown.

'Yeah. Place where the murders were. The Middleton place. Old Lady Middleton died. Old Wyghtham's daughter.'

Chapter Twenty-five

Stunned silence.

'Wyghtham?' Libby croaked finally.

'Yup.' The barman slid two glasses of wine and two brandies across the counter. 'Always swore it had been her family home.'

'Who exactly was she?' asked Fran, the first to recover properly. 'Was she Lady Middleton? Who was her husband?'

The barman looked up with a chuckle. 'Want to know a lot, don't you?'

The four of them looked at each other.

'Well, yes,' said Libby. 'We're – ah – involved in the investigation, you see.'

'You're not police.'

'No, we're ...' Libby stopped, not sure precisely what they were.

'We know Mrs Watson,' said Fran. 'We were called in to help her as she didn't have any local support.'

'No, she wouldn't.' The barman turned and put Ben's money in the till. 'Not much for being part of the village. Course,' he continued with a shrug, 'she weren't here mostly, and the old Middleton place isn't hardly in the village. More Keeper's Cob, to my way of thinking.'

'So,' said Libby, leaning cosily on the bar. 'This Lady Middleton. She owned the place?'

'Her old man did. Got his title back in the eighties. He got the house when his older brother died.'

'Is he still alive?' asked Ben.

'Nah. Died in the nineties. She stayed there until the last minute. Went into hospital kicking up a dust and died later the same day.'

'When was this?' asked Fran.

'Just before them Watsons bought it. They reckoned she'd been talking to him before she died.'

'Who do?' said Guy.

'Who do what?'

'Who reckon she'd been talking to Roland Watson?' elaborated Libby.

'Oh, everyone. "They" y'know?'

'Villagers,' said Fran.

'Yeah – just people. She weren't popular, see. Always had stuff delivered.'

'Didn't buy in the village,' said Libby.

'Even when we had a shop. Everything delivered. And only that Marilyn to help in the house.'

'Marilyn?' Libby and Fran both leant closer.

'Yeah.' The barman looked surprised. 'You know her?'

'Marilyn Fairbrass?

'Kevin's ma. Yeah.'

'Does she live on the farm with Kevin?' asked Fran.

Now the barman narrowed his eyes suspiciously. 'You don't know her.'

'Only as Adelaide Watson's housekeeper,' said Libby. 'So she stayed with the house.'

'You could say that.'

'So, Lady Middleton. She was a Wyghtham.'

'From over Cherry Ashton way. The Wyghthams been around here for ever.'

Edward appeared behind them.

'Wyghthams?' he repeated.

'We'll tell you outside,' said Libby. 'Are you going to have a drink?'

'No, I'm driving us back to Steeple Martin, aren't I?'

'How was Carl?' asked Fran.

'Subdued.' Edward glanced at the barman, who was looking interested.

'That Doctor Oxenford?' he asked. 'Poor bugger. Only been

187

here five minutes and goes and loses his wife. Mind, none of us know him, really.'

'Isn't he your doctor?' asked Guy.

'Well, no. Everyone goes to the Health Centre over in Steeple Mount. Always have. Haven't had a practice in the village since – before I were born, anyhow.'

'Did you know his wife?' asked Fran.

'Only saw her once. She were another one who never joined in. Never saw her about the place. Had things delivered.' He looked up at Edward. 'Sorry, mate, if she was a friend of yours.'

Edward shook his head with a slight smile.

'Come on, then,' said Libby, sliding off her bar stool. 'Time we were going.' She turned to the barman. 'Thanks for all the information. Let's hope it all gets cleared up soon, eh?'

She led a small company simmering with questions and tensions out of the bar and into the car park. 'What the –?'

'Wyghtham?'

'Middleton?'

'Cherry Ashton –?'

'No patients?'

Libby sat on the low wall that bordered the road. 'Do you realise we learnt more from that bloke than we've learnt in days. Well done for spotting that ad, Fran.'

'I wonder why the first barman was hostile?' mused Ben.

'I don't think he was hostile. He was just like those three blokes I saw the first time I came here. Wary.'

'Well Sammy the Second Barman certainly wasn't,' said Guy. 'I don't think I understood half the references you did.'

'And I haven't even heard them,' said Edward.

Libby rummaged in her bag and fished out a rather battered packet of cigarettes. 'I know I hardly ever have one of these now, but I feel the need,' she said. 'So don't anyone lecture me.' She lit the cigarette and proceeded to recount the barman's information, with frequent interruptions from Fran, Ben and Guy.

Edward looked positively lit-up. 'So there could be something there!'

188

'Not if old Lady Middleton-Wyghtham had been living there for twenty years or more. I wonder if she only married Mr Middleton to get back into the house?'

'They couldn't have had any children,' said Fran, 'or it would have been them who sold the house to Roland.'

'We just have to talk to Adelaide, now,' said Libby. 'I wonder if the police know this?'

'I don't suppose they'd think it was relevant,' said Ben.

'What about Carl?' asked Fran.

'He was just – subdued, as I said.' Edward frowned, leaning back against his car, his arms folded. 'He didn't say much.'

'In view of what the barman said, I wonder if he'll stay here,' said Guy,

'I don't understand it.' Edward shook his head. 'Why come here and start up a practice if there were going to be no patients?'

'He probably thought there would be, as there isn't a doctor in the village,' said Libby. 'How do you set up a practice? I thought there already had to be one you bought in to?'

'Quite a lot to look into,' said Fran. 'Go on, go home. We'll talk about it tomorrow.'

'And then,' said Libby, once they were in the car, 'there's Marilyn Fairbrass. We couldn't find a number for her, and it sounds as though we *really* need to talk to her. I wonder if the police have?'

'Of course they have,' said Ben. 'You know that.'

'But have they talked to her about *this*? About having been with Lady Middleton until the end?'

'I don't suppose they would even have thought about it,' said Ben.

'But she must know something,' said Edward.

'Maybe, maybe not,' said Libby, 'but someone needs to talk to her.'

'I really don't think the police are going to be interested, Libby.' Ben swivelled round from the front passenger seat. 'They only indulged you all about the treasure hunt while they

189

were casting around for something else.'

'You think this is involved with the treasure, then,' said Edward. 'This Lady Wyghtham – '

'Middleton,' said Libby.

'Lady Middleton knew about it … that's why she married?'

'I hope she wasn't quite that cynical,' said Libby. 'We'll see if Adelaide knows anything, and talk to Marilyn Fairbrass. At least we know her son's name now.'

'How will you find her?' asked Ben.

'Ask Adelaide,' said Libby.

But the next morning, Adelaide wasn't answering her phone.

While Libby was doing her Friday shop at the supermarket, her mobile rang.

'Can't hear you properly,' she said to the burbling voice. 'I'm in the supermarket.'

'Go to the door then,' came Ian's voice, and Libby, startled, did so.

'What's up?' She stood near enough to the doors to hear without setting off the alarms.

'Have you been in touch with Adelaide Watson since you saw her the day before yesterday?'

'No. I tried to ring her this morning but there was no reply.'

'Why? Why did you ring her?'

'To see how she was – if she'd got home all right.' Libby prevaricated. 'Why?'

'We can't get hold of her either. We sent Robertson up there yesterday, and according to the neighbours, no one's seen her.'

'What about Julian Watson?'

'Robertson tracked him down at work. According to him, he didn't even know his mother was coming back to London.'

'Do you believe him?'

'Apart from having had an affair with Ramani Oxenford while she was in London, he doesn't seem implicated in any way.'

'Oh, he's admitted that, has he?'

'Yes. He says he wasn't the only one.'

'Hmm. Ian, we learnt something else interesting yesterday.

190

At least, we thought it was interesting.'

DCI Connell sighed heavily. 'OK. What now?'

'Do you want to talk about it now? I'm in the middle of Sainsbury's and my frozen food's melting.'

'How urgent is it?'

'Not to say urgent, exactly.'

'I'll meet your at your place in – what? Half an hour?'

'OK,' said Libby meekly. She ended the call and phoned Fran.

'Can you meet me there, too?'

'I'm supposed to be shop-sitting, I can't really.'

'Oh, bugger,' said Libby, earning herself a dirty look from a passing grandmother with a toddler.

'You can call me while he's there if you need to,' said Fran. 'Go on, get a move on.'

Even though she hurried, Ian was still there before her, leaning on the bonnet of his long dark saloon looking Celtic and forbidding. He unbent enough to take her shopping bags while she opened the door, avoiding Sidney as he shot out of the door between their legs.

'Now, what's this all about,' he asked, as Libby began putting the frozen food away.

'Put the kettle on, will you?' said Libby. 'We can talk just as well with a cup of tea.'

Ian filled the electric kettle and switched it on. 'I don't trust your Rayburn. Now, go on.'

Libby told him everything they'd learnt the previous day, even her suspicions about the arts and antiquities racket.

'So you see, I really wanted to talk to Marilyn Fairbrass,' she finished, 'only we haven't got a number for her or her Kevin.'

Ian took his mug into the sitting room and sat in the armchair by the fireplace. 'To find out what?'

Libby sat opposite him. 'About old Lady Middleton. Did you know about her?'

'We knew Watson bought Dark House from the estate after probate, yes.'

'Who was her beneficiary?'

Ian raised his eyebrows. 'Her beneficiary? Why should we need to know that?'

'Ian!' Libby was shocked. 'Think about it. Someone might have been cross about the sale.'

'No, Libby. It would have been her beneficiary who authorised the sale.'

'Oh.' Libby deflated. 'Oh yes. Anyway, I'd still like to know. They might have found something out about the house after they'd sold it.'

'Why kill Ramani?'

'I don't know. I'm still thinking about this. It's a new theory. Anyway, what about Marilyn?'

'It's true we didn't know she was also with the previous owner. I suppose that bears further investigation.'

'Can't we talk to her?'

'If you can find her, I can't stop you,' said Ian with a sly smile.

'So you aren't going to tell me where she is?'

'No. But I will tell you the name of her son's farm.'

'Kevin. Does she live with him?

'The farm is Cob Farm. At the other end of Dark Lane.'

'Oh, lord,' said Libby gloomily. 'I hate that road. And what about Carl Oxenford and his ghost practice?'

'Just unlucky? From what we've heard over the last couple of weeks, his sole idea was to keep his wife away from temptation. I'll get on to the local Health Trust, see what I can find out.'

'You know,' said Libby, 'Adelaide was the one who told us Carl was their doctor. But was he NHS? Couldn't he have been private?'

'He could. That might make a difference.'

'Edward told us Carl was in practice in Leicester. Have you looked that up?'

'Libby,' said Ian, exasperated, 'we're the police. I am a Chief Detective Inspector. Of course we have!'

'And was that private?'

'No, although some of the doctors had private patients. Believe it or not, Carl Oxenford is still a partner of that practice, and personally owns the freehold of the property.'

'Blimey!' said Libby.

Chapter Twenty-six

Ian went away, promising to let Libby know if he heard anything about Adelaide. Libby rang Fran and told her what Ian had said.

'I want to see Marilyn Fairbrass,' she said. 'She's got to know something.'

'Did Ian say you could?'

'He said I could if I could find her. He also said she bears investigating.'

'When will you go?'

'I thought now. This afternoon. Before it gets dark.'

'Wouldn't it be better to wait until tomorrow morning? It gets dark so early in December.'

'But I want to speak to her as soon as possible!'

'Libby,' said Fran, with a patient sigh, 'suppose something happens? You get lost, or stuck in the mud or something?'

'Like Kevin turning out to be a mad axeman?'

'And it's dark. And you've got to get home again. You know what those lanes are like. They frightened you the first time you went there.'

'Oh, all right,' Libby grumbled. 'Will you be able to come with me tomorrow?'

'No, I'm still working in the shop. You ladies of leisure might be able to do what you like, but us workers can't.'

'You've got pots more money than I have!' said Libby indignantly.

'I also have a husband who won't take a penny of it and needs to make his business pay.'

'OK, OK. If Ben lets me, of course.'

'I thought he was off on his annual Christmas visit to the children tomorrow?'

Ben's grown-up children were now scattered over the country, but came together in London in order to see their father every Christmas. It wasn't an occasion either side relished.

'Oh, so he is. Bum. And it isn't Monday, so Harry can't come with me.'

'You've said you don't want Harry to come with you any more.'

'I could ask Pete.'

'You could ask Edward. He'd be game.'

'No.' Libby was firm. 'Much as I like him, I still don't quite trust him. He's got his own agenda. Pete hasn't got any agenda.'

'Ask him, then. But let me know when you leave, and text me every so often so I know where you are.'

Slightly unnerved by Fran's concern, Libby rang Peter.

'I'm sorry, me old trout,' he said, 'I'm off up Lunnon to do Christmas shopping and then go to a press dinner. I'm not coming home until Sunday.'

'Oh,' said Libby. 'Are you travelling up with Ben?'

'We are. And back on Sunday. We're even staying in the same hotel.'

'Why didn't I know any of this?'

'Because you don't listen, dear heart. Now, I shall tell Hal that you'll be in for supper on your own tomorrow night, shall I?'

'All right, thanks, Pete. Have a lovely time.'

Feeling forlorn, Libby wandered into the conservatory and peered out at the wintry garden. Low mist hung beyond the fence at the bottom, and the bare cherry tree dripped onto the dead leaves below. Libby sighed.

Christmas shopping, she pondered. Oh dear. She hadn't given it a thought. All she'd done was drag Ben off to get the tree. And now it was only two weeks until Christmas Day and a bit risky to rely on online shopping. However, if she made a start now, and paid for first class delivery, she supposed …

She went into the kitchen put a pan of soup on to heat and

went to light the fire in the sitting room. Ten minutes later, she was at the little table in the window, a bowl of steaming soup and the open laptop in front of her.

Half an hour later, her mobile ringing startled the life out of her.

'Is that Libby Sarjeant?' asked a strange masculine voice.

'Yes. Who's that? And how did you get my number?'

'It's Julian Watson here. Remember, we met in Canterbury?'

'Oh, yes. What can I do for you? I was actually trying to get hold of your mother this morning to see if she got back safely.'

'So were the police.' Julian sounded strained, and Libby decided not to tell him she knew that. 'So does that mean you don't know, either?'

'I'm afraid not. When did you last see her?'

'Last week in Canterbury, after she moved hotels. When did you see her?'

'The day before yesterday. She called me on Tuesday and asked me go to Dark House with her to help her pack, as she didn't want to go on her own. So I went on Wednesday morning. When she left she said she was driving straight to London.'

'Well, she didn't. None of her neighbours have seen her and I went with the police to the flat. There's no sign that she's been there.' Libby heard him take a deep, shuddering breath. 'Where can she be?'

'Julian, think. What do you know about your mother's private life? I'm not talking about the life she shared with your father.'

'That's just as well, because there wasn't much. He was hardly ever in the country.' Julian's voice was hard now. 'She wasn't happy, you know.'

'No. She changed a lot after he died, even in just a week.'

'Yes …' Julian trailed off.

'Was there something else? Something you've just thought of?'

'She was angry. I don't know what about, but it was as though she was expecting something to happen and it didn't.'

'Julian, I don't want to offend you, but – ' Libby stopped,

trying to work out exactly how to put her query.

He sighed heavily. 'I think I know what you're going to say. Was she having an affair.'

'Actually, yes. I was.'

'The truth is, I don't know. God knows, I wouldn't have blamed her if she'd had a dozen affairs, the way he treated her, but I truly don't know.'

'Even though you both lived in London most of the time? Didn't you see her then?'

'Sometimes, but we didn't move in the same circles. We'd have lunch or dinner together every now and then.'

'Do you think there's a possibility that she's gone to a lover? Sorry to put it like that.'

'If she has, why didn't she let me know?' Julian's voice was breaking, now. 'She didn't even tell me she was leaving the hotel.'

'What about your brother?'

'He hasn't heard anything either.' Julian took another deep breath. 'I know she wasn't everyone's idea of a good mother, but she was good to us.'

'Can I do anything to help?' asked Libby. 'Is there anyone down here you'd like me to go and see? Talk to? I'm going to see Marilyn Fairbrass tomorrow. Do you think she might know something?'

'I suppose so.' Now Julian sounded deflated. 'And that doctor, too. Ramani's husband.'

'Carl Oxenford.'

'Yes.' For a moment Libby thought she heard some other emotion in his voice. 'I'm pretty sure Mum knew him better than she let on.'

'I'll see them both,' promised Libby. 'What's your number? I'm no good at finding the numbers people are calling from.'

Julian reeled off two numbers, and also said he would let Libby know if he heard anything.

'Fran.' Libby took the phone with her into the kitchen, where she moved the big kettle on to the Rayburn hotplate.

'Has something happened?'

'Well, yes.' Libby recounted her conversation with Julian. 'Oh, and Pete's going up to London tomorrow with Ben, so I'll have to go to Cob Farm on my own. And I've promised Julian I'll see Carl Oxenford.'

'On your own?' Fran sounded doubtful. 'Is that wise?'

'I can't see Carl as a mad axe-wielding murderer, can you?''

'There's something not right about him, though,' said Fran. 'All the business of having no patients.'

'I'll risk it. It'll be broad daylight, and I'll ring you when I'm on his doorstep. So what do you think has happened to Adelaide?'

Fran was silent for a moment. 'I'm not feeling anything awful,' she said eventually. 'I wish we had something of hers, though.'

'Julian sounds frantic, poor boy.'

'I thought you'd stigmatised him as a money-grabbing ex-public-school trader?'

'I had. But he's still her son.'

Ben, as predicted, was dubious about the proposed expedition.

'But I've got to see if anyone knows where Adelaide might be,' argued Libby. 'Her son's worried stiff.'

'Shame he wasn't in touch with her more often, then,' said Ben with a scowl.

'He said they met in London, but when his father was home he wouldn't have wanted to come down here. And this wasn't their childhood home.'

'That isn't the only reason you're going, though, is it?'

'Well, no. I want to know about old Lady Middleton and the Wyghthams.'

'Can't you just ring up?'

'Neither of the Fairbrasses are listed in the directory. They must be mobile only.'

'Oh, all right.' Ben sighed. 'But promise me you'll keep in touch, at least by text.'

'I will. I told Fran the same thing.'

Peter collected Ben on Saturday morning, and, with many

dire warnings, they drove off towards Canterbury. Libby, having a sudden brainwave, went once again for the phone book and looked up Cob Farm. Sure enough it was there – under business listings. She took a deep breath and pushed the right buttons.

'Cob Farm,' said a female voice. 'How may I help you?'

'I'm awfully sorry to bother you,' said Libby, clearing her throat, 'but I'm trying to get in touch with Marilyn Fairbrass –'

'That's me,' broke in the voice. 'Who's asking?'

'My name's Libby Sarjeant,' said Libby, wishing she'd thought this through.

'Oh, are you young Adam's mother?'

'Yes,' said Libby in surprise. 'He didn't say he knew you.'

'Well, he doesn't, not really,' said Marilyn Fairbrass with a chuckle, 'but I know him. Johnny Templeton told me their names. The gardeners.'

'Oh, right. Well, I was actually wondering if I could talk to you at some point – '

'What about?'

'Adelaide Watson. She's disappeared.' Libby wondered if perhaps she shouldn't have let this out, but too late now.

'Disappeared? Oh. Bloody hell.'

'Exactly. Julian's really worried about her.'

'Julian? That the eldest boy? But he was hardly ever here. Mind, neither was she, much. Anyway, how can I help? I haven't seen her since before – before –'

'No, I realise that, but there were one or two things … You see, she asked my friend and me to help her after – well, after her husband …'

'Oh, hang on. Now I know who you are. That psychic woman.' Marilyn Fairbrass's voice changed.

'No, that's my friend, Fran. No, please don't hang up. You see, we know you worked for old Lady Middleton before the Watsons bought Dark House, and – and – well, we think something she knew was why the murders – er – happened.' Libby fanned herself with her hand and sat down abruptly on the stairs.

There was a short silence.

'All right,' said Marilyn Fairbrass eventually. 'Come along here – you know where we are? I usually have a cup of coffee about twelve, that do you?'

Libby ended the call with a sigh of relief and sent a text to both Fran and Ben telling them where she was going and when. She decided against fore-warning Carl Oxenford of her visit in the afternoon, just in case, as she was almost certain, Adelaide had gone into hiding with him, although she couldn't imagine why.

Dark Lane was as miserable as ever. Beyond Dark House, the trees closed in even more, until the lane bent round and on to an open area, almost obscured in the ever-present mist. However, on her left, she could just make out a metal sign announcing Cob Farm, and thankfully turned into the gateway.

A long, low metal building stood in front of her, with a light coming from behind a door at the far right end. She parked the car and went towards the door. As she approached, it was thrown open and a woman stood there.

'Saw you coming,' she said.

Marilyn Fairbrass was a surprise. Tall and broad-shouldered, she resembled nothing more than a seasoned county point-to-pointer. Her navy sweater had leather patches on the elbows, and her serviceable cord trousers were pushed into the top of rubber boots. Her iron grey hair was cut in a no-nonsense bob.

'Libby Sarjeant.' Libby held out her hand, which was taken in a firm, calloused grip.

'Come in. Kettle's on.'

The office, if that's what it was, smelt faintly of dog and horse. Marilyn Fairbrass indicated a chair on one side of the large desk while she went to a small area which held a sink, a kettle and a microwave oven.

'So what's all this about then?' She came back with two mugs of strong-looking coffee.

'No one knew you'd worked for Lady Middleton before you worked for the Watsons,' said Libby bluntly. 'And as it looks as though there may be a reason connected with the house that has a bearing on the deaths of Mrs Oxenford and Mr Watson, it seemed that you were the most likely person to know about it.'

'Oh?'

'Have the police been in touch with you today?'

'Yesterday.'

'And did they say the same thing?'

'I didn't speak to them. I was away. My son spoke to them.'

'Ah.' Libby looked down at the dark brown liquid and wondered if she dared drink it.

Marilyn Fairbrass sighed. 'I suppose it can do no harm.'

Libby looked up.

'Lady Middleton had a daughter, Olive. Back when Olive and I were young, we were friends.' Marilyn leant back in her chair. 'We rode together, you know, Pony Club, local gymkhanas.'

'Was this when the Middletons were at Cherry Ashton?'

'She wasn't Middleton then. Cherry Ashton was where the Wyghthams lived. Rachel Wyghtham married Tim Middleton and went to live at Dark House later. Olive, you see, was illegitimate.'

'Oh.' Libby was sympathetic. Illegitimacy was the worst blight on a young person's life in the fifties, when she supposed it would have been.

'Rachel used to talk to Olive and me about Dark House in the old days. Except she swore it should be called Wyghtham Hall.'

'She was right. What did she have to say about it?'

'Oh, she said her ancestor had left treasure behind, and it belonged to the Wyghtham family. It all sounded like a fairy story to me, but Olive believed it.' Marilyn shook her head. 'And then Rachel met Tim Middleton. She was a good-looking woman, and still young, of course. I don't know what went on, but within a year, she and Olive had moved to Dark House and she was Mrs Middleton. The Lady came later.'

'Is Olive still alive?' asked Libby, thinking maybe here was someone with a grudge against the Watsons.

'No.' Marilyn was silent for a moment. 'She was convinced about this story of treasure, and she kept looking for it. And then – you know that ridiculous Victorian grotto at the house?'

Libby nodded.

'She was poking about there and the ground gave way. Collapsed on top of her.'

Chapter Twenty-seven

Libby gasped. 'Underneath the grotto?'

Marilyn nodded.

After a moment, Libby said, 'How did Mrs Middleton take it?'

'Badly. She tried to blame Mr Middleton for not keeping it in good repair, but he'd always said the grotto was out of bounds. Anyway, she never got over it. Mr Middleton was knighted for services to business or something, and Rachel used to like me to come and sit with her to talk about Olive. And the treasure of course. I didn't believe in it any more than Mr Middleton did, but it became an obsession with Rachel. And when he died, I became a sort of companion to her. We had help in the house at first, but she wasn't happy with other people there, and gradually, they all went.' She shook her head. 'It was hard. I couldn't keep up with all the work in a house that size, especially as a lot of it was practically falling down by then.'

'Why did you come to work for the Watsons?'

'Because I knew the house. And I was hardly required. Only when she came down and the house wanted airing through. I employed a firm of cleaners to go through the place every now and then.'

'Did you? Who were they? That's the first I've heard of them.'

'Why should you?' Marilyn looked up at Libby suspiciously. 'I don't know why you want to know all this, or why I should tell you, come to that.'

'I was with Adelaide the day Ramani was found.' Libby crossed her fingers. 'And I've been trying to help ever since. I

203

even helped her pack up to move out of the house the other day.'

'You did?' Marilyn frowned. 'I wonder why she didn't tell me?'

'Well, the police are still in and out of the place, perhaps she thought you didn't need to know. Only now, no one can find her.'

The corners of Marilyn's mouth pulled down. 'Are you sure?'

Libby considered for a moment. 'It wouldn't have anything to do with Carl Oxenford, would it?'

'You're sharp,' Marilyn said.

'Despite both of them denying it vigorously, it looked to me as if they knew one another far better than they said. I was actually there when Carl phoned Adelaide to tell her Ramani was missing.'

'Which he wouldn't have done if they hardly knew one another.' Marilyn nodded. 'What's happened since?'

Libby gave her an edited version of events since Ramani's death, including the theory that Roland had seduced Ramani with tales of treasure somewhere in Dark House. Marilyn sighed.

'God, that bloody treasure. Caused two more deaths now. If it exists, which I doubt. If Rachel couldn't find it, despite having me searching the house every five minutes, it isn't there.'

Libby thought. 'Did you know,' she said at length, 'about the secret room?'

'Secret room?' Marilyn sat up. 'What secret room? Where? I never found one.'

'On the first floor,' said Libby, deciding to keep the secret staircase out of it for the moment. 'Well, on a half-landing, to be precise. And it's all right, there was nothing in it. No treasure. It was just a priest's hole. Nicholas Owen, we think,' she couldn't resist adding.

'Who?'

'Oh, someone who built priest's holes in the sixteen hundreds,' said Libby vaguely. 'Anyway, there was nothing there. Sir Godfrey didn't hide anything in there.'

'You know about Sir Godfrey?'

'Edward Hall, the old friend of Ramani's I told you about, he's an authority on the English civil wars, and he's including Sir Godfrey in a book.'

'Oh.' Marilyn looked thoughtful. 'I don't know.'

'Don't know?'

Marilyn came out of a brown study and looked at Libby. 'I've got something. I'm wondering if I should give it to this Edward Hall.'

Libby felt as if her heart had missed a beat. 'Shall I ask him to call you? He's staying in my village at the moment.'

'Can I trust you?'

Libby was taken aback. 'I hope so.'

'Would you give it to him?'

'Me? Well ...' Libby frowned. 'I would, of course, but don't you think he might want to talk to you about it? You could tell me, but I wouldn't know what to ask.'

'That's very honest.' Marilyn looked down at her clasped hands on her desk. 'In that case, could I come and see him, do you think?'

'Are you sure you want to?'

'He'll advise me, won't he?'

'Yes, I expect so,' said Libby, more puzzled than ever. 'Here, if you've got a phone directory, I'll look up the number of the pub for you.'

'Haven't you got his number in your phone?'

'Well, yes, of course, but it could be anybody. I thought you'd rather check.'

'Write it down for me and I'll call him.' Marilyn gave a wry smile. 'I'm more trusting than you think.'

Libby watched and listened.

'Mr Hall? My name is Marilyn Fairbrass. I worked for Mrs Watson – yes, I know – and for the previous owner. I have Mrs – er?' she frowned at Libby.

'Sarjeant.'

'Mrs Sarjeant with me and she gave me your number. I have something to show you on which I think you may be able to give advice. No, Mrs Sarjeant says you might want to ask me questions. No, I'll come to you, if that's all right. Would early evening be convenient?'

Marilyn finished the call. 'I'm meeting him in the pub at seven. Will you be there?'

'Only if you want me to be,' said Libby, burning with curiosity.

'I'm sure you want to be.' Marilyn smiled again. 'After all, you know so much about it already ...'

'I'd be delighted. But I'll check with Edward first.'

'I shall tell him I want you to be there. As insurance.'

'Right.' Libby stood up. 'Thank you for seeing me, Mrs Fairbrass. And I'll see you tonight.'

Feeling very confused, Libby drove out of the farmyard and headed back down Dark Lane towards Steeple Cross, barely even noticing the wet leaves and the lowering mist. Why hadn't Marilyn Fairbrass been questioned more thoroughly before? Why was this – whatever it was – only just coming out?

That's easy, said Libby's sensible inner voice. Because no one thought about it before. All she's been asked about is where she was on the night of November the something-or-other, and did she know the victim. But, wondered Libby, was she asked *before* Ramani had been identified, or after? And did it matter? Libby shook her head at herself and realised she was almost at Steeple Cross and Carl's house.

She pulled in to the car park of The Dragon and sat thinking. Was she right to just burst in on Carl, following an uneducated hunch that he knew where Adelaide was? She thought back to the last time Carl had been mentioned in front of Adelaide, when there had been noticeable tension. Adelaide hadn't looked happy. What was it Julian had said? "*She looked as though she was expecting something to happen and it hadn't.*" Had she been expecting Carl to come and take her away? To make good on a promise, perhaps?

Sighing, she got out of the car. At least she could call in, saying she'd been passing, which was more or less true, and wondered if he was all right.

206

'Come on then,' she told herself. 'Best foot forward.'

She went up the steps and knocked on the blue door. No one came. Suppressing a little surge of relief, she knocked again, before turning to go down the steps.

'Oh, Mrs – er. Sorry, I was at the back of the house.'

Libby nearly fell down the steps. 'Mr Oxenford! I mean, Doctor …'

The doctor gave a half smile. 'Don't worry. I don't insist on it. What can I do for you?'

Libby felt the heat coming into her cheeks. 'I didn't mean to intrude,' she said. 'I was, quite literally, passing, and I thought I'd see how you are.'

'How kind,' said Carl Oxenford, with an ironic little bow. 'Where were you passing from? Dark House?'

'Er – no, actually. Cob Farm.'

He raised his eyebrows. 'I don't think I know it.'

'The other end of Dark Lane,' said Libby. 'Past Dark House.'

'Ah. Of course, no one's there now, so I suppose you wouldn't have come from there.' There was a slight interrogative note in his voice.

'No.' Libby cleared her throat. 'The last time I was there was on Wednesday, when I helped Adelaide – Mrs Watson – to pack up before she went back to London.'

'Ah, yes. She hated being cooped up in the hotel.'

'Did you see her then?' Libby injected surprise into her voice. 'I didn't think you knew each other very well.'

'No,' he said, and sighed. 'Well, thank you for calling, Mrs – er –. I'm doing better as time goes on, but until I'm able to have the funeral …' he let his voice tail off and Libby felt guilty.

'No, of course. And I'm sure you have plenty of friends and family to turn to, but if there's anything I can do …'

The slight, dark man gave another little bow. 'Thank you.'

'Well – yes.' Libby smiled nervously and retreated down the steps. Carl Oxenford closed the door.

Chapter Twenty-eight

'Well, that didn't get me anywhere,' Libby said to Fran on the phone when she got home half an hour later.

'No, but he was evasive, wouldn't you say?' said Fran. 'And you more than made up for it with Marilyn Fairbrass.'

'I know. Talk about a turn-up for the books. I can't wait to find out what it is she wants to show Edward.'

'Something to do with the Wyghthams,' said Fran. 'It has to be, otherwise, why would Rachel and Olive be so keen to try and find this "treasure"? And how did Roland Watson know about it?'

'What was it the barman at The Dragon said? People thought he'd been talking to Lady Middleton before she died. I wonder why?'

'Perhaps he approached her about selling the house?'

'Sort of cold calling?' said Libby. 'I still wonder why.'

'Would he have found anything out about the house beforehand?' said Fran.

'He could have heard someone talking about it, I suppose. Perhaps he'd heard about the grotto.'

'Shame we can't ask her,' said Fran. 'Or him.'

'And do we think Adelaide really didn't know anything about it?'

'I certainly don't think Roland would have told her if there was anything underhand going on.'

'Or anything that might make him money,' said Libby, 'although I don't quite know how that fits in …'

'We've already thought about that, haven't we? Either some kind of forgery or arts and antiquities smuggling.'

'But could he have been planning it that long ago?'

'He was still working locally at that time, wasn't he? It wasn't until after they'd bought the house that he lost his job and got his new one abroad. That must have held him up.'

'I wonder ...' said Libby. 'If he didn't try and seduce Ramani with tales of the treasure, but recruited her for her knowledge. As we've already said.'

'That's a lot more likely, isn't it?' said Fran. 'Look, I've got to go, I've got customers.'

Libby sat for a while staring into the fireplace. Sidney appeared on the hearthrug and stared at it pointedly. Libby took the hint and lit the fire, then called Edward.

'What do you think?' she said when she'd recounted her meeting with Marilyn and the subsequent one with Carl Oxenford.

'I'm hoping she's got some artefact dating back to Sir Godfrey,' said Edward. 'I don't dare speculate as to what it is.'

'A document, I would have thought,' said Libby. 'But what about Carl and Adelaide?'

'Look, I don't know Carl any better than you do, nor Adelaide, come to that. And you're better at reading people than I am.'

'Well, I could hardly ask him, could I?' Libby sighed gustily. 'Oh, well, we'll just have to hope the police track her down.'

'And you're coming this evening, aren't you?'

'Try and stop me. I'm booked in at the caff for nine o'clock, though, so I shall have to leave then.'

'She's coming at seven, that should give us plenty of time.'

Libby arrived at the pub in time to see Marilyn Fairbrass staring in astonishment when Edward introduced himself. She hurried forward.

'Mrs Fairbrass – Marilyn. I hoped I'd be here in time to make the introductions.'

'How did you know who I was?' Marilyn looked nervously up at Edward.

'It wasn't hard.' He grinned. 'A woman of the right age who looked as if she was looking for someone – and looking nervous.'

'Oh.' Marilyn looked first at Libby, then back at Edward. 'Well, I hope you won't be too disappointed.'

'I'll be interested, I'm sure of it,' said Edward. 'Now, as there are no private rooms here, would you like to go up to my room here, or will you be all right in the bar?'

'It's quite quiet over there,' said Libby, pointing to the area which once had been the lounge bar, and the corner beyond the large fireplace.

'That'll be fine,' said Marilyn, and allowed herself to be led to the table in the corner. Edward went to order coffee for her, and drinks for himself and Libby. By the time he got back, she'd recovered her composure.

'So what do you want to show us?' he asked, settling himself in one of the large carver chairs.

Marilyn reached down into a capacious canvas bag and brought out a folder. 'This is the evidence Rachel and Olive had for believing there was treasure at Dark House. It's not very much, I'm afraid.' She looked apologetic as she handed the folder to Edward. 'And a bit fragile.'

Edward gave her a quick look, and pulled a pair of surgical gloves from his pocket.

'Always prepared,' Libby muttered to Marilyn, who gave an anxious half smile.

Edward drew a plastic document wallet out of the folder and placed it gently on table. They all leaned forward to look.

To Libby, it appeared to be an ancient document written in a script she couldn't read. It also looked as though it had been torn from something else. To Edward, it was obviously something else.

'And this is all there is?' He looked up at Marilyn. 'Did either of them ever say where they got it?'

'No. I gathered it had passed down through the family.'

'And Libby said the Wyghthams weren't living in the house when you first knew them? Do you know how they lost Wyghtham Hall?'

'No, I know nothing. Rachel was an unmarried mother when

210

I first met her, living with her old father in Cherry Ashton. It was a nice enough house, but I don't think they'd been there for generations.'

'And do you think she married Mr Middleton just to get Dark House?'

'It wouldn't surprise me,' said Marilyn dryly. 'I never heard her mourn him, only Olive and the bloody treasure.'

'We were told Roland Watson talked to Lady Middleton before she died,' said Libby.

'Who told you that?' Marilyn looked surprised.

'The barman at The Dragon,' admitted Libby.

Marilyn laughed. 'Gossip! Actually, it's true. And if you're right, that this has something to do with his murder, that must have been what started it.'

Edward and Libby looked at each other, confused.

'You see,' Marilyn went on, 'I didn't live in, but I went in every day to see that she was all right. Towards the end, I'd managed to persuade her to have what they call a care package, so she had a professional in twice a day, but she would only let them do the minimum. Anyway, one morning, I arrived and let myself in and found a strange man there.'

'Watson?' said Edward.

Marilyn nodded. 'Apparently, he'd knocked while the carer was there and she'd let him in.'

'That wasn't right, surely?' said Libby. 'He could have been anybody.'

'He asked for her by name.' Marilyn shrugged. 'It was common knowledge that Lady Middleton lived there.'

'What did he want?'

'He had the cheek to ask if she was thinking of selling the house, because he was looking in the area and it appealed to him.'

Libby gasped. '*Colossal* cheek!'

'She didn't mind, though. When I got there, she was in the middle of telling him all about her family's right to the place and sent me off to make coffee. She was going a bit – well – forgetful by this time, of course. After I brought the coffee, she

211

started hinting about the treasure. I could see he was interested. Anyway, when he'd gone, she told me to let him have first refusal of the house after she died. So I did. And that,' she pointed at the document, 'was in with all the deeds and her will. I decided he shouldn't have it. It had brought Rachel and Olive nothing but tragedy, and I didn't want anyone else to suffer.'

'So did you actually set up the sale?' asked Edward.

'I was her executor, so yes. And that was why I said I'd act as a sort of housekeeper-come-caretaker. Of course Johnny Templeton lives on the premises to keep a day-to-day eye on it.' She shook her head. 'I don't know why he didn't hear anything when – when the – er – the –'

'It's all right, we know what you mean,' said Libby. 'But it is strange that he didn't. Although he lives beyond the grotto, doesn't he? That would probably act as a sound break.'

'So would whatever he was smoking,' said Marilyn grimly. 'Have you met him?'

'No. Adam has, of course.' Libby turned to Edward. 'Johnny was the one who found the body.' She turned back to Marilyn. 'I'm surprised he's still there.'

'I don't suppose the police want him going anywhere.'

'So what is it, Edward?' Libby drew the document carefully towards her.

'I'm not absolutely sure. It could have been part of a will, or it could just be a letter. It's what it says that's surprising.' He looked at Marilyn. 'Do you know what it says?'

'No. I didn't see it until after Rachel died, although I knew this was what she called her evidence. The folder was always under lock and key in her desk. It's about Sir Godfrey, isn't it?'

'It appears to be *from* Sir Godfrey,' said Edward.

'Good God!' said Libby.

'And seems to be about his wife.'

'Rebecca? When did he write it? Was it during the war?'

Edward shook his head slowly. 'No, not Rebecca. His other wife.'

Chapter Twenty-nine

'What?' Libby almost shouted in shocked disbelief. Two drinkers in the other bar looked over curiously.

'"My wife Evelyn" it says.' Edward looked up.

'But –' Libby struggled to get her thoughts in order. 'It says in the church that Rebecca was the wife. And that note in the parish records.'

'I don't know what you're talking about,' said Marilyn, looking from one to the other.

'Do you know anything about Sir Godfrey Wyghtham at all?' asked Libby.

'Only that he was an ancestor who was supposed to have left some treasure at the house. Neither Rachel nor Olive explained why, although they went into great detail about how they'd traced their line back to him.'

'A mistress?' Libby turned to Edward.

'Addressed as "my wife"?' Edward shook his head. 'Let me see if I can decipher any more of this.' He took a notebook and pencil out of his jacket pocket and bent over the document.

Libby looked at Marilyn. 'What do you think?'

'I don't know what you've found out about this man so far,' said Marilyn. 'Or how – er – Edward got involved.'

Libby explained the circumstances of Edward's arrival, and all the background they had on Roland, Ramani and the Wyghthams.

'We did find a cross and a gimmel ring hidden in the attic, and Edward said they might be worth a bit, but they wouldn't be worth enough to murder for.'

Marilyn nodded. 'I did look in the attics, but to be honest, I

213

was scared of falling through the floor.'

'Lewis said it was in a state up there when he and his team went in.'

'That's the television person, isn't it?' Marilyn looked interested.

'Yes. He's the person who got me involved in the first place, except for Adam being there when the first body was found.'

'Is he a friend of yours?'

'Yes, I suppose so. And Adam works for him at his house – or garden, I should say.'

'I think I know what this is.' Edward looked up, leant back in his chair and took a healthy swig of beer. 'It's part of a letter. I don't know who to or when it was written, but it's talking about money and the house. It's just conceivable that it could be construed as proof that there was money hidden in the house, but it isn't very clear. I'd like Andrew to see it.'

'Professor Andrew Wylie. He's an Emeritus Professor of History,' Libby explained to Marilyn. 'He's been helping, too.'

'I don't know,' said Marilyn. 'I'm not sure I should let it out of my sight.'

Edward frowned. 'But strictly speaking, it isn't yours anyway. It really belongs to Rachel's heirs.'

'Family heirs, you mean? There was only a second cousin, who she'd never met. She left a small portion to her and the rest to me.'

Edward and Libby stared at her. 'So you're executor *and* beneficiary?' said Libby eventually.

Marilyn nodded, looking faintly embarrassed.

'In that case, may I take a copy of it?' asked Edward. 'And this complicates the matter even further.'

'Does it?' said Libby.

'If anything is found. Who it belongs to.'

'The Wyghtham family, really,' said Marilyn. 'If it was Godfrey who hid it.'

'But you said the only heir was a second cousin,' said Libby.

'But there are other Wyghtham lines.' Marilyn sighed. 'I know that, because Rachel was obsessive about the family

214

history.'

'She must have had a family tree, then,' said Edward.

'She just had her own notes. I used to tell her to get a proper family history done, but she never would.'

'Have you got the notes?' asked Libby.

'No, I never thought they'd be important. I only kept this because it looked old.'

'We're going to have to do a proper job on old Godfrey,' said Libby, 'out of interest's sake, if nothing else.'

'Andrew, then,' said Edward. 'May I take a copy, Mrs Fairbrass?'

'You can take it,' said Marilyn. 'You'll probably look after it better than I will.'

'Thank you,' said Edward. 'I'll give you a receipt for it.'

Marilyn waved a hand. 'No, no, it's fine. Just let me know what happens.' She stood up. 'I'm glad I brought it to you. I'll be even more glad if it's any help in finding a murderer.'

Libby walked her to the door. 'Can I ask you a question?'

'Yes?'

'You're not in the phone book, neither's your son. Only under Cob Farm. Do you both live there?'

Marilyn looked amused. 'Not exactly. Kevin does, but I have what used to be one of the tied cottages. I'm not in the phone book because I only give my number to people who need it. Here,' she rummaged in the large bag and found a pencil and an old receipt. 'You can have it. I don't always answer my mobile, but I've put both numbers. And you've already got Cob Farm's number.'

'Thank you,' said Libby. 'I'm in the book.'

She watched Marilyn walk back to the battered Land Rover that was obviously a farm vehicle, and then turned back into the pub.

'So what do we think of that?' she asked, sitting down and picking up her drink.

'I think,' said Edward, 'that Evelyn may have been a first wife. We may be wrong in thinking he left money for Rebecca in case he died in the war. If he left any, it would have been for

Evelyn.'

'Unless she had already died and he'd married Rebecca,' said Libby.

'We need a family tree,' said Edward impatiently. 'I'm going to ring Andrew.'

Libby watched while Edward made the call, recognising the relief in his face and voice when Andrew obviously agreed how important it was.

'I'm going over there now,' he said as he ended the call. 'Would you like to come?'

'No, thanks,' said Libby. 'I'm booked in at Harry's. Let me know how it goes. And do you think it will help catch a murderer?'

Edward shrugged. 'No idea. I can't see how it helps, frankly. All it confirms is that Roland must have genuinely believed Rachel's story of treasure. And that he must have done at least a bit of research – or Ramani did.'

'It looks more likely that the theory of getting Ramani to help with a scam is the right one, now, doesn't it?' Libby finished her drink and stood up.

'Maybe.' Edward put the plastic-covered document back in the folder. 'Anyway, I'll at least know a bit more about Sir Godfrey after this.'

Libby pulled a face at his back as he went out of the pub.

'I said he was selfish,' she said to Harry ten minutes later, as she sat in the little courtyard at the back of The Pink Geranium with one of her increasingly rare cigarettes. 'All he's really interested in is his seventeenth century research, not who killed Ramani and Roland.'

'Well,' said Harry reasonably, wiping his hands on his white apron, 'that's what he came down here for.'

'What puzzles me,' said Libby, 'is why, if Ramani really was doing research, and we know she went to the church, no notes were found. Nothing.'

'Do you know that?' asked Harry. 'The police might not have told you.'

'Considering that Ian authorised the search of the house, I

think he would have.' Libby stubbed out the cigarette. 'I'm sorry I turned up early, but with Edward dashing off to Nethergate, I didn't know what else to do.'

'Always happy to be a port in the storm,' said Harry. 'I'm going back to my kitchen. I'll send someone to fetch you when your table's ready.'

The table Harry had assigned to her was a small one tucked into a corner near the bar counter. It meant she could watch the other customers without being too conspicuous, however one group noticed her almost immediately.

Joe came over and leant on the table.

'All on yer own, then? Where's that Ben?'

'He and Peter have gone up to London. Family, and all that. Are you out for a Cattlegreen Nurseries Christmas do?'

'No, just fancied coming out. Young Owen doesn't get out much.' He sighed as he looked across at his beaming son. 'Anyhow, how're you getting on with those smugglers?'

'Oh, wow – I'd almost forgotten about them,' said Libby. 'We started on a different line of enquiry. At least,' she said frowning, 'I think we have.'

'Shame. I'd have loved to hear of one of them guineas being found.' He grinned at her and went back to his table. Nella and Owen waved.

By the time Libby had almost finished her pollo verde, Harry had finished in the kitchen and come to join her.

'Joe reminded me about the guineas and the prisoners of war,' Libby told him. 'In the excitement of finding out about Sir Godfrey, I'd forgotten them.'

'I think they were a red herring,' said Harry. 'I think it's much more likely that this Lady Middleton told him about her ancestor and he told Ramani. I still don't know why anyone should kill either of them, though. Unless it was Adelaide.'

'No.' Libby rested her chin on her hand. 'I'm sure the police haven't got so distracted by all these historical diversions. I know Ian's said he'll look into things when they've come up, but in reality I expect he'll be chasing suspects and looking for evidence and footprints and stuff.'

'And you won't know what that evidence is.'

'Or who the suspects are.' Libby sighed. 'And it's nearly three weeks since Ramani died. That's a long time.'

'Did you find out anything about that fake institute?'

'No.' Libby frowned. 'And that really was odd. I could bear to know a bit more about that.'

'That was one of the things Cuddly Connell was going to look into, wasn't it?'

Libby snorted into her wine. 'Cuddly Connell? You wait till I tell him.'

Harry beamed. 'Tell away.'

'And Sir Godfrey's family tree. That's what we need. When did his family sell to – what was his name? Goodman. William Goodman.'

'Who?'

'He was a magistrate who was involved in the smuggling trade. And then there was a vicar called the Reverend Mostyn – although Andrew thought that was a made-up person.'

'And then there was Middleton.'

'At some point, yes. It's fascinating, but doesn't actually get us any nearer the truth.'

'The truth of the murders, you mean?'

'Yes.' Libby sighed again and drained her wine glass. Harry topped it up. 'I expect it will turn out to be Carl and Adelaide after all. Or someone else involved with one of them that we don't know about.'

'Who are your suspects, exactly?'

'Carl and Adelaide, obviously. Er ... Julian, I suppose. Marilyn Fairbrass too, now, although I think that's pretty unlikely.'

'That's not very many suspects,' said Harry.

'No. That's why I'm pretty sure Ian's got lots of others. Carl and Adelaide have such good alibis.'

'What about your mate Edward?'

'I don't seriously think he's got anything to do with it. I've been a bit suspicious of him, but he's so focussed on his subject I think that's all he's really interested in, deep down.'

'But he's a self-confessed member of Libby's Loonies now,' said Harry. 'He's been enjoying looking into things.'

'Yes, because it's all been historical. And historians have to be detectives, don't they?'

'You're up a gum tree, then.' Harry stood up. 'Come on, come outside and have a last fag. I'll put the heater on.'

Libby pushed her chair back. 'We don't half suffer,' she said.

Later, walking back on her own to number 17, an activity frowned upon by Ben, who foresaw attacks round every corner, Libby thought about the conversation. If this was a detective story, there would be more than the two obvious suspects and two rather tenuous ones. There must be someone she and the others hadn't thought of. But then, if this *was* a detective story, that would be cheating because that person hadn't been there right at the beginning.

'Right,' she said to Sidney, as she let herself in. Sidney, wisely, decided not to make a dash for the great outdoors and instead walked pointedly to the fireplace, where he sat with his back to the room and his ears down.

'All right.' Libby took off her coat and came to stir up the ashes. 'Now, listen. I'll light you a fire if you'll help.' Sidney looked away. 'OK, I'll do it on my own.' She put a firelighter on the remnants of the earlier fire and loaded kindling on top. 'Who was there right at the beginning of the story? No, stupid, not Adam. No, not Mog, either. Johnny! He was the one who found the body. And no one's even thought about him since.'

Libby sat back on her heels and watched the flames curling round the wood. 'Well, perhaps the police have,' she told Sidney, who was now washing ostentatiously. 'I must see if I can't ask Ian about him. And tell him about Marilyn Fairbrass, although I doubt he'll be interested in that.'

Satisfied with the thought, she fetched herself a nightcap and a book and curled up on the sofa. It could all wait until morning. But it didn't.

Chapter Thirty

'Mum!'

Libby struggled awake and sat up. The fire had died down again, her book was on the floor and her glass was empty.

'Adam? What is it? What's the time?'

'I don't know. Mum, they've arrested Johnny.'

'Johnny? Oh, Johnny!' Libby's brain cleared fully. 'Um – why are you phoning me, though?'

'He didn't do it, Ma. I'm positive. You should have seen him when he found the body.'

'OK, I'm sure, but why are you telling me? And how do you know?'

'You know that one call you can have at the police station? Well, Johnny didn't have anyone else to call, so he called Mog.'

'What could Mog do?'

'I don't know. Neither did Mog. So he called me.'

'And you called me. But Ad, you know I haven't got any influence with the police. And this isn't an aspect of the investigation Fran and I have been concerned with, so we won't have Ian coming down on Wednesday for a cosy chat about it.'

'There must be something we can do! Poor sod hadn't got anyone else to turn to. It's so sad.'

'It is,' agreed Libby, feeling a sympathetic lump forming in her throat. 'Look, I can't possibly do anything tonight, not at – ' she peered at her watch ' – gawd, half past one, but in the morning I'll call Fran and we'll try and think of something.'

'Thanks, Ma.'

And what, exactly, can we do? Libby asked herself, as she went around turning off lights. She almost felt guilty for having thought about Johnny Templeton as a suspect earlier in the evening, even though she told herself that was stupid. But now she was wide awake, and without Ben beside her, she knew she would dwell on it for hours. Sighing, she climbed the stairs.

Sure enough, after a night of fitful sleep, she was up by seven o'clock, still wondering what evidence the police had against Johnny Templeton. At eight o'clock she was showered and dressed, unheard of on a Sunday, and wondering if it was too early to ring Fran. As she reached for the phone, it rang.

'What's wrong, Libby?'

'Fran? I was just going to ring you, but I thought it might be too early.'

'No, I've been awake for a while, and something's wrong, isn't it?'

Libby told her everything from what she now saw as traitorous thoughts about Johnny to her sleepless night after Adam's phone call.

'And I have no idea what we can do,' she finished. 'We can't possibly look into it, but Adam says Johnny's got no one else.'

'There must be some evidence,' said Fran. 'They wouldn't arrest someone out of the blue.'

'He was the one who found the body. And he lives on the premises,' said Libby. 'I suppose he could have killed Ramani the night before, and killed Roland because – what? Can't figure that one out.'

'And why did he kill Ramani? He doesn't sound the sort of man to be her type.'

'Well, as you said, there must be evidence of some kind, but it's just so unlikely. I wish I could think of somehow we could help.'

'You could try Adelaide,' said Fran slowly.

'Adelaide? But she's missing!'

'Try,' said Fran.

'But how could she help?'

'She might be allowed to see him, as his employer.'

'But if he's being questioned he won't be allowed to see her.'

'I just think it's worth a try, that's all.'

221

'But how do I find her?' cried Libby helplessly. 'We and the police have been trying for three days.'

'Try the phone.'

Libby ended the call and stared grumpily at the handset. Then, sighing, she punched in Adelaide's number. To her surprise, a recorded message answered her.

'Adelaide, we've been trying to get hold of you for days. Julian's looking for you as well and I thought you ought to know that Johnny – John – Templeton's been arrested. And I spoke to Marilyn Fairbrass yesterday. Er – bye.'

She rang Fran back. 'I've done it and left a message. That was different, too. There was no recorded message the last time I tried.'

'I think you might hear from her. Or the police might.'

'Really? She's definitely not dead, then?'

'Why should she be dead?'

'Well, Ramani and Roland are. It just seemed to follow.'

'Unless someone else has turned on her voicemail – unlikely – she's still alive and using her phone.'

'In that case, the police should have traced her. They can do that, can't they?'

'If they've been taking her disappearance that seriously, yes. But no one seems to have been that worried about her.'

'Her son is.'

'That's different.'

'I suppose it is.' Libby thought for a moment. 'Oh, well, there's nothing else we can do, is there. I wish there was.'

'For once, the police have beaten us to it, Lib. Or rather, they've known a lot more than we have. We didn't pay any attention to Johnny, even though they always say the person who finds the body is statistically most likely to be the murderer.'

'But he didn't find Roland's body.'

'No,' Libby could almost hear Fran frowning. 'And that's a very odd thing. The grotto was still taped off as a crime scene. Whoever put Roland's body there was very determined.'

'And we don't even know when that was,' said Libby. 'All the police would have to go on would be the last time they were

222

there themselves.'

'There'll have been a post mortem by now,' said Fran. 'I'm sure they know.'

'But Ian hasn't told us.'

'No, all he'll talk about is the parts of the investigation we've been involved in. You know that.'

Libby sighed. 'I know. It just comes as a shock when you realise how much dogged police work has been going on while we've been enjoying ourselves doing historical research.'

'That's what the police always say about crime dramas on TV, isn't it? If they showed all the real routine they'd be too boring to watch.'

'Well, they must have been doing a hell of a lot of boring stuff. We'll just have to wait.'

Libby ended the call and found Adam's number.

'Hey, Ma.' He sounded as though he'd just woken up.

'Oh, sorry, darling, I forgot how early it is was,' said Libby. 'Just calling to say I've talked to Fran about Johnny, and she suggested I try to call Adelaide.'

'Adelaide?' Adam stifled a yawn. 'But I thought she'd gone missing?'

'She has, but Fran seemed to think she'd surface again. I'm also going to ring Marilyn Fairbrass. She must know Johnny better than we do.'

'OK. Let me know if anything happens before I see you at lunchtime.'

'Lunch – ? Oh, bloody hell, it's Sunday! Thanks for reminding me, Ad. I hope Pete and Ben are back in time.'

Unable to settle, Libby suddenly decided to make a Christmas cake. It would still have two weeks to mature, she thought, and even if she didn't like it herself, it would be a welcome addition to the Boxing Day open house she and Ben held at number 17.

Having covered herself and the kitchen liberally with flour and dripped egg white, the phone ringing came as an unwelcome interruption. Trying to pick it up without transferring putative cake, she muttered 'Hello,' and wiped her hands on a tea towel.

'Libby, this is Adelaide Watson.'

Libby practically dropped the phone.

'I'm sorry I've been out of contact. Carl told me you'd been looking for me.'

'Carl …' began Libby.

'Yes. I'm afraid I went straight to his house when I left you on Wednesday.'

'So you've been there all the time?' Libby began to get angry. 'While your poor son was thinking the worst? His father murdered and you disappeared – what was he supposed to think?'

'I know. I didn't think. I just wanted to get away.'

'Well, you didn't get very far, did you? Have you called the police?'

'Not yet. Carl – er – we – er – *I* thought I'd ask you what was going on first.'

'Have you called Julian?'

'Yes. Before I got your message. He wanted to come down, but I told him not to.'

'Well, that's something, I suppose. Now, I suggest you call the police. They'll be bound to want to ask you questions about Johnny Templeton – how you knew him, how long he'd worked for you. All that sort of thing.' Libby decided not to say anything about the other questions the police might want to ask about fake Napoleonic Institutes and priest holes, in case Adelaide took off again.

Adelaide sighed. 'All right. They'll want to see me, I suppose.'

'I expect they'll want you at the station,' said Libby. 'If I were you, I'd not bother to ring, I'd go straight there.'

'I'll think about it,' said Adelaide. 'I'll ask Carl.'

'He hasn't given you much good advice so far, has he?' said Libby. 'Did you get so used to giving in to Roland you've lost any willpower of your own? Really, Adelaide.'

'I'll do what I like,' said Adelaide, and cut the connection.

Libby immediately called Ian's private mobile number, where she left a message, then his work line.

'Connell,' he barked.

'Ian, it's me – listen.' Libby broke across the stifled expletive. 'Adelaide Watson. She's been hiding out with Carl Oxenford and –'

'What?' Ian shouted. 'How do you know?'

'She just called me. I tried her mobile again after I heard about Johnny Templeton and her voice mail was switched on, so I left a message. She's just called me back. I told her to come into the police station, but she said she's asking Carl.'

'Are they at his house?'

'I assume so. He was there yesterday. I saw him.'

'Right. I'll get someone out there straight away. Thanks, Libby. Oh – and how did you know about Templeton?'

'He called Mog after he was arrested. He doesn't have anyone else.'

'Hmm,' said Ian. 'If I have a moment, I'll call you later.'

'Oh, bugger,' said Libby to Sidney. 'I still don't know why Johnny was arrested.'

She called Fran to bring her up to date, and went back to the cake mix without enthusiasm, where Ben discovered her half an hour later.

'You have been busy,' he said, when she'd finished recounting the events of Saturday and Sunday. 'And making a cake, too.'

'I didn't know what to do with myself while I was waiting for you,' Libby admitted, sliding the cake tin into the Rayburn. 'I've had enough of cooking now. I'm glad we're going to Hetty's.'

'I think Flo and Lenny are coming today, too,' said Ben. 'Flo has a bottle of something special that needs opening, apparently.'

Lenny was Hetty's brother, Flo her oldest friend. After years apart, they had found each other again and Lenny had moved into Flo's sheltered accommodation with her. Flo's late husband had been something of a wine buff and left her the contents of his cellar, which she now guarded with the devotion of a connoisseur.

'That's something to look forward to,' said Libby, brightening. 'And now tell me how your day went.'

By the time Libby and Ben arrived at The Manor, Peter, Adam, Flo and Lenny were all assembled round the huge kitchen table, while Hetty transferred trays of vegetables into old blue and white dishes. On top of the Aga, the roast beef rested quietly under its overcoat of tea-towels.

Supplied with aperitifs of gin and tonic (for a change), they all exchanged news. Adam was most concerned with the plight of Johnny Templeton, but Libby was able to console him with the news that now she had helped Ian find Adelaide Watson, she might be able to get something out of him.

'You'd think she'd 'ave stopped all this lark by now, wouldn't you?' Flo said to Hetty. 'Yer gettin' too old, gal.'

'Oh, thanks, Flo,' said Libby. 'No offence taken, I'm sure.'

'We're all younger at our age than you were when you were our age,' explained Ben, putting an arm round Libby. 'If you know what I mean.'

'I was always young fer me age,' said Lenny, brushing his little white moustache proudly.

'Specially when you was nineteen,' said Flo, giving him a dig in the ribs. 'Wouldn't look at yer twice.'

It was while they were all laughing at this that Libby's phone rang. About to switch it off she looked at the caller.

'Ian,' she said to the table, and answered it.

'Libby, I think I'm going to have to talk to you officially. I don't want to have to bring you in to the station, so I'm coming round now.'

'What?'

'I think we may have found the source of your stories of treasure.'

Chapter Thirty-one

'You what?' Libby gasped.

'I'm not saying any more over the phone. I'll see you in half an hour.'

'But Hetty's just dishing up lunch!' wailed Libby.

'Bloody hell, it's Sunday,' said Ian. 'Oh, all right. An hour then, and we'll come to The Manor.'

'We?'

'I'll have a sergeant with me, of course. And I'm sure,' he finished sardonically, 'that the rest of the party will be on tenterhooks to find out what we've been talking about.'

Libby pulled a face at the people round the table. 'All right. I'm sure Hetty will let us use the drawing room. See you in an hour.'

She relayed what Ian had said while Hetty brought the beef to the table to carve.

'Treasure?' said Lenny. 'What treasure?'

'We don't know,' said Libby. 'And Ian said "the source of the stories" so it sounds as if there isn't any. Does anyone mind if I send Fran a text to tell her? Then I promise I'll turn the phone off.'

Lunch was enlivened, as would be expected, by all sorts of speculations about the treasure. Hetty, Flo and Lenny were filled in regarding Sir Godfrey's possible hoard and the Napoleonic guineas, the fake insitute and the French prisoners of war. As none of them had come from the area originally, but arrived as hop pickers during the last war, they'd heard nothing of the local stories and were fascinated.

'Joe at Cattlegreen says we've probably got a tunnel under

The Manor, Mum,' said Ben, helping himself to more roast parsnips.

Hetty grunted. 'Don't you go diggin' no holes in my floorboards.'

'There's a tunnel under the church,' said Flo.

They all turned to her. 'How do you know?' asked Libby.

'Go ter church, don't I? It's in the booklet. Vicar a few years ago wrote it. Smugglin', it says.'

'Yes, that's it. They must have stored the contraband under the church,' said Peter. 'I nearly wrote a play about it once.'

'Good job you didn't,' said Hetty.

'Oh, don't remind him,' said Libby. 'It's hardly Pete's fault that people kill each other off during his plays!'

Ben was pouring them all brandies at the end of the meal when there was a knock at the big oak door.

'Come in,' shouted Ben, and Chief Detective Inspector Connell, followed by a still surprised DC Robertson, emerged into the kitchen.

Ian was greeted familiarly by everyone, and Hetty offered coffee.

'I think we'd better go into the other room, Hetty,' said Libby. 'They won't want to waste time.'

'I'll bring coffee in,' said Ben. 'Use the office.'

Seated in the office, Libby having allowed Ian to sit in Ben's chair behind the desk, she explained the situation to DC Robertson. 'He told you he knew the family, didn't he? Well, he knows all of us, you see. Perhaps he shouldn't have been allowed to come and question me, should you, Ian?' She grinned mischievously. Reluctantly, he smiled back.

'No, probably I shouldn't, but as you aren't a suspect and have been giving me useful information, I think we can overlook it this time.'

Ben arrived with a tray of coffee and quirked an eyebrow at Libby. She shrugged, and he left.

'Now,' said Ian, pouring himself a cup, and indicating that DC Robertson should do the same. 'First of all, I want you to tell me how you first became aware of the stories about the treasure.'

Libby was surprised. 'But you know all this,' she said.

'Indulge me.'

'OK.' She frowned. 'Blimey, it's quite difficult. We seem to have known about it for ever. Well. The first we heard about it was when Edward arrived. Wasn't it?' She looked up at Ian. 'When he told us that Ramani had told him that there was Civil War treasure buried somewhere inside Dark House.'

'Yes. Was there any confirmation of that story?'

A cold hand gripped Libby's stomach. 'Er, no.'

'So, what happened next?'

'Edward looked up the records and came to see me and Fran. That's right, isn't it?'

'Did anyone else say anything about the treasure?'

'No. But then we went to the church and found Sir Godfrey's grave, or plaque, whatever it was, and found out when he and his wife Rebecca died.'

'And then Mr Watson was found dead.'

'And then you had to authorise the search after he was dead, because you couldn't get hold of him before.' Libby was watching Ian closely. 'You're not telling me that Edward had something to do with this after all? That he killed Roland in order to search the premises?'

'I'm not telling you anything,' said Ian. 'Go on. When did the story of the Napoleonic treasure arise?'

'Oh, Lord, I can't remember! Oh, wait. Yes, I do. Andrew found it, after we asked him to do some research for us.'

'Dr Hall didn't find it?'

'No.' Libby shook her head emphatically. 'It isn't his period, is it?'

'His university don't seem to know that he has a speciality,' said Ian. 'He's a history lecturer pure and simple.'

Libby felt a certain amount of relief. At least Edward was a real historian. Perhaps the civil wars were a private obsession.

'And has Dr Hall had access to Dark House at any time that you know of, other than when you were with him?'

'Not as far as I know.' Libby was bewildered. 'But he does

know – well, we both saw Marilyn Fairbrass yesterday. And he's got a document she gave him that belonged to the previous owner. A descendant of the Wyghtham family.'

'What document?'

'I'm not sure. He called Andrew and was going over there last night to see if they could sort it out.'

'What did it say?'

'I couldn't make any of it out, but apparently it said that Sir Godfrey had another wife, Evelyn.'

Ian frowned. 'Why does that matter?'

'Because in the church the slab says "his wife Rebecca". Anyway, it was this document that made old Lady Middleton – you know who she was?'

'The previous owner.'

'Well, made her and her daughter, who died years ago – guess where?'

Ian closed his eyes. 'Don't tell me. The grotto.'

'Exactly. Anyway, this mother and daughter both believed that this document, whatever it is, proved there was treasure somewhere in Dark House. Which was why Lady Middleton married her husband, who was living in the house.'

'And Edward Hall has gone off with this document.'

'You could check with Andrew,' suggested Libby. 'And please tell me why you're suddenly so interested in Edward?'

'We've been interested in him from the beginning.' Ian picked up his phone and punched in a number. 'We'll see. Ah – Professor Wylie. Yes it's DCI Connell. Mrs Sarjeant tells me Dr Hall brought a document to you yesterday evening. Oh, you have?' Ian's gaze flicked to Libby. 'Yes, of course. No, that's fine. As soon as you have.' He ended the call.

'Dr Hall left the document with Professor Wylie. As soon as he has something definite, he'll tell us before he tells Dr Hall.'

'Did he say if it mentioned treasure?'

'No.'

'So why are you interested in Edward? You still haven't told me. And you've been fine about letting him help with the searches and everything.'

'Easier to keep a check on him if he was with all of you.'

'But you actually called him in and told him he could have a look at the grotto.'

Ian smiled. 'And he was just about to go back to London, wasn't he?'

'Oh!' Libby gasped. 'You wanted to keep him here!'

'And right under your nose, too. You remember what he said that night in the pub? Hadn't I ever let something out in front of the wrong person?'

'And he blushed when you asked him if he was the wrong person.' Libby shook her head and groaned. 'Oh, no. I've been an idiot, haven't I?'

'No. Think about it. Was Fran worried?'

'No. She wanted to come to my house to meet him the first time he came over, to see if he was a suspect, but she said he wasn't.'

'He was. But although his main idea was to find a seventeenth-century treasure, he didn't have anything to do with the murders.'

'You've just led me up the garden path!' said Libby indignantly.

'No. We needed to find out – still do – if his main interest was the supposed treasure or simply the evidence.'

'Do you honestly think he came here to steal it? The treasure, I mean.'

'I don't know. It was the coincidence of his turning up after Ramani Oxenford died which was so suspicious.'

'He thought it was because he was black you took him in,' said Libby darkly, turning to DC Robertson, who went pink.

'He has got a bit of a chip on his shoulder about that,' said Ian. 'Anyway, we'll still keep an eye on him. Are you seeing him today?'

'No idea. I imagine he might stay around while Andrew does his research on the document. And now, please tell me what you meant about the treasure. You said it was urgent.'

Ian leant back in his chair and took a sip of coffee. 'Johnny Templeton.'

'Yes. You've arrested him. And what has it got to do with Edward?'

'Nothing, we hope. You've just told me that you only found out about the Napoleonic connection from Professor Wylie.'

'Yes.'

'We went to talk to John Templeton about the possibility of a different type of treasure.'

'Why? I don't understand.' Libby's brow was wrinkled.

'You remember your Institute of Napoleonic Studies? You were right about that scrap having come from one of the online printing companies. His was the name on the order form.'

'What? That's nonsense.'

'It looks like it, doesn't it?'

'And this was – when?'

'Over a year ago.'

Libby gaped. 'OK. It still doesn't make sense.'

'Particularly when you discover that John Templeton has no computer, no smart phone, no modern technology at all, other than a very old mobile phone.'

'So he couldn't have ordered it?'

'He could, using a public computer.'

'He'd need a credit or debit card.'

'Indeed. The order at the print company was paid by credit card in his name.'

'So you arrested him?'

'We went to talk to him. He wasn't exactly co-operative, so we took him to the station to help with our enquiries.'

'Late at night?'

'No, it was quite early in the evening.'

'But he didn't call Mog until after one in the morning.'

'No, because he was being, as I said, unco-operative. In the end, we decided to keep him and have another go this morning. He asked if he could call someone to let them know where he was.'

'So what's his explanation? And why did you want to talk to me about it?'

'Because we needed to know who knew that there was a

possibility of smuggled gold somewhere in Dark House.'

Chapter Thirty-two

'*Gold?*' repeated Libby. 'You mean the Napoleonic guineas?'

Ian nodded. 'Now, this part is off the record. Robertson, put your notebook away. We searched Templeton's cottage, which we hadn't done before, and eventually we found a stack of stationery, all with this fake Institute's heading. I must say, it looked good. He'd used a very good quality paper.'

'And what was it for? And why had he used his own credit card?'

'All he's said this morning is that it was nothing to do with him. Last night he was considerably under the influence of something, which the doctor confirmed, so it was no wonder he was unco-operative and belligerent.'

'I thought it always made people rather – well – benign.'

'Depends on the circumstances. He was fine when we first got there.'

'So what does it mean?'

'We aren't sure, but there was a standard form letter among the stationery informing the addressee that their property was the possible location of a hoard of guineas dating from the Napoleonic wars.'

'Which addressee? Who?'

'I just said,' explained Ian patiently, 'it's a form letter. Something that could be sent out to many.'

'And it was sent to the Watsons?'

'I'm not saying that. We've looked at the credit card account that was used to buy the stuff, and it's only ever been used for that one transaction. The card account was one of those that could be opened online, and the security doesn't appear to have been that tight. The account was paid off with cash over a bank counter. It looks as though Templeton was used by whoever initiated the scam, or whatever it is, but without his own bank account being compromised, so it may not come to light.'

'Sneaky. So he's nothing to do with it, as he said?'

'Not quite,' said Ian. 'But he's storing the evidence. And he won't say who told him to.'

Libby frowned. 'Presumably it was delivered to him? So he really might not know who did it. And they could have kept him quiet by some sort of blackmail? He looks as if he might have something dodgy in his past.'

'It's a possibility. But you see why I had to know who knew about the smuggled gold in the area. I had to know if Edward Hall knew.'

'It's even more puzzling now. The local families – the old ones – they knew. And I would have thought a historian would know. Andrew probably knew but hadn't connected it up. Edward didn't seem to know at all. And I'd swear he didn't know anything about the fake Institute.'

'Thanks for your help.' Ian put his coffee cup back on the tray. 'You'll also be glad to know that we went to have a chat with Mrs Watson this morning.'

'At Carl Oxenford's house?'

'Yes, although he tried to tell us she wasn't there.'

'Have they been having an affair?'

'It would appear so, but for how long we don't know. Neither of them is being very forthcoming about it.'

'Did she say anything about the Institute? That's what you were going to ask her, wasn't it?'

'She'd never heard of it, and didn't recognise the piece of envelope. She knows nothing about Napoleonic gold, smugglers or civil wars, according to her. History has no interest for her. As for Doctor Oxenford, he just looked bemused about the whole thing.'

'What about this false practice of his, though?'

'I did just touch on that,' said Ian, with a grin, 'but he simply looked mournful and said it hadn't worked out. All the villagers were registered with a practice at Steeple Mount and didn't want to change.'

'So how come the Watsons were his patients? Were they private?'

'I don't know. And we've enough to do trying to work out who knew, or thought they did, about the so-called treasure and who would have murdered for it.'

'Are we allowed to talk to Edward?'

'I'm going to see him now. He's expecting us at the pub. After that, yes.'

'And what about Johnny and the Institute?'

'We can't hold him. And there was nothing else at his house to suggest that he was involved in anything more than looking after the stationery and purchasing it. If he did. We will look into the blackmail aspect, of course.'

'And do you think it might lead to the murderer?' Libby stood up.

'As I said as soon as we heard about it, just the rumour of it might be enough, if someone thought it was worth it.' Ian went to the door and DC Robertson held it open. 'I'll just say goodbye to the family.'

'So,' said Peter, as soon as they'd seen the two policemen off the premises. 'What was that all about?'

'I think we ought to help Hetty clear the table and let her have a rest,' said Libby diplomatically. 'She won't want us sitting round her table holding her up.'

Hetty stood up. 'Come on, then. Just get the plates in the dishwasher. I'll do the pots meself.'

When the big kitchen was suitably tidied, Peter, Adam, Ben and Libby said their farewells and left Hetty, Flo and Lenny sitting round the fire in the drawing room.

'Come back to ours,' said Peter. 'Hal should be back by now. Coming, Adam?'

'Thanks, but I'm going out later. I'll call you, Ma. I need to know about Johnny.'

'He's OK. They're going to let him go,' said Libby. 'But he's still got questions to answer. Not directly about the murders, though.'

Adam looked relieved. He kissed Libby's cheek and loped off to the flat above The Pink Geranium.

Harry had already prepared his drinks tray when Peter let them in to the cottage. Libby slumped in her favourite chair and accepted a whisky.

'Sunday seems to be a day of drink after drink,' she said sipping appreciatively.

'Come on, then, what's going on,' said Harry, sitting beside Peter on the sofa and swinging his legs onto his partner's lap. 'I need to know.'

Libby related everything that had happened that day. 'So as far as I can make out, Ian's now following a trail that someone was out to – oh, I don't know – con people into thinking they had a hoard of Napoleonic gold in their house.'

'Why?' Harry looked puzzled.

'To gain access for burglary?' suggested Ben. 'That would be the most obvious thing.'

'But they were looking into a civil war hoard,' said Libby. 'I know we only got that from Edward, who now seems to be a most suspicious character, but the Rev. Toby confirmed it when he told us Ramani went in looking for Sir Godfrey's tomb.'

'This credit card business,' said Peter thoughtfully. 'How much do you think Templeton was involved?'

'I don't think he was, really. I think someone borrowed his identity to get a card and have a delivery address for the stationery,' said Libby.

'In that case, he must have had some knowledge of it.'

'Because of the stuff being delivered?'

'Yes. And who would know enough about him to get the credit card?'

'We don't know, do we?' said Libby. 'We don't know anything about his social circle. He doesn't drink in The Dragon, but I bet he's known in The Feathers.'

'The Feathers?' said Harry.

'The pub in Keeper's Cob. It's a dive. Lewis said not to go near it, but Fran and I did go in there a couple of weeks ago

237

when we got lost. The tunnel that leads away from Dark House under the grotto goes to Keeper's Cob, which borders the end of the estate, and we've made the assumption it comes up to the pub.'

'So if Templeton drinks in there he's likely to have fairly unsavoury connections?' said Peter.

'You're making a lot of assumptions here,' said Ben.

'I know.' Libby sighed. 'We can't really know, can we?'

'And this letter. You think it was sent to the Watsons?' said Peter.

'That's what I think,' said Libby. 'And it makes sense. If Roland received that letter, he would immediately want to look for it. And, depending on whether he'd already started his affair with Ramani, he would either use the knowledge to tempt her or ask for her help.'

'Why did she go and look for that tomb, though, or whatever it was?' asked Harry.

'And why did she tell Edward there was Civil War treasure buried there? And when?' said Peter.

'Golly,' said Libby. 'I don't know.' She wrinkled her brow. 'I assume it must have been not long before she died, or Edward would have got in touch before.'

'You are the only person I know who says "Golly",' said Harry. 'I feel I ought to be serving you lashings of ginger beer.'

'Did you know she never actually wrote that?' said Libby. 'It was from *Five Go Mad In Dorset*, the Comic Strip film.'

'Was it?' Harry turned to Peter. 'Have I seen that?'

Peter patted his arm. 'I'll find it on DVD for you. You'll love it.'

'This is all speculation,' said Ben.

'About the Famous Five?' said Libby.

'About Edward, Templeton and everything else. You don't actually know anything.'

'No, I know.' Libby sighed. 'But all this has put a whole new slant on things. I really wish I could talk to Edward, now. I need to know if he's trustworthy, or a criminal.'

'Tell you what,' said Harry, swinging his legs off Peter's lap.

'Why don't we ask him here this evening?'

'What?' said three voices together.

'I could do a little snacky supper. We could be saving him from another lonely evening in the pub. If he accepts, it probably means he's kosher. If he doesn't – well.'

'Or, if he's been hauled off to the nick,' said Ben with a grin.

'What do you think, Pete?' said Libby. 'It's your house, and your evening off with Hal.'

Peter shrugged. 'I'm fine with it. If Hal wants to get back in the kitchen on his night off.'

'I've got another night off tomorrow.' Harry beamed. 'Go on, Lib. Ring him.'

'Ian might still be with him,' demurred Libby.

'Send him a text, then,' said Ben.

Libby laboriously sent a text to Edward's number, and put the phone on the coffee table.

'Well, now we wait,' said Peter.

'And if we don't hear in the next – what? Hour?' said Harry.

'We'll go home and normal service will be resumed,' said Ben.

'Meanwhile, you can carry on dicussing who might be the murderer,' said Peter. 'Tell us more about the enigmatic Mrs Fairbrass, Lib.'

'I must say, it came as a bit of a surprise. She's not exactly a housekeeper and turns out to be the beneficiary of the last owner of Dark House.'

'And knew all about the supposed treasure,' said Harry. 'I told Peter all about it this morning before he went up to The Manor.'

'Well, I did recap for the benefit of Hetty, Flo and Lenny,' said Libby. 'It's that document I'm worried about now.'

'Andrew's got it, didn't you say?' said Ben.

'Yes. Ian called him and he said Edward had left it with him.'

'That doesn't sound as though he's a crook, does it?' said Harry. 'And I liked him, anyway.'

'Just as well,' said Libby, as her phone told her there was a message. She read it and grinned. 'Because Edward's looking forward to coming here this evening!'

Chapter Thirty-three

Libby and Ben decided to go home, have a cup of tea and possibly a nap before what could be an interesting evening. Harry had pressed them to stay, offering more whisky, but, as Libby said, if they were all as drunk as skunks by the time Edward arrived at seven thirty it rather negated the purpose of the evening.

Accordingly, the four of them gathered at seven fifteen feeling less sleepy than they might have done. Libby and Ben handed over two bottles of wine, and Peter handed them glasses of red.

At exactly seven thirty, Edward arrived.

'This is lovely,' he said looking round. 'Love the fire.'

'Ours is a proper one,' said Harry. 'Not like Libby's piddling little Victorian one.'

Edward laughed. 'But at least it's a real fire.'

'Sit down,' said Peter, 'and tell us how your interview with DCI Connell went.'

Libby frowned at him, but Peter was unabashed.

'Edward will know we want to know. He could hardly not.'

Edward sighed and leant forward in his chair, elbows on his knees. 'Of course you want to know. And you'll have quite a few questions for me. Haven't you, Libby?'

Libby nodded. 'Ian left me feeling deeply suspicious of you earlier today. And I must say I felt a bit mortified, having introduced you and – '

'Allowed me into Libby's Loonies,' interrrupted Edward, with a small smile. 'I know. But it really wasn't like that.'

'So what was it like? Come on, Edward – full story. When

241

did Ramani get in touch with you and what exactly did she say?'

Edward sighed. 'I've been all through this with your inspector already, so at least I know the answers. The first time she mentioned the house and the possibility of treasure was when she was up in town and I managed to get down to see her. This would have been – oh, a year ago. I wasn't particularly interested. She didn't say anything about the Watsons. Then, about six weeks ago, she told me she'd found out that it could possibly be connected with the civil wars. That did interest me. So I asked if I could come down and have a look at the house. She was very evasive.'

'Did she say anything about the Watsons this time?' asked Libby.

'Not a lot. I have to say, I almost thought that she'd made up the civil war connection to get me interested. Anyway, I kept trying to get hold of her, and she'd return the odd text, but then went silent. So I came down. I knew where she lived, and I had actually met Carl some time ago in Leicester.'

'Didn't you feel awkward about seeing him, knowing you'd continued a relationship with his wife?'

'I did, a bit.' Edward lowered his eyes.

'So you arrived and knew nothing about Ramani's death?' said Ben.

Edward nodded. 'I arrived on the doorstep as the police were leaving and they swept me off to the police station in Canterbury. And that's it, really.'

'When she first mentioned treasure, did she say anything about the Napoleonic wars or the gold?' asked Libby.

'She said something about smuggling, but that was all. I got the impression she rather dismissed the story.'

'So what do you think happened?'

'I don't know. I wanted to look into it, so I stayed around. There was honestly nothing underhand about it. Your inspector seems to think I knew something about what was going on – perhaps even involved with some sort of scam.'

'Yes. Because of the fake Institute and your sudden appearance on the scene,' said Libby. 'I didn't entirely trust you,

242

either.'

'Do you now?'

'I think so.' Libby smiled. 'As long as you've told us everything now. Mind you, it didn't amount to much more than we knew already.'

'Except that Ramani had told you about treasure a year ago and mentioned smugglers,' said Peter.

'That will have interested Cuddly Connell,' said Harry.

'Who?' Edward looked bewildered.

'The chief inspector,' said Peter. 'I think he is rather suspicious, and thinks you may well have known the story of the guinea boats before arriving here. Did he tell you what they found – when, Lib? Yesterday?'

'I assume so.' She looked at Edward. 'Did he?'

'Did he what?'

'Tell you what the police found yesterday?'

'No? I have no idea what you're talking about. He asked me a lot of questions that seemed to relate to this fake institute, and if I studied that period.' Libby thought she saw that faint flush on Edward's dark cheeks. 'In fact, he almost seemed not to believe I'm a historian. He said he'd been in touch with the university.'

'Yes, he told me that,' said Libby. 'And had you studied that period?'

'How do you imagine one becomes a history lecturer?' Edward's tone became peremptory. 'I have an Honours Degree, a Master's and a doctorate. The eighteenth and nineteenth centuries haven't been my particular interest, but of course I've studied them. I wasn't aware of the guinea boats, I have to say, nor did I know about the escape routes of the French prisoners. They are small areas of special interest.'

'Well,' said Harry. 'That told us.'

'Sorry.' Edward looked anything but repentant.

'Edward,' said Ben gently, 'do you know anything about architecture?'

'Architecture? Well – a bit. When it's Tudor.'

'And do you know how long it takes to become an architect?'

243

'No …'

'Seven years. Five at university and two under the direct supervision of a qualified architect.'

Edward was looking at him warily. 'Yes,' he said.

'So we don't really want your academic credentials. Just a simple answer would have done.'

Edward seemed to collapse into his chair. 'Oh, I'm sorry.' He looked at Libby. 'It's the "me, me, me" syndrome again, isn't it?'

'As long as you recognise it.' Libby patted his arm. 'Now. Get off your high horse and try and help us with sorting out this mess. What you don't know is that Johnny Templeton was arrested and stationery with the institute's heading found in his cottage. And it was purchased with a credit card in his name. So I expect Ian was trying to find out if you'd had any contact with him.'

'He did mention the name. Who is he?'

'You must have heard us mention him,' said Libby. 'He's the person who found Ramani's body.' She went on to explain about the form letter and the theory that one had been sent to the Watsons which piqued Roland's interest.

'When was that?' Edward frowned. 'Only, as I said, Ramani mentioned smugglers to me a year ago.'

'I didn't ask!' said Libby. 'Oh, how silly!'

'That fragment of envelope you found. Did it look old?' asked Peter.

'Well it wasn't brand new. And it was stuck in the back of a drawer, so it hadn't been put there recently.'

'Unless it was purposely hidden,' said Ben.

'But from whom? I thought it was one of Adelaide's drawers, but we think the letter was sent to Roland, don't we?'

'And didn't she say she didn't know nuffink about anyfink?' said Harry, getting up. 'Another drink, anyone? And I'll get me little dainties out of the oven.'

While Harry bustled about being a host, the rest of them tried to make sense of a situation they really knew nothing about.

'Ian says Johnny won't say who told him to store the

244

stationery,' said Libby.

'It sounds too clever to be a ruffian from The Feathers,' said Peter.

'Ooh, what a lovely word, "ruffian",' said Harry, bringing in a tray of food and ruffling Peter's hair on the way back to the kitchen.

'So, some devious character who we've never heard of,' said Libby gloomily. 'And why, anyway? Why tell Roland he might have a hoard of guineas hidden in his house?'

'Why tell anyone, frankly?' said Ben. 'Unless you really thought there *was* a hoard.'

'And why alert the owners if you wanted to nick it?' said Harry, pouring wine all round.

They all looked at each other. Edward shook his head slowly. 'None of it makes any sense,' he said.

'Let's go back to the civil wars,' said Peter, ten minutes later, when they'd all partaken of Harry's dainties. 'Could the letters be to allow someone to search the houses and then regretfully say they'd been mistaken, while actually looking for a civil war treasure?'

Everyone looked at Edward.

'Don't look at me,' he said in alarm. 'It wasn't me!'

'No, but could that be a reason?' said Libby. 'It sounds quite likely to me.'

'I suppose so, but it seems like an inordinate amount of trouble to go to,' said Edward. 'All the expense of printing fake letters, not to mention Templeton's credit card, just to search a house?'

'And why couldn't you go to an owner and say "'Ere, mate, I reckon you've got some old treasure, can I look for it?" They'd be only too happy, wouldn't they?' said Harry.

'Not if you planned to steal it,' said Peter. 'And listen. If you said a hoard of guineas, that would belong to the Crown because it was stolen from the Crown in the first place – more or less – so the owner wouldn't be so keen to interfere. If you said it was something buried by a former owner it could well be a different matter.'

'That's true, but you'd have to be absolutely certain there really was something to find,' said Ben.

'But that's what Ramani was doing,' said Libby excitedly. 'Looking into the Civil War treasure. She went to the church, didn't she?'

'So we're back where we started,' said Edward. 'A war treasure hidden by Sir Godfrey Wyghtham. Which we haven't found.'

'Except for the ring and the cross you found in the chimney in the attic,' said Libby.

'And back to wondering who also knew and killed both Ramani and Roland for it.' said Edward. He looked round the room. 'And it wasn't me.'

'The other person who knew, possibly, was your new friend Mrs Fairbrass,' said Harry.

'She says she didn't believe in the treasure. It was Lady Middleton and her daughter who did,' said Libby.

'And what was it happened to the daughter?' asked Ben.

'She fell into the grotto and was killed. Years ago.'

The sudden silence meant that everybody had the same idea at once.

'She found it!' said Harry, voicing the one thought.

'If she did,' said Libby carefully, 'why wasn't it found with her body?'

'Because whoever discovered her body made away with it,' said Peter. 'Does that make sense?'

'Except that the grotto wasn't built until two hundred years after the civil wars,' said Libby.

'But the tunnels weren't,' said Edward, beginning to look interested. 'They were only bricked up in the late nineteenth.'

'Were they bricked up when the grotto was built, do you think?' mused Libby. 'And if Godfrey's treasure – assuming that was what was hidden – was there when that was done, why didn't the Victorians find it?'

'That's true. Or – the daughter could have discovered the hiding place, not necessarily the treasure,' said Edward.

'And there's the other thing. About Godfrey's wife.' Libby

looked across over the rim of her wine glass.

'Rebecca? What?'

'No – Evelyn. The other wife.'

Edward looked round at the four faces staring at him. 'Yes. So – what?'

'This document Andrew's got – will it explain that?'

'I don't know. And I don't know if it makes a difference anyway.'

'Well, it is that document that started the story of the treasure,' said Ben. 'So was the Middleton daughter looking for a treasure left for Evelyn or Rebecca?'

'It's another red herring,' said Libby, sighing. 'It doesn't make any difference at all. All we really need to know is who made up the Institute and the letter. And why.'

'And is it the same person who killed Ramani and Roland?' said Ben.

'And why are we bothering?' said Harry.

Chapter Thirty-four

On Monday morning, Adam called his mother with the surprising news that he and Mog were allowed back to the Dark House gardens.

'Mog called Mrs Watson,' he said.

'And she answered?'

'Yes. Shouldn't she have?'

'Never mind. So what did she say?'

'She wants us to finish off the work and give her an invoice for work done so far. And an estimate of the end result.'

'And will she pay for all the making good of the police investigation?'

'She won't know, will she? Anyway, she's going to sell the house as soon as she's able, so she'll have pots.'

'Not if she wants to buy a house on Wimbledon Common,' said Libby, 'which is what she told me she wanted to do. Nine million for a house there. I looked it up.'

'Bloody hell!' said Adam. 'Didn't you used to live near there?'

'Not far,' said Libby. 'Your father and I had our wedding reception in that famous pub in Wimbledon village.'

'Think if you'd stayed there,' said Adam wistfully.

'I'd never have had you lot,' said Libby. 'We had a studio flat in Streatham. Not ideal for bringing up a family. So when are you going back?'

'This morning,' said Adam. 'Mog's picking me up in half an hour.'

'Can I come over?' asked Libby, on the spur of the moment. 'Johnny's home and I'd like to meet him.'

'Oh?' Adam sounded wary. 'Would Ian like that?'

'I'm sure he wouldn't mind,' said Libby cheerily. 'Johnny isn't a suspect.'

'You said he still had questions to answer.'

'He does, but not about the murders.'

'And what are you going to talk to him about?'

'His cottage,' said Libby, thinking on her feet. 'How old it is.'

'Isn't it the same age as the house?' said Adam.

'I don't know, do I? I've never seen it.'

'All right, then, I suppose I can't stop you,' said Adam, 'but don't get me into trouble.'

'Great! I'll see you later, then.' Libby ended the call and pressed Fran's number.

'Lots to tell you, and do you want to come to meet Johnny Templeton with me in about an hour?'

'I'll meet you there,' said Fran. 'You can tell me then.'

Although still grey, there was no mist and Dark Lane had lost its mysterious and ghostly aspect. Libby drove in to the forecourt and parked behind Mog's van. Almost immediately, Fran's Smart car turned in beside her.

'So what exactly are we doing here?' asked Fran, when Libby had regaled her with the events of Sunday afternoon and evening.

'I wanted to see if Johnny Templeton would open up to me – or us – more than he did to Ian. And – oh, I don't know. See if we could pick up on anything else?'

'Tell me again,' said Fran, as they walked over the lawn to where Adam and Mog were trying to get their work site back in order, 'why you all thought the girl who died in the grotto –'

'Olive Wyghtham,' put in Libby.

'Olive – why she'd found the treasure?'

'I don't know. It's just that the grotto has featured so heavily in all of this, and she was looking there, when it wasn't even in existence in the sixteen hundreds.'

'Hmm.' Fran stopped and looked towards the arch in the hedge that led to the grotto. 'Have you heard from Andrew about that document yet?'

'No. Should we ring him, do you think?'

'Perhaps later. He'll ring Ian first, won't he?'

'Yes, and then perhaps Marilyn Fairbrass. It's hers, after all.'

But before they could speak to Adam, Libby's phone rang.

'Libby, I thought you might want to know,' said Ian. 'A couple of pieces of information.'

'That's very kind, Ian.' Libby raised her eyebrows at Fran.

'First, you remember the jewellery Edward found in the chimney?'

'Yes.'

'Apparently, they are – er – quite valuable. If they were in an auction today, their joint value would be around twenty-five thousand pounds.'

'Twenty-five thousand!' echoed Libby.

'Yes, but is that enough to murder for? And how much would they have been worth in the sixteen fifties? Anyway, that's one thing. The other is that Andrew has some interesting information from that document. We're holding the original in case it proves to be relevant, but he has a modern translation for you to give Mrs Fairbrass. Give him a ring.'

'And I'm allowed to do that?' said Libby.

'Yes, Libby, you are.'

'Well, how about that!' said Libby, and related the conversation to Fran. 'Shall we go to Andrew's now?'

'No, we'll go and see Johnny Templeton. Adam may well have told him we're coming.'

'OK, but then we ring Andrew?'

'I'll ring him while you speak to Adam, and say we'll come over when we've finished here, if that's convenient.'

Adam, looking awkward, led them through the arch in the hedge and down to the grotto. The pallet the constable had placed over the hole was still there. Looming over them either side were artistically place rough boulders planted with ferns and running with water. Above them, straddling the path, was a bridge.

'Can you get to that bridge?' asked Libby.

'Where does the water come from?' asked Fran.

'I don't know to both questions,' said Adam. 'All I know is the water runs into a little stream, look, over there. That feeds the fishpond further down the garden.'

'Is that new?' said Libby.

'How do I know?' said Adam, exasperated. 'All we've done here is this bloody swimming pool.'

'All right, all right,' soothed Libby. 'Come on, where's Johnny's house?'

Adam led them under the bridge, after which the path sunk down between even higher artistic walls. Libby shivered.

'Unpleasant,' said Fran.

Suddenly the path emerged into daylight and in front of them stood a cottage that looked as though there should be girls in bonnets with kittens playing outside.

Adam looked at his mother and Fran, then nervously knocked on the door.

Nothing happened. Adam turned away.

'He's not there.'

'He is,' said Fran, and stepped past him. 'Mr Templeton! May we speak to you for a moment?'

There was a pause, then the door opened a crack.

'Johnny,' said Adam, 'this is my mother and a friend. They just want to speak to you for a minute.'

The door opened wider and Johnny Templeton appeared, looking as though he'd stepped out of a squat in the early seventies.

'What?' he said.

'May we come in, Mr Templeton?' asked Libby stepping forward. 'We've been looking into the history of Dark House and we wondered if your cottage was the same date.'

'Why?'

Libby was stumped.

'Because of the treasure,' said Fran smoothly, and Libby gasped.

'I'm going back to work, Ma,' said Adam. 'Check in before you leave.'

'We will,' said Libby.

Johnny Templeton half closed the door, but Fran was too quick for him.

'Mr Templeton – Johnny – we know you know about the treasure. You do, don't you?'

'Might do.'

'You do, because of all that stationery the police found here.'

'That was made up,' said Johnny.

'I know. Who made it up?'

Johnny looked shifty. 'I dunno, do I? I told the police.'

'Why did you keep the stuff then, after it had been delivered?'

'Didn't know what to do with it, did I? Could'a chucked it out.'

'But someone didn't want you to, did they?' said Fran, who was obviously on a roll. 'And they must have told you about that treasure. Did you know about the treasure before that stationery arrived? About the golden guineas?'

An avaricious gleam showed briefly in Johnny's muddy eyes. 'No.'

'What about the other treasure?'

He frowned. 'What other treasure?'

Fran looked up at the cottage. 'From when your cottage was built.'

'Eh?' Johnny looked round as if expecting jewellery to fall out of the walls.

'Johnny, who rented you this cottage?'

'Watson.' Johnny was frowning again.

'No, before Mr Watson.'

Libby looked at her friend in surprise.

'Middleton.'

'Lady Middleton? For how long?'

He shrugged. 'Must be twenty years.'

'Twenty years!" said Libby. 'You've been here twenty years?'

'Why shouldn't I?'

Fran suddenly switched tack.

'When did you meet Mr Watson?'

Johnny looked confused for a moment.

'Was it when he moved in?'

'Can't remember.'

'Did you know him before he bought Dark House?'

Johnny stepped backwards into the house, but Fran was right after him. Libby followed into the dark interior, which smelled of rotting food and something else indefinable.

'Look Johnny,' said Fran, fixing him with an intense eye, probably trying to ignore the surroundings, thought Libby, 'we aren't the police. This is Adam's mother. Adam's all right, isn't he?'

'Maybe.'

'So why don't you talk to us? The police are still interested in you, you know that, but maybe we could help you.'

'How?' Johnny fumbled on the untidy table for tobacco. 'What do you want?'

'Who told you about the guineas and who got you to buy that stationery?'

'No one. I dunno. Nothing to do with me. Been here all year.'

'What, the stationery?' asked Libby. 'Been here for a year?'

'When Ramani first told Carl about the treasure,' said Fran.

'Look, I told that copper – I don't know nothing. It's nothing to do with me. I never done nothing.'

'And you don't know anything about any other treasure?'

'No, I swear,' said Johnny, and for the first time sounded as though he was telling the truth.

Fran sighed. 'Come on, Libby. He's not going to let us help him.'

They went out into the fresh air.

''Ere.'

They turned round.

'Why d'you want to know if this place is the same as the big house?'

'In case the treasure is hidden here, of course,' said Fran, and turned on her heel.

Libby hurried after her, back through the sunken lane and

253

under the fake bridge. 'Do you really think that?' she panted.

'It's a thought,' said Fran. 'Let's see what Andrew's document has to say.'

'What? What's that got to do with it?'

'I don't know, but we ought to find out. Are we going in separate cars?'

Andrew's flat stood at the top of Nethergate, looking out over the town and the bay. Rosie's cat Talbot greeted them at the door.

'Doesn't he try to get away?' asked Libby, as Talbot sniffed the air and turned to stroll back into the flat, tail held high.

'No.' Andrew smiled after his black and white companion. 'Considering how much space he had to roam at Rosie's place, it's quite surprising.'

'Have you heard from Rosie?' asked Fran, as they followed Andrew into his large, light sitting room, where armchairs were arranged round a table in the window.

'Oh, yes. She's still in the States, having now been invited to Canada and Hawaii.'

'Having the time of her life, then?' said Libby.

'And good luck to her,' said Andrew with a grin. 'I told her that she will have to fight me for the custody of Talbot when she gets back.'

'What did she say?' asked Fran, amused.

'That I could have him and welcome, as she had no idea when she might come back to England.' Andrew laughed. 'So I offered to put the house on the market for her. That shook her.'

Fran and Libby laughed.

'What did she say?' asked Libby.

'She was rather peeved that I didn't seem to mind. Now, I'll just fetch tea – or would you rather have coffee?'

They both opted for coffee, which Andrew served with home-made apple cake, once again bought from the local farmers' market.

'So this document. Edward was right, it is part of a letter. There's no indication of who it was sent to, but it appears to be giving instructions to someone to look after Sir Godfrey's wife,

254

Evelyn, in the event of his death. It says he has made provision for her, and that the recipient knows where to find whatever it is. That's really all, it's just the very difficult and flowery language of the time. So then, I decided to look for a record of Evelyn Wyghtham.'

'Where? At the county archives?' said Libby.

'No, first I looked up the records of listed houses, but no mention there. So I took myself off to your church at Steeple Cross and saw the Reverend Toby.'

'On a Sunday? Gosh, I bet he was pleased!'

'He didn't mind a bit. Charming chap. We had a look at the parish records, and the old marriage registers, which are even harder to read than that letter, and then we had a cup of coffee at the rectory.'

'What did you find?' asked Fran.

'Godfrey married Evelyn in 1640. There is no record of a marriage to Rebecca.'

'What?' said Libby and Fran together.

'But the slab in the church says "wife", and what about the children?' said Libby.

'There are no records for them, either. The only reference is on the slab in the church,' said Andrew. 'Which means, I think, and so does Toby, that Rebecca was Godfrey's mistress and the children by him were illegitimate. At some point before Godfrey died, Evelyn must have passed away, too. Whether he really did marry Rebecca after that isn't clear. They could have got a licence and got married somewhere else, or even had a clandestine marriage.'

'A clandestine marriage? An underhand one?' asked Fran.

'Quite common for a long time,' said Andrew. 'The Fleet and Newgate held most of them. There are specific records for those.'

'Oh, I can see that.' Libby frowned. 'But why do you think that one page gave rise to the treasure theory? It doesn't actually say anything.'

'I've no idea,' said Andrew. 'I suppose someone at some point formulated the theory that "provision" meant money and it was hidden somewhere. But it could just as well have meant it was being kept by a lawyer. I also think that it's a possibility, given the language in the letter, that it was written to Rebecca.'

'Telling her to look after Evelyn? What a cheek!' gasped Libby.

'It's only an opinion,' said Andrew, with a smile, 'but it would be quite likely that Rebecca was a maid, and maids were often seen to be legitimate targets for their masters' lusts.'

'Only this time he actually loved her.' Fran nodded. Andrew and Libby looked at her. She smiled. 'So she wouldn't have to wear a white sheet in the church door.'

'She what?' Libby was startled.

'Often a punishment by the villagers,' said Andrew, 'when a maid got herself pregnant by the lord of the manor. The woman was always punished, never the man.'

Libby made a sound between a snort and an explosion.

'Anyway,' said Fran. 'Andrew's right, I'm sure of it. It's a working premise, at any rate.'

'So,' said Libby, looking between Fran and Andrew, 'Godfrey marries Evelyn – pity we don't know more about her. She could have been an ugly old crab, couldn't she?'

'She could,' agreed Andrew with a grin.

'So, Rebecca comes as a maid and he exerts his *droit du seigneur*, gets her pregnant with the eldest child – you told us the estate went to his eldest son, didn't you? – and at some point asks her to make sure his wife's provided for. Do we know the date of the letter?'

'No. But it would make sense if it was during the civil wars, probably just before the Battle of Maidstone, if he went to that.'

'He did,' said Fran with assurance.

Andrew shook his head. 'I wish we could just take all your statements and use them as fact.'

Fran sighed. 'I wish you could, too. Anyway, it looks as though Evelyn was still alive then, if that's the case.'

'Poor woman,' said Libby. 'What a life. So do we take it that there wasn't any treasure?'

'Apart from that little note in the parish record there's

nothing to suggest it,' said Andrew. 'Whether or not it's Rebecca he's writing to, there's nothing to suggest that whatever his provisions were they weren't used, or reclaimed after the war. I think your Middleton ladies worked it up into a story.'

'But why did that particular sheet of paper survive all the way down to them?'

'We'll never know,' said Andrew. 'I think it's a mystery you'll never solve. All you need to know is if Roland Watson and the Doctor's wife believed it.'

'Or if they believed in the story of the guineas,' said Libby.

'Ramani told Edward about the civil war connection,' said Fran. 'And went to the church, so it looks as if they believed it.'

'And we think old Lady Middleton told Roland before she died,' said Libby. 'But he didn't get the piece of paper, so he may have dismissed the whole idea.'

'And then – what? This letter turns up from the fake Institute saying he might have a load of guineas tucked away?' Fran shook her head. 'None of it makes any sense or gets us any nearer to who murdered them both.' She turned to Andrew. 'But thank you, Andrew. It's a little bit clearer now.'

'Where now?' asked Libby as they left Andrew's flat. 'Take this translation back to Marilyn Fairbrass?'

Fran leant on the railing on the other side of the road to the block of flats and stared out over a wintry Nethergate. Her dark hair blew gently across her face.

'I keep coming back to Ramani. She was a historian. She wouldn't get taken in, or believe a tale passed down to gullible women.'

Libby leant beside her. 'What do you mean? Don't forget she was also a bit of a good-time girl.'

'That doesn't mean she wasn't a good historian. And she went to the church. Why do we think that was *all* the research she did? It stands to reason she did more than that. So where is it?'

Chapter Thirty-five

Libby stared. 'Do you mean we've been looking at this the wrong way round from the start?'

'Not necessarily. But we've assumed Roland used the treasure story to tempt Ramani into an affair. It could have been the other way round if Ramani knew anything about the family.'

'But she couldn't have,' said Libby.

'No, I agree that's unlikely, but think about it. She told Carl about it a year ago. What else has come up? The guineas.'

'But we all agreed that she'd never be taken in by that letter. Roland, maybe, but not Ramani.'

Fran turned to face her friend, pulling her scarf up round her ears. 'So, think about it again. She wouldn't be taken in, but who would?'

'The owners of houses where there might be smuggled goods? Old houses?'

'Exactly. And who better to write a convincing letter than a historian?'

Libby's mouth fell open. '*Ramani* wrote that letter?'

'Doesn't it make sense?'

'She wrote it to Roland?'

'I would have said they were both in it together.' Fran stood up straight. 'I'd give anything to know if the police have found anything in her belongings. If she was trying, probably with Roland's help, to con people somehow, that could be a motive, couldn't it?'

'I still don't see what the game was, though,' said Libby.

'Neither do I.' Fran turned towards her car. 'How about a visit to Carl Oxenford? Do you think he might answer some questions about Ramani?'

'He was a bit off when I called in on Saturday,' said Libby. 'And Adelaide might be there.'

'Let's see.' Fran opened her car door. 'Coming?'

'I haven't had any lunch yet,' grumbled Libby, going towards her battered Renault.

'You've had apple cake,' said Fran. 'Don't complain.'

Libby sighed and started the car.

They parked in the car park of The Dragon and Libby climbed into Fran's passenger seat to discuss tactics.

'It's hardly going to endear us to him if we say we think his wife was a crook,' said Libby.

'No, but we can ask about her work as a historian,' said Fran.

'But she didn't work, did she? Not that we heard.'

'All right, her history as a historian, then.'

'Why will we say we're interested?'

'Everyone knows now about the treasure theory, and that's why Edward came to see Carl. It's reasonable that we might ask if Ramani knew anything about it and would she have done any research into it.'

'I'm sure the police have already asked that,' said Libby. 'And I still don't think that's reason enough to be questioning Carl. I think it just makes us look like nosy old bats.'

'We could ask to talk to Adelaide,' said Fran.

'But Ian said when he finally spoke to her she knew nothing about nothing, as Harry said.'

'Let's try anyway,' said Fran, opening her door. 'I've got a feeling about this.'

'A proper feeling?' asked Libby, hurrying after her as she walked briskly towards the Oxenford house.

Fran stopped. 'I don't know. I'm almost sure there's something in this. It answers a lot of questions.'

Libby scowled. 'I don't see it. I still think it's a complete muddle that will never be sorted out.'

Carl Oxenford opened the door to them, looking surprised.

'Have you come to see Adelaide?' he asked.

'Yes!' said Libby hurriedly, before Fran could ask anything

awkward. 'Is she here?'

'She is. The police tracked her down after all.' He sounded resigned. 'I'm afraid our relationship rather muddied their waters.' He led them through to the room at the back where they had first met Edward.

'Libby!' Adelaide stood up, looking harassed.

'It's all right, Adelaide. We just wanted to make sure you were all right,' said Libby. 'I was worried about you when I couldn't get hold of you. Have you seen Julian?'

'Yes, he came down yesterday.' Adelaide sat down again and waved a vague hand at the other chairs. 'Carl said you came on Saturday?'

'Yes. Just after I'd been to see Marilyn Fairbrass.' Libby caught Fran's eye and gave her a warning frown. Fran stayed silent.

'Marilyn? Whatever for?'

'To ask her about the history of the house. After all, she was with Lady Middleton before you, wasn't she?'

Adelaide opened her mouth but nothing came out.

'And Roland talked to Lady Middleton before she died, didn't he?' said Fran, seeing where Libby had been heading.

Adelaide looked uncomfortable. 'Yes. But honestly, I didn't know anything about any treasure. I told you.'

'Doctor Oxenford, Ramani would have been interested, wouldn't she?' said Libby.

Carl frowned. 'Yes, she would, but I don't see –? You know all this, surely. And what business is it of yours, anyway?'

'Well, we got into it because Adelaide asked us,' said Libby, 'and now we've seen the original letter that we think gave rise to the myth of the treasure –'

'What letter?' said Adelaide.

'Myth?' said Carl.

'We think so,' said Fran. 'But that just made us wonder what research Ramani would have done. Did she leave any notes or anything?'

Carl shook his head slowly. 'Not that I found – or the police, come to that. But I wouldn't, would I? It was all to do with her affair with Roland.' He darted a look at Adelaide.

'Why was it necessary to lie about your affair, though?' asked Libby, looking genuinely interested. 'Adelaide's already admitted part of the reason I was there that night was to provide back-up to the story that you hardly knew each other.'

'That's not quite right –' said Adelaide.

'How could she have known –' said Carl. They looked at each other. 'You go ahead,' said Carl.

'It wasn't like that,' said Adelaide. 'I didn't know Carl would ring.'

'But you *had* recognised Ramani, hadn't you? Despite the very good act you put on,' said Libby.

'I don't see what this has to do with her murder, or indeed, what it has to do with you?' said Carl, sounding increasingly exasperated.

'Maybe it hasn't anything to do with me or the murder,' said Libby, 'but I was involved from the start – for God's sake, Adelaide asked me – us – to look into it! – So I think it has got something to do with me. And all Fran and I have tried to do is help find out who the murderer is. And finding a motive is essential, as the police will tell you. All the way through this investigation, again, as the police will tell you, the treasure has been a possible motive, even if it doesn't exist.'

'Doesn't exist?' Carl frowned. 'But why, in that case?'

'If someone did believe it,' said Fran, 'then a lot of money is a powerful motive. Imagine how annoyed the murderer would be if he found out after killing someone that his efforts were in vain.'

'So you think,' said Carl slowly, 'that my wife was looking into the story of this treasure? What – to validate it?'

'Isn't that a possibility?' said Fran.

He nodded. 'In that case ...' He stopped. 'The police never looked in the shed. We could see if she left anything in there.'

'In a shed?' Libby frowned. 'Would she?'

'She actually quite liked gardening,' said Carl, looking sheepish. 'She spent a lot of time in there.'

'I didn't know that,' said Adelaide. Carl gave her a look that said quite plainly "You don't know everything".

'Come on, then,' said Libby, standing up. 'You never know.' She caught sight of Fran looking dubious. 'Fran? Will you come?'

The four of them trooped down the small walled garden to where an ancient shed stood in one corner. Carl opened the door.

'It's not even locked!' said Libby.

'Nothing to steal,' said Carl, and showed them inside.

Indeed, at first glance there were only sacks of peat-free compost, a lot of pots of various sizes and some gardening tools. But there were cardboard boxes, and some piles of what looked like newspaper. Libby sighed.

'Let's make a start, then,' she said.

It didn't take long to search the boxes and piles of paper. There were no notes anywhere. Carl looked disappointed, Adelaide puzzled and Fran resigned.

'I can't think of anywhere else,' Carl said as he led the way back to the house. 'The second time the police searched the house they went everywhere, even the attics and the cellar.'

'Cellar?' said Libby. 'You've got a cellar?'

'Yes, every house along this ginnel has. It's said they were once joined up as a tunnel used by the smugglers. It went as far as the church.'

Libby looked excited, Fran unsurprised.

'But Ramani would have known that!' said Libby.

'I'm not sure that she did.' Carl was cautious. 'I never heard her talk about it.'

Libby's phone rang in her pocket. The screen showed an unfamiliar number.

'That Adam's mum? 'E gave me yer number. Johnny Templeton here. Got something to show yer. Don't say nothin' to anyone.'

'Er – right. Fran and I will be along soon.' Libby darted a glance at Fran, who stood aside looking composed. She turned off the phone and turned to Carl and Adelaide. 'Well, thank you for showing us the shed, and I'm sorry if we've seemed intrusive.'

Adelaide shrugged. 'Pity there isn't any treasure,' she said.

'We don't know there isn't,' said Fran, suddenly coming to life. 'If Ramani was researching it, which I'm sure she was, it's probably still wherever it was hidden.'

Libby stared at her in amazement, while Adelaide looked excited.

Carl shook his head. 'I don't think so. Even if she researched it, you said it was probably a myth. And no one's found any notes.'

'No. Come on, Fran, we must be going. I'm sure we'll see you both again soon.' Libby took Fran's arm, bestowing a smile on Carl and Adelaide as they stood aside to let them through the house.

'And just what was that all about?' said Libby breathlessly, as she rushed them across the road to the car park. 'Why say there *is* treasure?'

'There still could be,' said Fran. 'And where are we going?'

'Back to Johnny. That was him on the phone. Can we go in your car? I'll leave mine here.'

'What did Johnny want?' asked Fran, as she swung the little car into Dark Lane.

'He wants to show us something and said not to tell anyone.'

'Ah.' Fran's smile was smug.

'What?' shrieked an exasperated Libby. 'You've been acting funny for the last half an hour. And I'm still hungry.'

'Ramani was researching the treasure. At a guess, both sorts. Also at a guess, she found out as much, if not more, than we have about the guineas. We've just heard about the tunnel under her house to the church. What's the betting she went to St Mary's more than once to see if she could find evidence of a tunnel there.'

'And there was a tunnel at Dark House,' said Libby.

'And Roland had been tantalised by the hint of treasure from old Lady Middleton.' Fran negotiated a bend. 'And what if Ramani realised if she could get into people's houses to look for a spurious nineteenth-century treasure that actually sounded genuine, and had good sound research and reasoning behind it,'

263

she took a deep breath, 'she could help herself to anything she found.'

'So plain old burglary, then?' said Libby.

'Not plain. Very fancy, I'd have said.' Fran turned into the drive of Dark House.

'So what about Roland, then?' said Libby, climbing out of the car and following Fran towards the back of the house. Adam and Mog looked up in surprise. Libby waved as Fran disappeared through the arch in the hedge.

'Purely supposition,' said Fran as Libby caught her up, 'but if you think about it logically – if Roland told Ramani about the possibility of a civil war treasure when he was first seducing her, she may well have decided to look into it. And while doing so, came across all the information about the guinea boats and the prisoners. Especially as she knew about her own cellar.'

'But Carl said she didn't.'

'Of course she did.' Fran was scornful.

'So she wrote the fake letter to Roland?'

'I rather think, as I said earlier, it was a joint venture. After all, did Ramani know Johnny well enough to get the credit card and get him to store the stationery? No. So who did?'

'Roland!' Libby gasped. 'I say, Fran, you're too bloody good at this.'

'It's only specualtion, but it fits the facts,' said Fran, 'and I have a feeling we're just about to have it confirmed.'

'You've been having these "feelings" all day,' said Libby. 'Good job that part of your brain's working again!'

Fran grinned. 'It's just got into practice, that's all. I ought to give it more to do.'

Johnny was looking out for them, his eyes even more furtive.

'What is it, then, Johnny?' said Fran.

He led them into the malodorous kitchen once again. On the table there was a large box, which by the labelling, had once held a pair of boots. Johnny pointed to it.

'He brought it in 'ere,' he said.

'Who did? When?' said Libby.

'Mr Watson. Day after she died.'

264

Chapter Thirty-six

Libby was thunderstruck. 'Mr Watson did?' she repeated.

Johnny shrugged. 'Day after he got home.'

'Why didn't you show the police when they found the box of stationery?' asked Fran.

'Forgot.'

'May we look?'

He shrugged again and turned away. Libby lifted the lid.

Inside were books, papers, copies of documents, some material they had already seen and lists of names and addresses.

'Look,' whispered Libby. 'Stone House, Maple Farm, Hall Park ...'

'And here they are.' Fran held out the booklet on the Prisoners of War and the guineas. 'All houses along the smugglers' route.'

'Do you think they were all sent letters?' said Libby.

'I expect so, but it does seem awfully chancy.'

Johnny turned at this, 'Nah. Knew what they was doin'. Knew where there was stuff.'

Fran and Libby both gasped. 'You *knew* about it?' said Libby.

He looked uncomfortable. 'I knew people. I 'ad to store the stuff.'

'How did Watson manage to get you to do that?' asked Fran.

'Knew stuff. About me.' Johnny fidgeted.

'Where did the stuff go from here?' asked Libby. 'Please don't say through a tunnel.'

'Well, yeah, actually.' He pointed to a door. 'Leads down into the tunnel to Keeper's Cob.'

'But the rock fall?' said Libby.

'We 'ad to, didn't we? Didn't want no one findin' it.'

'A deliberate rock fall.' Fran shook her head. 'So it was a scam, all along. A very sophisticated scam.'

'How did Roland manage to kill Ramani, though?' said Libby. 'He was in France – or was it Belgium?'

'He didn't kill Ramani,' said Fran.*

Johnny nodded. 'Nah. 'E didn't.'

'How do you know?' asked Libby suspiciously. 'Did you kill her?'

Johhny looked sick. 'No, I fuckin' didn't.'

'Do you know who did?' asked Fran.

'Nah.' Johnny looked down at the table, and Fran narrowed her eyes.

'Why have you decided to show us this now?' she asked.

Johnny's eyes swivelled from side to side. 'Police,' he said.

'Police? What do you mean?' said Libby.

'You can tell 'em.'

Fran looked shocked. 'No, we can't! You must tell them yourself.'

'Can't.' Now Johnny was looking really frightened.

Libby moved a little closer to Fran. 'Who are you frightened of, Johnny?'

He looked cornered.

'The police?' suggested Fran. Johnny hesitated, then nodded. She shook her head. 'No. You're frightened of the person who killed Ramani and Roland, aren't you? And if you tell the police he'll know, and he'll kill you? But they might get to him or her first, as long as you tell them everything you know.'

'But not if I kill him first,' said a voice behind them.

Fran and Libby whirled round to see Carl Oxenford standing behind them.

'And now I'm going to have to kill you,' he said pleasantly. 'I knew you were a couple of interfering old biddies the moment I saw you. Walking clichés, the pair of you.'

Johnny had edged round the table.

'Oh, not you. You'll keep quiet as always.' Carl moved

towards Fran. She backed up against the table.

'Just how do you propose to kill us?' asked Libby. 'You may not have noticed, but my son and his colleague are outside. And what with? There are three people in here, you can't get us all.'

'Sorry to disappoint you,' said Carl, and drew a small gun from his pocket. Libby's jaw dropped and she thought she might faint.

'It's a gun!' she stuttered.

'Very bright,' said Carl.

'You can't possibly think you'll get away with this,' said Fran.

'Another cliché! You have been watching too much bad television, haven't you? I'm sure you don't need reminding that Johnny just pointed out the entrance to the tunnel? I have nothing to come back for.'

'Were you in on it, too? The scam?' asked Fran, sounding much calmer than Libby, whose heart was beating so hard she was sure everyone in the room could hear it. Added to that was a pair of legs which felt that they might give way any moment and she couldn't have framed an intelligent question if her life depended on it.

'I found out. They were going to leave. After Ramani died, Watson tried to talk me into going in with him. Bastard. Stole my wife, then tried to compensate me. It's all right, though. I know where everything is. Clever, my wife. Had all the documentation filed.'

'Why didn't the police find it?' blurted Libby.

'Oh, it was gone before she died.' Carl smiled again. 'Anyway, we're wasting time here. This isn't a story where the murderer explains everything away at the end just to show off. Open that door, Templeton.'

Johnny shuffled over to the door he'd shown them earlier.

'Now, you two, get in there.' He pointed the gun straight at Libby, and she stumbled backwards towards the door. 'And you.' He pointed the gun at Fran. 'And that'll be the last anyone sees of you for a very long time.'

'Really, Doctor Oxenford?' said a calm voice, and,

miraculously, Ian appeared in the doorway behind Carl.

'Genie from the bottle,' whispered Fran, as she caught Libby's sagging body.

Peter cancelled rehearsal that night. Libby spent the next day lying on the sofa with Sidney recovering from shock and embarrassment, but by Wednesday was feeling bright enough to take the rehearsal and hope that Ian would be able to join them at the pub afterwards. Also in hope, Fran and Guy had come to Steeple Martin and booked in for a meal at The Pink Geranium with Patti and Anne.

After a rehearsal spent mainly responding to eager questions about "her ordeal", Libby, Ben and Peter went to the pub. Ben had barely taken a drinks order when Ian appeared. To his discomfiture, everyone round the table clapped.

'First of all,' said Peter, 'how did you know where they were?'

'We were, believe it or not, on our way to talk to Doctor Oxenford about his wife's empty bank account. When there was no reply at his house, I remembered seeing Libby's car in the car park. Quite distinctive, your car.' He grinned at her. 'And then, your very intelligent son, wondering why you two had suddenly reappeared to be followed by someone he didn't know, had the sense to ring me. Oxenford followed you because he overheard the call you had from Johnny Templeton and surmised he was about to spill the beans. Simple really.'

'But you were only just in time,' said Libby. 'I've promised Adam washing for life, if he likes.'

'So it was all a scam?' said Ben. 'The guineas, and everything?'

'Fran got it almost right. Roland asked Ramani if she could find this treasure. She used to go and prowl round the house when Adelaide was in London, but, of course, she found nothing.'

'She missed the jewellery,' said Edward, who had joined them.

'She did. But she found the priest's hole. Some of the stuff they stole was stored there, before being transferred to Johnny, before going through the tunnel to Keeper's Cob – yes, we've been along it now – and away. We were right when we said he was in the right place on the arts and antiques trail. It all went to Europe. He and Ramani had new accounts, new names, the lot.'

'So they were definitely going?' said Fran.

'Oh, yes. Then Carl found out. What he found he hasn't yet said, but then he decided he might as well take it for himself. She wasn't interested in him, and he couldn't really have cared less about Adelaide – '

'Poor woman,' said Libby.

'So, he killed her.'

'But how?' asked Ben. 'I thought he was away the night she was killed.'

'He was a doctor,' said Ian. 'He cut her throat – sorry,' he grinned round at the expressions on the faces around him, 'but very carefully, so that she didn't die immediately. He wrapped her in a blanket, put her in the car, carried the body to the grotto, knowing that neither Adelaide nor Roland would be there. He'd already begun to blackmail Templeton about his involvement with the scam and the fact that he was being supplied with drugs by Watson. In fact, that was why he chose the grotto, so Templeton could be on the spot to find the body when he, Oxenford, told him to. He probably put Watson's body there too for the same reason, then he left her to bleed out, drove the car away and dumped it, claiming it had been stolen and she was the victim of a burglary gone wrong. So she died some hours later, by which time his colleague had collected him and he was miles away in Hertfordshire. If the weather had been colder she might have survived for longer, but it's doubtful.'

There was silence round the table for a moment, then Guy asked: 'What about the Watson man?'

'He was busy trying to get rid of any trace of their little business. Carl confronted him about the escape plan and Carl just killed him. Simple as that. He hasn't given us much detail about that so far. He's a very clever man and completely unfazed by his arrest.'

'He's a bloody good actor, too,' said Libby.

'So there never were any golden guineas?' said Anne.

'No. Ramani came across the story of them, she and Roland rigged up the fake Institute and wrote to all the people on or near the smugglers' routes who could just have had guineas stored in their cellars, but only those houses identified by Johnny's circle of "friends" as having items worth stealing. Then Ramani would go along and present her – quite genuine – credentials and be given licence to poke around the house. Often the burglaries weren't noticed for some time. She never took anything large. We've matched up a lot of the reports of theft, now. All from those houses you saw listed.'

'Well, I'm glad it's all over,' said Fran. 'I've never been so scared in my life.'

'You?' cried Libby. 'You were as cool as a cucumber, while I was going completely to pieces!'

'I'm a good actor, too,' said Fran, giving her a grin.

'Well,' said Ben, 'now that our women have survived yet another almost disastrous adventure, Guy, I suggest we keep them away from each other until Christmas.'

'I'll drink to that,' said Ian.

Burham Heath, May 30th 1648

Godfrey Wyghtham leant on his musket and surveyed the tents and horses gathered in a disorganised rabble. They'd done it now. The Earl of Norwich had been proclaimed leader of the Royalists here only yesterday; leader of a largely untrained, poorly-equipped army, who were going to – what? To march on the capital and demand that the King be set free and the bloody Parliamentarians banished? Oh, yes, he could see that happening.

And who were they up against? General Fairfax, commander-in-chief of the New Model Army. Godfrey sighed. They might just as well turn tail and flee now in his opinion, not that his opinion was often sought. He thought of his Rebecca as he'd last seen her, standing at the gate with little Tom in her arms, Mary and Elizabeth clinging to her skirts. He was thankful that at least he'd hidden the money she might need should he fail to return to her. She knew where to find it, but who knew what renegades might be roaming the county looking to steal and – God forbid – rape. If she could get to his little hoard, she and the children would be able to make for the coast, Dover, Deal or Walmer, where she'd be safe. Evelyn was taken care of, her lawyer father made sure of that.

He turned to go inside the tent he shared with Knivetton and Fleetwood, who were both snoring already. He wondered which, of the three of them, would survive this debacle. Which of their names would be written in history. Or would they all three be unrecorded, their bodies in unmarked graves, unknown victims of a dreadful conflict. He put down his musket and began to pray.

271

An excerpt from

MURDER IN A DIFFERENT PLACE

The next Libby Sarjeant Mystery

by

LESLEY COOKMAN

Chapter One

The watcher on the cliff stood hidden against the backdrop of trees, as the sea turned into a boiling, mud-coloured devastation; the wind wrenched the tiles from the roofs and flung them into the air like playing cards. Satisfied, the watcher turned away.

'It's such a gorgeous place,' said Libby Sarjeant, leaning back in her deck chair. 'Pity we had to come here for a funeral.'

'Pity old Matthew had to die,' said her friend Peter Parker reprovingly.

'Yes, of course. What I meant was –'

'It would have been better if we'd come here for a nicer reason,' her significant other, Ben Wilde, replied for her.

'Thanks, Ben, I would have managed that on my own.' Libby looked over the shaded deck towards a figure standing at the edge looking out to sea. 'What's up with Harry?'

'Are you being deliberately insensitive this morning or what?' said Peter, standing up. 'What do you *think's* wrong with him?'

Libby looked towards Ben. 'I am being a bit stupid, aren't I?'

'Yes, darling, you are.' Ben patted her hand.

'Sorry, Pete. Harry knew Matthew before any of the rest of us, didn't he?'

'Not exactly. We knew Matthew as a leading light in the Kent drama scene. Harry knew him in London. Matthew introduced us.'

'Yes, I knew that,' said Libby. 'At that press club. I didn't realise Matthew was a journalist at the time.'

'He was a fairly influential editor by that time,' said Peter.

'And he came from the Isle of Wight,' said Ben. 'I never

knew that, either. Although I didn't know him as well as you did.'

'I love his cousins,' said Libby. 'Priceless, all of them.'

'And obviously very close,' said Peter, casting an anxious glance at his partner, Harry, who still stood surveying the sea. 'They're coming down here for tea, you said?'

'So they said yesterday.' Libby stood up and peered up towards the house halfway up the cliff. 'It's a bit of a climb for them.'

'They must be used to it. Didn't one of them say they had a beach house down here as well?'

'They used to.' Libby frowned. 'It seemed to be a subject to be avoided, though.'

Harry turned away from the sea.

'He loved his cousins,' he said. 'They were brought up together, apparently, in the big house.'

'The big house?' repeated Peter.

'It used to stand up there.' Harry pointed. 'It was called Overcliffe Castle. An early Victorian folly, really.'

The other three looked at him in surprise.

'How do you know?' said Peter, eventually.

Harry shrugged. 'Matthew told me. Told me all about the cousins.'

'Why didn't you tell me when we were organising the trip?' Peter was frowning, now.

'Well, it wasn't as if I actually knew the cousins, was it?' He turned back to his contemplation of the sea.

The other three looked at each other.

'He's been more affected by it than we have,' said Libby. 'He must have known him better than we did.'

Peter nodded. 'He did. I think Matthew looked out for him when he was in London, and I know they kept in touch after Harry moved down to Steeple Martin with me. He was a lovely old boy.'

'So Harry's lost a sort of father figure?' said Ben.

'I think so. It's so unlike him to be this ... I can't think of the word.' Peter shook his head.

'Reserved. Buttoned-up. Down.' Libby sighed. 'All those things. And he got worse at the reception.'

'Wake, dear, wake,' said Peter. 'It wasn't a wedding.'

'Well, it's a shame. Poor Matthew dying, and now Harry's upset. Perhaps we shouldn't have come.'

Ben cocked his head on one side. 'Now, why do you say that? You know you were as intrigued as we all were when we got the invitation.'

'Well, that's just it,' said Libby uncomfortably. 'Why on earth did these women invite us out of the blue? We hadn't been in touch with Matthew for years. At least I hadn't.'

'Only Harry had, I think,' said Peter. 'And you couldn't wait to find out why we were invited, admit it.'

'I know,' admitted Libby reluctantly, 'but now, however beautiful the Island is, and however lovely Overcliffe is, I think it might have been a mistake.'

'Well, don't say it in front of them,' said Harry, suddenly appearing beside her, as a clatter of stones on the wooden steps announced the arrival of three ladies looking remarkably like characters from an Agatha Christie novel, complete with long strings of beads hanging over their long floral frocks.

'Yoo-hoo!' said the first one. 'Here we are at last! Come on Honoria, sit over there. Amelia, you can go next to Libby – Harry, dear boy, sit next to me.'

'Do stop organising us, Alicia,' said the one referred to as Honoria, in a deep, thundery rumble. 'We're not in the classroom now.'

'No, dear, I know,' said Alicia, 'but I'm sure these good people have been wondering why we asked them to Matthew's funeral in the first place. And I want to get on with it.'

'We all liked Matthew,' said Libby, unsure what she was expected to say.

'Yes, dear, we know. He used to tell us all about the plays and pantomimes you put on in Kent, and he was terribly excited about your lovely theatre. He came to the opening, didn't he?'

'Yes, he did, although that was rather overshadowed –'

'By a murder. Yes, we know.' The third member of the trio,

Amelia, spoke in a soft, fluttery voice, that Libby was certain held a hint of steel.

'Um.' Harry's voice, unnaturally hesitant, broke in. 'I hope I'm not going to upset anyone, but Matthew always spoke about four of you.' He looked questioningly at the three sisters.

They all nodded, and Honoria and Amelia looked at Alicia. 'Go on, dear,' they said together.

'That's just it, you see,' said Alicia. 'Celia was our youngest sister. And we think she was murdered.'

THE END

More titles in the Libby Sarjeant Series

For more information on **Lesley Cookman**
and other **Accent Press** titles, please visit

www.accentpress.co.uk

277

G